SO-BEH-588

Brain-twisters, spine-chilling perils, secret codes, daring deductions, well-hidden clues, suspicious-looking characters—these are just a few of the tantalizing ingredients Miss Christie measures out for her insatiable fans in

13 FOR LUCK

With over 200 million copies of her books sold, Agatha Christie is unequaled as a renowned and distinguished author of ingenious tales of mystery and suspense.

13 FOR LUCK

AGATHA CHRISTIE

A DELL BOOK

Published by
DELL PUBLISHING CO., INC.
750 Third Avenue
New York, N.Y.

Copyright © 1961 by Christie Copyrights Trust

All rights reserved. The characters, places, incidents and
situations in this book are imaginary and have no relation to
any person, place or actual happening

Dell ® TM 681510, Dell Publishing Co., Inc.
Reprinted by arrangement with
Dodd, Mead & Company
New York, N.Y.

Printed in U.S.A.
Previous Dell Edition #8753
New Dell Edition
First printing—December 1968
Second printing—June 1969
Third printing—November 1969

ACKNOWLEDGMENTS

THE VEILED LADY and THE MARKET BASING MYSTERY © 1925 by Dodd,
   Mead & Company, Inc. © 1925 by Agatha Christie.
   Renewal © 1953 by Agatha Christie Mallowan
THE NEMEAN LION © 1944 by Agatha Christie
THE GIRDLE OF HYPPOLITA © 1939 by Agatha Christie
TAPE-MEASURE MURDER © 1941 by Agatha Christie
THE FOUR SUSPECTS and THE BLUE GERANIUM © 1933 by Agatha
   Christie Mallowan. Renewal © 1960 by Agatha Christie Mallowan
THE FACE OF HELEN © 1927 by Agatha Christie. Renewal ©
   1954 by Agatha Christie Mallowan
THE BIRD WITH THE BROKEN WING © 1930 by Dodd,
   Mead & Company, Inc. Renewal © 1957 by Agatha Christie Mallowan
THE REGATTA MYSTERY and PROBLEM AT POLLENSA BAY ©
   1936 by Agatha Christie
THE UNBREAKABLE ALIBI © 1929 by Dodd, Mead &
   Company, Inc. Renewal © 1957 by Agatha Christie Mallowan
ACCIDENT © 1943 by Agatha Christie

PREFACE

THROUGH THE PAGES of this book you will enter a delightful new world of entertainment and excitement. As you move through this land of enchantment, your guide and hostess will be Agatha Christie, the acknowledged queen of the mystery writers. Do you like thrillers, baffling mysteries, spine-chilling perils, secret codes, surprise endings? Agatha Christie has all of these in her many stories and novels.

Here are thirteen of her short stories for your pleasure, introducing six of her most famous detectives. And when you have finished reading them and have fallen under the spell of Agatha Christie, a new series of fascinating adventures awaits you in her many other books. Then, for you, this introductory collection of her stories will truly have been **13 for Luck!**

CONTENTS

HERCULE POIROT: MASTER DETECTIVE

JANE MARPLE: SPINSTER OF ST. MARY MEAD

HARLEY QUIN: THE INVISIBLE

MR. PARKER PYNE: PERSONAL CONSULTANT

TOMMY AND TUPPENCE: PARTNERS IN CRIME

INSPECTOR EVANS: SCOTLAND YARD

13 FOR LUCK

HERCULE POIROT

MASTER DETECTIVE

Hercule Poirot, the dapper little Belgian of the magnificent moustaches and "the little grey cells," is among the most famous and formidable of the world's literary sleuths. He came to London at the close of World War I with his friend Captain Hastings and set up there as a private detective. Like most of his profession, Poirot has his eccentricities. Although he is only five feet four in height, he considers himself quite imposing and takes pride in his moustaches, which are the finest in all Europe. His eyes are greenish and his egg-shaped head is carried to one side—the left. Order and method are his gods. At breakfast, for instance, his toast must be cut into neat little squares and his two eggs must be identical in size. In his bookcase, the tallest book is at the end, then the next tallest, and so on. Anything the least crooked and disorderly is a torment to him.

To a like degree, in his pursuit of crime, Poirot has an emphatic disdain for tangible evidence—the analysis of cigarette ashes, for instance, and such matters. Quite otherwise, he prefers to sit quietly and think, employing his little grey cells. He arranges the facts of each of his cases neatly, each in its proper place. With method and logic he can accomplish anything.

In spite of his grandiloquent opinion of his own abilities, Hercule Poirot is a formidable antagonist for any criminal. And woe to the evildoer, no matter how clever, who attempts to conceal the facts of the case from him. Particularly is he adept in last-minute surprises. When the local constable and Scotland Yard have concluded their criminal investigations and have laid their official hands on the protesting culprit, watch for the matchless Poirot to play his ace—and to unmask the real and unexpected villain.

Hercule Poirot's exploits are legion. He appears in many nov-

els, of which the most famous is **The Murder of Roger Ackroyd,**
and in a large number of short stories, among the best of which
are **Poirot Investigates** and **The Labors of Hercules.** This last collection of stories, which parallels the labors assigned to the
great Hercules of Greek mythology, has for the title of each
story the name of one of the fabulous exploits of the ancient
hero. The first of these was the pursuit of the Nemean lion; in
Agatha Christie's version the Pekinese plays the leading part because of his great courage and his leonine mane.

THE VEILED LADY

I HAD NOTICED that for some time Hercule Poirot had been growing increasingly dissatisfied and restless. We had had no interesting cases of late, nothing on which my little friend could exercise his keen wits and remarkable powers of deduction. This July morning he flung down the newspaper with an impatient *"Tchah!"*—a favorite exclamation of his which sounded exactly like a cat sneezing.

"They fear me, Hastings—the criminals of your England, they fear me! When the cat is there, the little mice, they come no more to the cheese!"

"I don't suppose the greater part of them even know of your existence," I said, laughing.

Poirot looked at me reproachfully. He always imagines that the whole world is thinking and talking of Hercule Poirot. He had certainly made a name for himself in London, but I could hardly believe that his existence struck terror into the criminal world.

"What about that daylight robbery of jewels in Bond Street the other day?" I asked.

"A neat *coup*," said Poirot approvingly, "though not in my line. *Pas de finesse, seulement de l'audace!* A man with a loaded cane smashes the plate-glass window of a jeweler's shop and grabs a number of precious stones. Worthy citizens immediately seize him; a policeman arrives. He is caught red-handed with the jewels on him. He is marched off to the police station, and then it is discovered that the stones are paste. He has passed the real ones to a confederate—one of the aforementioned worthy citizens. He will go to prison—true; but when he comes out, there will be a nice little fortune awaiting him. Yes, not badly imagined. But I could do better than that. Sometimes, Hastings, I regret that I am of such a moral disposition. To work against the law, it would be pleasing, for a change."

"Cheer up, Poirot. You know you are unique in your own line."

"But what is there on hand in my own line?"

I picked up the paper. "Here's an Englishman mysteriously done to death in Holland," I said.

"They always say that—and later they find that he ate the tinned fish and that his death is perfectly natural."

"Well, if you're determined to grouse!"

"Tiens!" said Poirot, who had strolled across to the window. "Here in the street is what they call in novels a 'heavily veiled lady.' She mounts the steps; she rings the bell—she comes to consult us. Here is a possibility of something interesting. When one is as young and pretty as that one, one does not veil the face except for a big affair.

A minute later our visitor was ushered in. As Poirot had said, she was indeed heavily veiled. It was impossible to distinguish her features until she raised her veil of black Spanish lace. Then I saw that Poirot's intuition had been right; the lady was extremely pretty, with fair hair and large blue eyes. From the costly simplicity of her attire, I deduced at once that she belonged to an upper stratum of society.

"Monsieur Poirot," said the lady in a soft, musical voice, "I am in great trouble. I can hardly believe that you can help me, but I have heard such wonderful things of you that I come literally as a last hope to beg you to do the impossible."

"The impossible, it pleases me always," said Poirot. "Continue, I beg of you, mademoiselle."

Our fair guest hesitated.

"But you must be frank," added Poirot. "You must not leave me in the dark on any point."

"I will trust you," said the girl suddenly. "You have heard of Lady Millicent Castle Vaughan?"

I looked up with keen interest. The announcement of Lady Millicent's engagement to the young Duke of Southshire had appeared a few days previously. She was, I knew, the fifth daughter of an impecunious Irish peer, and the Duke of Southshire was one of the best matches in England.

"I am Lady Millicent," continued the girl. "You may have read of my engagement. I should be one of the happiest girls alive, but, but, oh, Monsieur Poirot, I am in terrible trouble! There is a man, a horrible man—his name is Lavington; and he—I hardly know how to tell you. There was a letter I wrote—I was only sixteen at the time; and he—he——"

"A letter that you wrote to this Mr. Lavington?"

"Oh, *no*—not to him! To a young soldier—I was very fond of him—he was killed in the war."

"I understand," said Poirot kindly.

"It was a foolish letter, an indiscreet letter, but indeed, Monsieur Poirot, nothing more. But there are phrases in it which—which might bear a different interpretation."

"I see," said Poirot. "And this letter has come into the possession of Mr. Lavington?"

"Yes, and he threatens, unless I pay him an enormous sum of money, a sum that it is quite impossible for me to raise, to send it to the Duke."

"The dirty swine!" I exclaimed. "I beg your pardon, Lady Millicent."

"Would it not be wiser to confess all to your future husband?"

"I dare not, Monsieur Poirot. The Duke is a very jealous man, suspicious and prone to believe the worst. I might as well break off my engagement at once."

"Dear, dear," said Poirot with an expressive grimace. "And what do you want me to do, milady?"

"I thought perhaps that I might ask Mr. Lavington to call upon you. I would tell him that you were empowered by me to discuss the matter. Perhaps you could reduce his demands."

"What sum does he mention?"

"Twenty thousand pounds—an impossibility. I doubt if I could raise even a thousand."

"You might perhaps borrow the money on the prospect of your coming marriage—but, *eh bien*, it is repugnant to

me that you should pay! No, the ingenuity of Hercule
Poirot shall defeat your enemies! Send me this Mr. Lavington. Is he likely to bring the letter with him?"

The girl shook her head.

"I do not think so. He is very cautious."

"I suppose there is no doubt that he really has it?"

"He showed it to me when I went to his house."

"You went to his house? That was very imprudent,
milady."

"Was it? I was so desperate. I hoped my entreaties might
move him."

"Oh, *lá lá!* The Lavingtons of this world are not moved
by entreaties! He would welcome them as showing how
much importance you attached to the document. Where
does he live, this fine gentleman?"

"At Buona Vista, Wimbledon. I went there after dark"—
Poirot groaned—"I declared that I would inform the police
in the end, but he only laughed in a horrid, sneering manner.
'By all means, my dear Lady Millicent, do so if you wish,'
he said."

"Yes, it is hardly an affair for the police," murmured
Poirot.

" 'But I think you will be wiser than that,' he said. 'See,
here is your letter—in this little Chinese Puzzle box!' He
held it so that I could see. I tried to snatch at it, but he was
too quick for me. With a horrid smile he folded it up and replaced it in the little wooden box. 'It will be quite safe here,
I assure you,' he said, 'and I keep the box itself in such a
clever place that you would never find it.' My eyes turned
to the small wall safe and he shook his head and laughed.
'I have a better safe than that,' he said. Oh, he was odious!
Do you think you can help me?"

"Have faith in Papa Poirot. I will find a way."

These reassurances were all very well, I thought, as Poirot
gallantly ushered his fair client down the stairs, but it
seemed to me that we had a tough nut to crack. I said as
much to Poirot when he returned. He nodded ruefully.

"Yes—the solution does not leap to the eye. He has the

whip hand, this Mr. Lavington. For the moment I do not see how we are to circumvent him."

Mr. Lavington duly called on us that afternoon. Lady Millicent had spoken truly when she described him as an odious man. I felt a positive tingling in the end of my foot, so keen was I to kick him down the stairs.

He was blustering and overbearing in manner, laughed Poirot's gentle suggestions to scorn, and generally showed himself as master of the situation. I could not help feeling that Poirot was hardly appearing at his best. He looked discouraged and crestfallen.

"Well, gentlemen," said Lavington as he took up his hat, "we don't seem to be getting much farther. The case stands like this: I'll let the Lady Millicent off cheap, as she is such a charming young lady. We'll say eighteen thousand. I'm off to Paris today—a little piece of business to attend to over there. I shall be back on Tuesday. Unless the money is paid by Tuesday evening, the letter goes to the Duke. Don't tell me Lady Millicent can't raise the money. Some of her gentlemen friends would be only too willing to oblige such a pretty woman with a loan—if she goes about it the right way."

I took a step forward, but Lavington had wheeled out of the room as he finished his sentence.

"Something has got to be done. You seem to be taking this lying down, Poirot," I cried.

"You have an excellent heart, my friend—but your grey cells are in a deplorable condition. I have no wish to impress Mr. Lavington with my capabilities. The more pusillanimous he thinks me, the better."

"Why?"

"It is curious," murmured Poirot reminiscently, "that I should have uttered a wish to work against the law just before Lady Millicent arrived!"

"You are going to burgle his house while he is away?" I gasped.

"Sometimes, Hastings, your mental processes are amazingly quick."

"Suppose he takes the letter with him?"

Poirot shook his head. "That is very unlikely. He has evidently a hiding place in his house that he fancies to be impregnable."

"When do we—er—do the deed?"

"Tomorrow night. We will start from here about eleven o'clock."

At the time appointed I was ready to set off. I had donned a dark suit and a soft dark hat. Poirot beamed kindly on me.

"You have dressed the part, I see," he observed. "Come, let us take the underground to Wimbledon."

"Aren't we going to take anything with us? Tools to break in with?"

"My dear Hastings, Hercule Poirot does not adopt such crude methods."

It was midnight when we entered the small suburban garden of Buona Vista. The house was dark and silent. Poirot went straight to a window at the back of the house, raised the sash noiselessly, and bade me enter.

"How did you know this window would be open?" I whispered, for really it seemed uncanny.

"Because I saw through the catch this morning."

"What?"

"But yes, it was the most simple. I called, presented a fictitious card and one of Inspector Japp's official ones. I said I had been sent, recommended by Scotland Yard, to attend to some burglarproof fastenings that Mr. Lavington wanted fixed while he was away. The housekeeper welcomed me with enthusiasm. It seems they have had two attempted burglaries here lately—evidently our little idea has occurred to other clients of Mr. Lavington's—with nothing of value taken. I examined all the windows, made my little arrangements, forbade the servants to touch the windows until tomorrow, as they were electrically connected up, and withdrew gracefully."

"Really, Poirot, you are wonderful."

"*Mon ami*, it was of the simplest. Now, to work! The servants sleep at the top of the house, so we will run little risk of disturbing them."

"I presume the safe is built into the wall somewhere?"

"Safe? Fiddlesticks! There is no safe. Mr. Lavington is an intelligent man. You will see, he will have devised a hiding place much more intelligent than a safe. A safe is the first thing everyone looks for."

Whereupon we began a systematic search. But after several hours' ransacking of the house, our search had been unavailing. I saw symptoms of anger gathering on Poirot's face.

"*Ah, sapristi,* is Hercule Poirot to be beaten? Never! Let us be calm. Let us reflect. Let us reason. Let us—*en fin!*—employ our little grey cells!"

He paused for some moments, bending his brows in concentration; then the green light I knew so well stole into his eyes.

"I have been an imbecile! The kitchen!"

"The kitchen," I cried. "But that's impossible. The servants!"

"Exactly. Just what ninety-nine people out of a hundred would say! And for that very reason the kitchen is the ideal place to choose. It is full of various homely objects. *En avante,* to the kitchen!"

I followed him, completely skeptical, and watched while he dived into bread bins, tapped saucepans, and put his head into the gas oven. In the end, tired of watching him, I strolled back to the study. I was convinced that there, and there only, would we find the *cache.* I made a further minute search, noted that it was now a quarter past four and that therefore it would soon be growing light, and then went back to the kitchen regions.

To my utter amazement, Poirot was now standing right inside the coal bin, to the utter ruin of his neat light suit. He made a grimace.

"But yes, my friend, it is against all my instincts so to ruin my appearance, but what will you?"

"Lavington can't have buried it under the coal!"

"If you would use your eyes, you would see that it is not the coal that I examine."

I then saw that on a shelf behind the coal bunker some logs of wood were piled. Poirot was dexterously taking them down one by one. Suddenly he uttered a low exclamation.

"Your knife, Hastings!"

I handed it to him. He appeared to insert it in the wood, and suddenly the log split in two. It had been neatly sawn in half and a cavity hollowed out in the center. From this cavity Poirot took a little wooden box of Chinese make.

"Well done!" I cried.

"Gently, Hastings! Do not raise your voice too much. Come, let us be off before the daylight is upon us."

Slipping the box into his pocket, he leaped lightly out of the coal bunker, brushed himself down as well as he could, and, after leaving the house by the same way as we had entered, we walked rapidly in the direction of London.

"But what an extraordinary place!" I expostulated. "Anyone might have used the log."

"In *July*, Hastings? And it was at the bottom of the pile— a very ingenious hiding place. Ah, here is a taxi! Now for home, a wash, and a refreshing sleep."

After the excitement of the night, I slept late. When I finally strolled into our sitting room just before twelve o'clock, I was surprised to see Poirot, leaning back in an armchair, the Chinese box open beside him, calmly reading the letter he had taken from it.

He smiled at me affectionately and tapped the sheet he held.

"She was right, the Lady Millicent—never would the Duke have pardoned this letter! It contains some of the most extravagant terms of affection I have ever come across."

"Really, Poirot," I said, "I don't think you should have read the letter. That's the sort of thing that isn't done."

"It is done by Hercule Poirot," replied my friend imperturbably.

"And another thing," I said. "I don't think using Japp's official card yesterday was quite playing the game."

"But I was not playing a game, Hastings. I was conducting a case."

I shrugged—one can't argue with a point of view.

"A step on the stairs," said Poirot. "That will be Lady Millicent."

Our fair client came in with an anxious expression on her face which changed to one of delight on seeing the letter and box which Poirot held up.

"Oh, Monsieur Poirot, how wonderful of you! How did you do it?"

"By rather reprehensible methods, milady. But Mr. Lavington will not prosecute. This is your letter, is it not?"

She glanced through it.

"Yes. Oh, how can I ever thank you! You are a wonderful, wonderful man. Where was it hidden?"

Poirot told her.

"How very clever of you!" She took up the small box from the table. "I shall keep this as a souvenir."

"I had hoped, milady, that you would permit me to keep it—also as a souvenir."

"I hope to send you a better souvenir than that—on my wedding day. You shall not find me ungrateful, Monsieur Poirot."

"The pleasure of doing you a service will be more to me than a check—so you permit that I retain the box."

"Oh, no, Monsieur Poirot, I simply must have that," she cried laughingly.

She stretched out her hand, but Poirot's closed over it. "I think not." His voice had changed.

"What do you mean?" Her voice seemed to have grown sharper.

"At any rate, permit me to abstract its further contents. You observe that the original cavity has been reduced by half. In the top half, the compromising letter; in the bottom——"

He made a nimble gesture, then held out his hand. On the palm were four large glittering stones and two big milky-white pearls.

"The jewels stolen in Bond Street the other day, I rather fancy," murmured Poirot. "Japp will tell us."

To my utter amazement, Japp himself stepped out of Poirot's bedroom.

"An old friend of yours, I believe," said Poirot politely to Lady Millicent.

"Nabbed!" said Lady Millicent with a complete change of manner. "You nippy old devil!" She looked at Poirot with almost affectionate awe.

"Well, Gertie, my dear," said Japp, "the game's up this time—fancy seeing you again so soon! We've got your pal, too, the gentleman who called here the other day *calling himself* Lavington. As for Lavington himself, alias Corker, alias Reed, I wonder which of the gang it was who stuck a knife into him the other day in Holland? Thought he'd got the goods with him, didn't you? And he hadn't. He double-crossed you properly—hid 'em in his own house. You had two fellows looking for them, and then you tackled Monsieur Poirot here, and by a piece of amazing luck he found them."

"You do like talking, don't you?" said the late Lady Millicent. "Easy there, now. I'll go quietly. You can't say that I'm not the perfect lady. *Ta-ta*, all!"

"The shoes were wrong," said Poirot dreamily while I was still too stupefied to speak. "I have made my little observations of your English nation, and a lady, a born lady, is always particular about her shoes. She may have shabby clothes, but she will be well shod. Now, this Lady Millicent had smart, expensive clothes and cheap shoes. It was not likely that either you or I should have seen the real Lady Millicent; she has been very little in London, and this girl had a certain superficial resemblance, which would pass well enough. As I say, the shoes first awakened my suspicions, and then her story—and her veil—were a little melodramatic, eh? The Chinese box with a bogus compromising letter in the top must have been known to all the gang, but the log of wood was the late Mr. Lavington's own idea. *Eh, par exemple*, Hastings, I hope you will not again wound my feelings as you did yesterday by saying that I am unknown to the criminal classes. *Ma foi*, they even employ me when they themselves fail!"

THE NEMEAN LION

"ANYTHING OF INTEREST this morning, Miss Lemon?" Hercule Poirot asked as he entered the room.

He trusted Miss Lemon. She was a woman without imagination, but she had an instinct. Anything that she mentioned as worth consideration usually was worth consideration. She was a born secretary.

"Nothing much, Monsieur Poirot. There is just one letter that I thought might interest you. I have put it on the top of the pile."

"And what is that?" He took an interested step forward.

"It's from a man who wants you to investigate the disappearance of his wife's Pekinese dog."

Poirot paused with his foot still in the air. He threw a glance of deep reproach at Miss Lemon. She did not notice it. She had begun to type. She typed with the speed and precision of a quick-firing tank.

Poirot was shaken—shaken and embittered. Miss Lemon, the efficient Miss Lemon, had let him down! A Pekinese *dog*. A *Pekinese* dog! And after the dream he had had last night. He had been leaving Buckingham Palace after being personally thanked when his valet had come in with his morning chocolate!

Words trembled on his lips—witty, caustic words. He did not utter them because Miss Lemon, owing to the speed and efficiency of her typing, would not have heard them.

With a grunt of disgust he picked up the topmost letter from the little pile on the side of his desk.

Yes, it was exactly as Miss Lemon had said. A city address —a curt, businesslike, unrefined demand. The subject—the kidnapping of a Pekinese dog. One of those bulging-eyed, overpampered pets of a rich woman. Hercule Poirot's lip curled as he read it.

Nothing unusual about this. Nothing out of the way or— but yes, yes, in one small detail, Miss Lemon was right. In one small detail there *was* something unusual.

Hercule Poirot sat down. He read the letter slowly and carefully. It was not the kind of case he wanted, it was not the kind of case he had promised himself. It was not in any sense an important case, it was supremely unimportant. It was not—and here was the crux of his objection—it was not a proper Labor of Hercules.

But unfortunately he was curious. . . .

Yes, he was curious. . . .

He raised his voice so as to be heard by Miss Lemon above the noise of her typing.

"Ring up this Sir Joseph Hoggin," he ordered, "and make an appointment for me to see him at his office as he suggests."

As usual, Miss Lemon had been right.

"I'm a plain man, Monsieur Poirot," said Sir Joseph Hoggin.

Hercule Poirot made a noncommittal gesture with his right hand. It expressed (if you chose to take it so) admiration for the solid worth of Sir Joseph's career and an appreciation of his modesty in so describing himself. It could also have conveyed a graceful depreciation of the statement. In any case, it gave no clue to the thought then uppermost in Hercule Poirot's mind, which was that Sir Joseph certainly was (using the term in its more colloquial sense) a very plain man indeed. Hercule Poirot's eyes rested critically on the swelling jowl, the small pig eyes, the bulbous nose, and the close-lipped mouth. The whole general effect reminded him of someone or something—but for the moment he could not recollect who or what it was. A memory stirred dimly. A long time ago . . . in Belgium . . . something, surely, to do with *soap*. . . .

Sir Joseph was continuing.

"No frills about me. I don't beat about the bush. Most

people, Monsieur Poirot, would let this business go. Write it off as a bad debt and forget about it. But that's not Joseph Hoggin's way. I'm a rich man—and in a manner of speaking two hundred pounds is neither here nor there to me——"

Poirot interpolated swiftly: "I congratulate you."

"Eh?"

Sir Joseph paused a minute. His small eyes narrowed themselves still more. He said sharply: "That's not to say that I'm in the habit of throwing my money about. What I want I pay for. But I pay the market price—no more."

Hercule Poirot said: "You realise that my fees are high?"

"Yes, yes. But this," Sir Joseph looked at him cunningly, "is a very small matter."

Hercule Poirot shrugged his shoulders. He said: "I do not bargain. I am an expert. For the services of an expert you have to pay."

Sir Joseph said frankly: "I know you're a tiptop man at this sort of thing. I made inquiries and I was told that you were the best man available. I mean to get to the bottom of this business and I don't grudge the expense. That's why I got you to come here."

"You were fortunate," said Hercule Poirot.

Sir Joseph said "Eh?" again.

"Exceedingly fortunate," said Hercule Poirot firmly. "I am, I may say so without undue modesty, at the apex of my career. Very shortly I intend to retire—to live in the country, to travel occasionally to see the world—also, it may be, to cultivate my garden—with particular attention improving the strain of vegetable marrows. Magnificent vegetables—but they lack flavour. That, however, is not the point. I wished merely to explain that before retiring I had imposed upon myself a certain task. I have decided to accept twelve cases— no more, no less. A self-imposed 'Labors of Hercules,' if I may so describe it. Your case, Sir Joseph, is the first of the twelve. I was attracted to it," he sighed, "by its striking unimportance."

"Importance?" said Sir Joseph.

"*Un*importance was what I said. I have been called in for varying causes—to investigate murders, unexplained deaths, robberies, thefts of jewelry. This is the first time that I have been asked to turn my talents to elucidate the kidnapping of a Pekinese dog."

Sir Joseph grunted. He said: "You surprise me! I should have said you'd have had no end of women pestering you about their pet dogs."

"That, certainly. But it is the first time that I am summoned by the husband in the case."

Sir Joseph's little eyes narrowed appreciatively.

He said: "I begin to see why they recommended you to me. You're a shrewd fellow, Monsieur Poirot."

Poirot murmured: "If you will now tell me the facts of the case. The dog disappeared when?"

"Exactly a week ago."

"And your wife is by now quite frantic, I presume?"

Sir Joseph started. He said: "You don't understand. The dog has been returned."

"Returned? Then, permit me to ask, where do *I* enter the matter?"

Sir Joseph went crimson in the face.

"Because I'm damned if I'll be swindled! Now then, Monsieur Poirot, I'm going to tell you the whole thing. The dog was stolen a week ago—nipped in Kensington Gardens, where he was out with my wife's companion. The next day my wife got a demand for two hundred pounds. I ask you— two hundred pounds! For a yapping little brute that's always getting under your feet anyway!"

Poirot murmured: "You did not approve of paying such a sum, naturally?"

"Of course I didn't—or wouldn't have if I'd known anything about it! Milly, my wife, knew that well enough. She didn't say anything to *me*. Just sent off the money—in one-pound notes as stipulated—to the address given."

"And the dog was returned?"

"Yes. That evening the bell rang and there was the little brute sitting on the doorstep. And not a soul to be seen."

"Perfectly. Continue."

"Then, of course, Milly confessed what she'd done and I

lost my temper a bit. However, I calmed down after a while
—after all, the thing was done and you can't expect a woman
to behave with any sense—and I daresay I should have let
the whole thing go if it hadn't been for meeting old Samuelson at the Club."

"Yes?"

"This thing must be a positive racket! Exactly the same
thing had happened to him. Three hundred pounds they'd
rooked his wife of! Well, that was a bit too much. I decided
the thing had got to be stopped. I sent for you."

"But surely, Sir Joseph, the proper thing (and a very much
more inexpensive thing) would have been to send for the
police?"

Sir Joseph rubbed his nose.

He said: "Are you married, Monsieur Poirot?"

"Alas," said Poirot, "I have not that felicity."

"H'm," said Sir Joseph. "Don't know about felicity, but if
you were, you'd know that women are funny creatures. My
wife went into hysterics at the mere mention of the police—
she'd got into her head that something would happen to her
precious Shan Tung if I went to them. She wouldn't hear of
the idea—and I may say she doesn't take very kindly to the
idea of your being called in. But I stood firm there and at
last she gave way. But, mind you, she doesn't like it."

Hercule Poirot murmured: "The position is, I perceive,
a delicate one. It would be as well, perhaps, if I were to
interview Madame your wife and gain further particulars
from her whilst at the same time reassuring her as to the
future safety of her dog."

Sir Joseph nodded and rose to his feet. He said: "I'll take
you along in the car right away."

In a large, hot, ornately furnished drawing room two
women were sitting.

As Sir Joseph and Hercule Poirot entered, a small Pekinese
dog rushed forward, barking furiously and circling danger-
ously round Poirot's ankles.

"Shan—Shan, come here. Come here to mother, lovey
——Pick him up, Miss Carnaby."

The second woman hurried forward and Hercule Poirot murmured: "A veritable lion, indeed."

Rather breathlessly, Shan Tung's captor agreed.

"Yes, indeed, he's such a *good* watchdog. He's not frightened of anything or anyone. There's a lovely boy, then."

Having performed the necessary introduction, Sir Joseph said: "Well, Monsieur Poirot, I'll leave you to get on with it." And with a short nod he left the room.

Lady Hoggin was a stout, petulant-looking woman with dyed henna-red hair. Her companion, the fluttering Miss Carnaby, was a plump, amiable-looking creature between forty and fifty. She treated Lady Hoggin with great deference and was clearly frightened to death of her.

Poirot said: "Now tell me, Lady Hoggin, the full circumstances of this abominable crime."

Lady Hoggin flushed.

"I'm very glad to hear you say that, Monsieur Poirot. For it was a crime. Pekinese are terribly sensitive—just as sensitive as children. Poor Shan Tung might have died of fright if of nothing else."

Miss Carnaby chimed in breathlessly: "Yes, it was wicked —wicked!"

"Please tell me the facts."

"Well, it was like this. Shan Tung was out for his walk in the park with Miss Carnaby——"

"Oh, dear me, yes, it was all my fault," chimed in the companion. "How could I have been so stupid—so careless——"

Lady Hoggin said acidly: "I don't want to reproach you, Miss Carnaby, but I do think you might have been more alert."

Poirot transferred his gaze to the companion.

"What happened?"

Miss Carnaby burst into voluble and slightly flustered speech.

"Well, it was the most extraordinary thing! We had just been along the flower walk—Shan Tung was on the lead, of course—he'd had his little run on the grass—and I was just about to turn and go home when my attention was caught

by a baby in a pram—such a lovely baby—it smiled at me—
lovely rosy cheeks and such curls. I couldn't just resist speaking to the nurse in charge and asking how old it was—seventeen months, she said—and I'm sure I was only speaking to
her for about a minute or two, and then suddenly I looked
down and Shan wasn't there any more. The lead had been
cut right through——"

Lady Hoggin said: "If you'd been paying proper attention
to your duties, nobody could have sneaked up and cut that
lead."

Miss Carnaby seemed inclined to burst into tears. Poirot
said hastily: "And what happened next?"

"Well, of course I looked everywhere. And called! And I
asked the park attendant if he'd seen a man carrying a
Pekinese dog, but he hadn't noticed anything of the kind—
and I didn't know what to do—and I went on searching, but
at last, of course, I had to come home——"

Miss Carnaby stopped dead. Poirot could imagine the
scene that followed well enough. He asked: "And then you
received a letter?"

Lady Hoggin took up the tale.

"By the first post the following morning. It said that if I
wanted to see Shan Tung alive I was to send two hundred
pounds in one-pound notes in an unregistered packet to
Captain Curtis, 38 Bloomsbury Road Square. It said that if
the money were marked or the police informed, then—then
—Shan Tung's ears and tail would be—cut off!"

Miss Carnaby began to sniff.

"So awful," she murmured. "How people can be such
fiends!"

Lady Hoggin went on: "It said that if I sent the money at
once, Shan Tung would be returned the same evening alive
and well, but that if—if afterwards I went to the police, it
would be Shan Tung who would suffer for it——"

Miss Carnaby murmured tearfully: "Oh, dear, I'm so
afraid that even now—of course, Monsieur Poirot isn't
exactly the police——"

Lady Hoggin said anxiously: "So you see, Monsieur Poirot, you will have to be very careful——"

Hercule Poirot was quick to allay her anxiety.

"But I, I am not of the police. My inquiries, they will be conducted very discreetly, very quietly. You can be assured, Lady Hoggin, that Shan Tung will be perfectly safe. That I will guarantee."

Both ladies seemed relieved by the magic word. Poirot went on: "You have here the letter?"

Lady Hoggin shook her head.

"No, I was instructed to enclose it with the money."

"And you did so?"

"Yes."

"H'm, that is a pity."

Miss Carnaby said brightly: "But I have the dog lead still. Shall I get it?"

She left the room. Hercule Poirot profited by her absence to ask a few pertinent questions.

"Amy Carnaby? Oh, she's quite all right. A good soul, though foolish, of course. I have had several companions and they have all been complete fools. But Amy was devoted to Shan Tung and she was terribly upset over the whole thing —as well she might be—hanging over perambulators and neglecting my little sweetheart! These old maids are all the same, idiotic over babies! No, I'm quite sure she had nothing whatever to do with it."

"It does not seem likely," Poirot agreed. "But as the dog disappeared when in her charge one must make quite certain of her honesty. She has been with you long?"

"Nearly a year. I had excellent references with her. She was with old Lady Hartingfield until she died—ten years, I believe. After that she looked after an invalid sister for a while. She is really an excellent creature—but a complete fool, as I said."

Amy Carnaby, returned at this minute, slightly more out of breath, and produced the cut dog lead, which she handed to Poirot with the utmost solemnity, looking at him with hopeful expectancy.

Poirot surveyed it carefully.

"Mais oui," he said. "This has undoubtedly been cut."

The two women still waited expectantly. He said: "I will keep this."

Solemnly he put it in his pocket. The two women breathed a sigh of relief. He had clearly done what was expected of him.

It was the habit of Hercule Poirot to leave nothing untested.

Though on the face of it it seemed unlikely that Miss Carnaby was anything but the foolish and rather muddleheaded woman that she appeared to be, Poirot nevertheless managed to interview a somewhat forbidding lady, who was the niece of the late Lady Hartingfield.

"Amy Carnaby?" said Miss Maltravers. "Of course, remember her perfectly. She was a good soul and suited Aunt Julia down to the ground. Devoted to dogs and excellent at reading aloud. Tactful, too; never contradicted an invalid. What's happened to her? Not in distress of any kind, I hope, I gave her a reference about a year ago to some woman— name began with H——"

Poirot explained hastily that Miss Carnaby was still in her post. There had been, he said, a little trouble over a lost dog.

"Amy Carnaby is devoted to dogs. My aunt had a Pekinese. She left it to Miss Carnaby when she died and Miss Carnaby was devoted to it. I believe she was quite heartbroken when it died. Oh, yes, she's a good soul. Not, of course, precisely intellectual."

Hercule Poirot agreed that Miss Carnaby could not, perhaps, be described as intellectual.

His next proceeding was to discover the park keeper to whom Miss Carnaby had spoken on the fateful afternoon. This he did without much difficulty. The man remembered the incident in question.

"Middle-aged lady, rather stout—in a regular state she was —lost her Pekinese dog. I knew her well by sight—brings the dog along most afternoons. I saw her come in with it. She was in a rare taking when she lost it. Came running to me to know if I'd seen anyone with a Pekinese dog! Well, I ask you! I can tell you, the Gardens is full of dogs—every kind—terriers, Pekes, German sausage dogs—even them Borzoys—all kinds we have. Not likely as I'd notice one Peke more than another."

Hercule Poirot nodded his head thoughtfully.

He went to 38 Bloomsbury Road Square.

Numbers 38, 39, and 40 were incorporated together as the Balaclava Private Hotel. Poirot walked up the steps and pushed open the door. He was greeted inside by gloom and a smell of cooking cabbage with a reminiscence of breakfast kippers. On his left was a mahogany table with a sad-looking chrysanthemum plant on it. Above the table was a big baize-covered rack into which letters were stuck. Poirot stared at the board thoughtfully for some minutes. He pushed open a door on his right. It led into a kind of lounge with small tables and some so-called easy chairs covered with a depressing pattern of cretonne. Three old ladies and one fierce-looking old gentleman raised their heads and gazed at the intruder with deadly venom. Hercule Poirot blushed and withdrew.

He walked further along the passage and came to a staircase. On his right a passage branched at right angles to what was evidently the dining room.

A little way along this passage was a door marked "Office."

On this Poirot tapped. Receiving no response, he opened the door and looked in. There was a large desk in the room, covered with papers, but there was no one to be seen. He withdrew, closing the door again. He penetrated to the dining room.

A sad-looking girl in a dirty apron was shuffling about with a basket of knives and forks with which she was laying the tables.

Hercule Poirot said apologetically: "Excuse me, but could I see the manageress?"

The girl looked at him with lacklustre eyes.

She said: "I don't know, I'm sure."

Hercule Poirot said: "There is no one in the office."

"Well, I don't know where she'd be, I'm sure."

"Perhaps," Hercule Poirot said, patient and persistent, "you could find out?"

The girl sighed. Dreary as her day's round was, it had now been made additionally so by this new burden laid upon her. She said sadly: "Well, I'll see what I can do."

Poirot thanked her and removed himself once more to the hall, not daring to face the malevolent glare of the occupants of the lounge. He was staring up at the baize-covered letter rack when a rustle and a strong smell of Devonshire violets proclaimed the arrival of the manageress.

Mrs. Harte was full of graciousness. She exclaimed: "So sorry I was not in my office. You were requiring rooms?"

Hercule Poirot murmured: "Not precisely. I was wondering if a friend of mine had been staying here lately. A Captain Curtis."

"Curtis," exclaimed Mrs. Harte. "Captain Curtis? Now where have I heard that name?"

Poirot did not help her. She shook her head vexedly.

He said: "You have not, then, had a Captain Curtis staying here?"

"Well, not lately, certainly. And yet, you know, the name is certainly familiar to me. Can you describe your friend at all?"

"That," said Hercule Poirot, "would be difficult." He went on: "I suppose it sometimes happens that letters arrive for people when in actual fact no one of that name is staying here?"

"That does happen, of course."

"What do you do with such letters?"

"Well, we keep them for a time. You see, it probably means that the person in question will arrive shortly. Of course, if letters or parcels are a long time here unclaimed, they are returned to the post office."

Hercule Poirot nodded thoughtfully.

He said: "I comprehend." He added: "It is like this, you see. I wrote a letter to my friend here."

Mrs. Harte's face cleared.

"That explains it. I must have noticed the name on an envelope. But really we have so many ex-Army gentlemen staying here or passing through——Let me see now."

She peered up at the board.

Hercule Poirot said: "It is not there now."

"It must have been returned to the postman, I suppose. I am so sorry. Nothing important, I hope?"

"No, no, it was of no importance."

As he moved towards the door, Mrs. Harte, enveloped in her pungent odour of violets, pursued him.

"If your friend should come——"

"It is most unlikely. I must have made a mistake. . . ."

"Our terms," said Mrs. Harte, "are very moderate. Coffee after dinner is included. I would like you to see one or two of our bed-sitting rooms. . . ."

With difficulty Hercule Poirot escaped.

The drawing room of Mrs. Samuelson was larger, more lavishly furnished, and enjoyed an even more stifling amount of central heating than that of Lady Hoggin. Hercule Poirot picked his way giddily amongst gilded console tables and large groups of statuary.

Mrs. Samuelson was taller than Lady Hoggin and her hair was dyed with peroxide. Her Pekinese was called Nanki Poo. His bulging eyes surveyed Hercule Poirot with arrogance. Miss Keble, Mrs. Samuelson's companion, was thin and scraggy where Miss Carnaby had been plump, but she also was voluble and slightly breathless. She, too, had been blamed for Nanki Poo's disappearance.

"But really, Monsieur Poirot, it was the most amazing thing. It all happened in a second. Outside Harrods it was. A nurse there asked me the time——"

Poirot interrupted her.

"A nurse? A hospital nurse?"

"No, no—a children's nurse. Such a sweet baby it was, too! A dear little mite. Such lovely rosy cheeks. They say children don't look healthy in London, but I'm sure——"

"Ellen," said Mrs. Samuelson.

Miss Keble blushed, stammered, and subsided into silence.

Mrs. Samuelson said acidly: "And while Miss Keble was bending over a perambulator that had nothing to do with her, this audacious villain cut Nanki Poo's lead and made off with him."

Miss Keble murmured tearfully: "It all happened in a second. I looked round and the darling boy was gone—there was just the dangling lead in my hand. Perhaps you'd like to see the lead, Monsieur Poirot?"

"By no means," said Poirot hastily. He had no wish to make a collection of cut dog leads. "I understand," he went on, "that shortly afterwards you received a letter?"

The story followed the same course exactly—the letter—the threats of violence to Nanki Poo's ears and tail. Only two things were different—the sum of money demanded—three hundred pounds—and the address to which it was to be sent; this time it was to Commander Blackleigh, Harrington Hotel, 76 Clonmel Gardens, Kensington.

Mrs. Samuelson went on: "When Nanki Poo was safely back again, I went to the place myself, Monsieur Poirot. After all, three hundred pounds is three hundred pounds."

"Certainly it is."

"The very first thing I saw was my letter enclosing the money in a kind of rack in the hall. Whilst I was waiting for the proprietress I slipped it into my bag. Unfortunately——"

Poirot said: "Unfortunately, when you opened it, it contained only blank sheets of paper."

"How did you know?" Mrs. Samuelson turned on him with awe.

Poirot shrugged his shoulders.

"Obviously, *chère* madame, the thief would take care to recover the money before he returned the dog. He would then replace the notes with blank paper and return the letter to the rack in case its absence should be noticed."

"No such person as Commander Blackleigh had ever stayed there."

Poirot smiled.

"And of course, my husband was extremely annoyed about the whole thing. In fact, he was livid—absolutely livid!"

Poirot murmured cautiously: "You did not—er—consult him before despatching the money?"

"Certainly not," said Mrs. Samuelson with decision.

Poirot looked a question. The lady explained.

"I wouldn't have risked it for a moment. Men are so extraordinary when it's a question of money. Jacob would have insisted on going to the police. I couldn't risk that. My poor darling Nanki Poo. Anything might have happened to him! Of course, I *had* to tell my husband afterwards, because I had to explain why I was overdrawn at the bank."

Poirot murmured: "Quite so—quite so."

"And I have really never seen him so angry. Men," said Mrs. Samuelson, rearranging her handsome diamond bracelet and turning her rings on her fingers, "think of nothing but money."

Hercule Poirot went up in the lift to Sir Joseph Hoggin's office. He sent in his card and was told that Sir Joseph was engaged at the moment but would see him presently. A haughty secretary sailed out of Sir Joseph's room at last with her hands full of papers. She gave the quaint little man a disdainful glance in passing.

Sir Joseph was seated behind his immense mahogany desk.

"Well, Monsieur Poirot? Sit down. Got any news for me?"

Hercule Poirot said: "The whole affair is of a pleasing simplicity. In each case the money was sent to one of those boarding houses or private hotels where there is no porter or hall attendant and where a large number of guests are always coming and going, including a fairly large preponderance of ex-servicemen. Nothing would be easier than for anyone to walk in, abstract a letter from the rack, either take it away, or else remove the money and replace it with blank paper. Therefore, in every case, the trail ends abruptly in a blank wall."

"You mean you've no idea who the fellow is?"

"I have certain ideas, yes. It will take a few days to follow them up."

Sir Joseph looked at him curiously.

"Good work. Then, when you've got anything to report ———"

"I will report to you at your house."

Sir Joseph said: "If you get to the bottom of this business, it will be a pretty good piece of work."

Hercule Poirot said: "There is no question of failure. Hercule Poirot does not fail."

Sir Joseph Hoggin looked at the little man and grinned.

"Sure of yourself, aren't you?" he demanded.

"Entirely with reason."

"Oh, well." Sir Joseph Hoggin leaned back in his chair. "Pride goes before a fall, you know."

Hercule Poirot, sitting in front of his electric radiator (and feeling a quiet satisfaction in its neat geometrical pattern), was giving instructions to his valet and general factotum.

"You understand, Georges?"

"Perfectly, sir."

"More probably a flat or maisonette. And it will definitely be within certain limits. South of the Park, east of Kensington Church, west of Knightsbridge Barracks, and north of Fulham Road."

"I understand perfectly, sir."

Poirot murmured: "A curious little case. There is evidence here of a very definite talent for organisation. And there is, of course, the surprising invisibility of the star performer—the Nemean Lion himself, if I may so style him. Yes, an interesting little case. I could wish that I felt more attracted to my client—but he bears an unfortunate resemblance to a soap manufacturer of Liège who poisoned his wife in order to marry his secretary. One of my early successes."

Georges shook his head gravely.

It was three days later when the invaluable Georges said: "This is the address, sir."

Hercule Poirot took the piece of paper handed to him.

"Excellent, my good Georges. And what day of the week?"

"Thursdays, sir."

"Thursdays. And today, most fortunately, is a Thursday. So there need be no delay."

Twenty minutes later Hercule Poirot was climbing the stairs of an obscure block of flats tucked away in a little street leading off a more fashionable one. Number 10 Rosholm Mansions was on the third and top floor and there was no lift. Poirot toiled upwards round and round the narrow cork-screw staircase.

He paused to regain his breath on the top landing and from behind the door of Number 10 a new sound broke the silence—the sharp bark of a dog.

Hercule Poirot nodded his head with a slight smile. He pressed the bell of Number 10.

The barking redoubled—footsteps came to the door—it was opened. . . .

Miss Amy Carnaby fell back; her hand went to her ample breast.

"You permit that I enter?" said Hercule Poirot, and entered without waiting for the reply.

There was a sitting-room door open on the right and he walked in. Behind him, Miss Carnaby followed as though in a dream.

The room was very small and much overcrowded. Amongst the furniture a human being could be discovered, an elderly woman lying on a sofa drawn up to the gas fire. As Poirot came in, a Pekinese dog jumped off the sofa and came forward, uttering a few sharp, suspicious barks

"Aha," said Poirot. "The chief actor! I salute you, my little friend."

He bent forward, extending his hand. The dog sniffed at it, his intelligent eyes fixed on the man's face.

Miss Carnaby murmured faintly: "So you know?"

Hercule Poirot nodded.

"Yes, I know." He looked at the woman on the sofa. "Your sister, I think?"

Miss Carnaby said mechanically: "Yes, Emily, this—this is Monsieur Poirot."

Emily Carnaby gave a gasp. She said: "Oh!"

Amy Carnaby said: "Augustus . . ."

The Pekinese looked towards her—his tail moved—then he resumed his scrutiny of Poirot's hand. Again his tail moved faintly.

Gently, Poirot picked the little dog up and sat down with Augustus on his knee. He said: "So I have captured the Nemean Lion. My task is completed."

Amy Carnaby said in a hard, dry voice: "Do you really know everything?"

Poirot nodded.

"I think so. You organised this business—with Augustus to help you. You took your employer's dog out for his usual walk, brought him here, and went on to the Park with Augustus. The park keeper saw you with a Pekinese as usual. The nurse girl, if we had ever found her, would also have agreed that you had a Pekinese with you when you spoke to her. Then, while you were talking, you cut the lead and Augustus, trained by you, slipped off at once and made a beeline back home. A few minutes later you gave the alarm that the dog had been stolen."

There was a pause. Then Miss Carnaby drew herself up with a certain pathetic dignity. She said: "Yes. It is all quite true. I—I have nothing to say."

The invalid woman on the sofa began to cry softly.

Poirot said: "Nothing at all, mademoiselle?"

Miss Carnaby said: "Nothing. I have been a thief—and now I am found out."

Poirot murmured: "You have nothing to say—in your own defence?"

A spot of red showed suddenly in Amy Carnaby's white cheeks. She said: "I—I don't regret what I did. I think that you are a kind man, Monsieur Poirot, and that possibly you might understand. You see, I've been so terribly afraid."

"Afraid?"

"Yes, it's difficult for a gentleman to understand, I expect. But you see, I'm not a clever woman at all, and I've no training, and I'm getting older—and I'm so terrified for the future. I've not been able to save anything—how could I, with Emily to be cared for?—and as I get older and more incompetent there won't be anyone who wants me. They'll want somebody young and brisk. I've—I've known so many people like I am —nobody wants you and you live in one room and you can't have a fire or any warmth and not very much to eat, and at last you can't even pay the rent of your room. . . . There are institutions, of course, but it's not very easy to get into them unless you have influential friends, and I haven't. There are a good many others situated like I am—poor companions—untrained, useless women with nothing to look forward to but a deadly fear. . . ."

Her voice shook. She said: "And so—some of us—got together and—and I thought of this. It was really having Augustus that put it into my mind. You see, to most people, one Pekinese is very much like another. (Just as we think the Chinese are.) Really, of course, it's ridiculous. No one who knew could mistake Augustus for Nanki Poo or Shan Tung or any of the other Pekes. He's far more intelligent, for one thing, and he's much handsomer, but, as I say, to most people a Peke is just a Peke. Augustus put it into my head—that, combined with the fact that so many rich women have Pekinese dogs."

Poirot said with a faint smile: "It must have been a profitable—racket! How many are there in the—the gang? Or perhaps I had better ask how often operations have been successfully carried out?"

Miss Carnaby said simply: "Shan Tung was the sixteenth."

Hercule Poirot raised his eyebrows.

"I congratulate you. Your organisation must have been indeed excellent."

Emily Carnaby said: "Amy was always good at organisation. Our father—he was the Vicar of Kellington in Essex—always said that Amy had quite a genius for planning. She always made all the arrangements for the socials and the bazaars and all that."

Poirot said with a little bow: "I agree. As a criminal, mademoiselle, you are quite in the first rank."

Amy Carnaby cried: "A criminal. Oh, dear, I suppose I am. But—but it never felt like that."

"How did it feel?"

"Of course, you are quite right. It was breaking the law. But you see—how can I explain it? Nearly all these women who employ us are so very rude and unpleasant. Lady Hoggin, for instance, doesn't mind what she says to me. She said her tonic tasted unpleasant the other day and practically accused me of tampering with it. All that sort of thing." Miss Carnaby flushed. "It's really very unpleasant. And not being able to say anything or answer back makes it rankle more, if you know what I mean."

"I know what you mean," said Hercule Poirot.

"And then seeing money frittered away so wastefully—that is upsetting. And Sir Joseph, occasionally he used to describe a *coup* he had made in the city—sometimes something that seemed to me (of course, I know I've only got a woman's brain and don't understand finance) downright dishonest. Well, you know, Monsieur Poirot, it all—it all unsettled me, and I felt that to take a little money away from these people who really wouldn't miss it and hadn't been too scrupulous in acquiring it—well, really, it hardly seemed wrong at all."

Poirot murmured: "A modern Robin Hood! Tell me, Miss Carnaby, did you ever have to carry out the threats you used in your letters?"

"Threats?"

"Were you ever compelled to mutilate the animals in the way you specified?"

Miss Carnaby regarded him in horror.

"Of course, I would never have dreamed of doing such a thing! That was just—just an artistic touch."

"Very artistic. It worked."

"Well, of course, I knew it would. I know how I should have felt about Augustus, and of course I had to make sure these women never told their husbands until afterwards. The plan worked beautifully every time. In nine cases out of ten the companion was given the letter with the money to post. We usually steamed it open, took out the notes, and replaced them with paper. Once or twice the woman posted it herself. Then, of course, the companion had to go to the hotel and take the letter out of the rack. But that was quite easy, too."

"And the nursemaid touch? Was it always a nursemaid?"

"Well, you see, Monsieur Poirot, old maids are known to be foolishly sentimental about babies. So it seemed quite natural that they should be absorbed over a baby and not notice anything."

Hercule Poirot sighed. He said. "Your psychology is excellent, your organisation is first-class, and you are also a

very fine actress. Your performance the other day when I
interviewed Lady Hoggin was irreproachable. Never think
of yourself disparagingly, Miss Carnaby. You may be what
is termed an untrained woman but there is nothing wrong
with your brains or with your courage."

Miss Carnaby said with a faint smile: "And yet I have been
found out, Monsieur Poirot."

"Only by Me. That was inevitable! When I had interviewed Mrs. Samuelson I realised that the kidnapping of
Shan Tung was one of a series. I had already learned that
you had once been left a Pekinese dog and had an invalid
sister. I had only to ask my invaluable servant to look for a
small flat within a certain radius occupied by an invalid lady
who had a Pekinese dog and a sister who visited her once a
week on her day out. It was simple."

Amy Carnaby drew herself up. She said: "You have been
very kind. It emboldens me to ask you a favour. I cannot, I
know, escape the penalty for what I have done. I shall be
sent to prison, I suppose. But if you could, Monsieur Poirot,
avert some of the publicity. So distressing for Emily—and
for those few who knew us in the old days. I could not, I
suppose, go to prison under a false name? Or is that a very
wrong thing to ask?"

Hercule Poirot said: "I think I can do more than that.
But first of all I must make one thing quite clear. This racket
has got to stop. There must be no more disappearing dogs.
All that is finished!"

"Yes! Oh, yes!"

"And the money you extracted from Lady Hoggin must be
returned."

Amy Carnaby crossed the room, opened the drawer of a
bureau, and returned with a packet of notes which she
handed to Poirot.

"I was going to pay it into the pool today."

Poirot took the notes and counted them. He got up.

"I think it possible, Miss Carnaby, that I may be able to
persuade Sir Joseph not to prosecute."

"Oh, Monsieur Poirot!"

Amy Carnaby clasped her hands. Emily gave a cry of joy. Augustus barked and wagged his tail.

"As for you, *mon ami*," said Poirot, addressing him, "there is one thing that I wish you would give me. It is your mantle of invisibility that I need. In all these cases nobody for a moment suspected that there was a *second* dog involved. Augustus possessed the lion's skin of invisibility."

"Of course, Monsieur Poirot, according to the legend, Pekinese were lions once. And they still have the hearts of lions!"

"Augustus is, I suppose, the dog that was left to you by Lady Hartingfield and who is reported to have died? Were you never afraid of him coming home alone through the traffic?"

"Oh, no, Monsieur Poirot. Augustus is very clever about traffic. I have trained him most carefully. He has even grasped the principle of one-way streets."

"In that case," said Hercule Poirot, "he is superior to most human beings!"

Sir Joseph received Hercule Poirot in his study. He said: "Well, Monsieur Poirot? Made your boast good?"

"Let me first ask you a question," said Poirot as he seated himself. "I know who the criminal is and I think it possible that I can produce sufficient evidence to convict this person. But in that case I doubt if you will ever recover your money."

"Not get back my money?"

Sir Joseph turned purple.

Hercule Poirot went on: "But I am not a policeman. I am acting in this case solely in your interests. I could, I think, recover your money intact, if no proceedings were taken."

"Eh?" said Sir Joseph. "That needs a bit of thinking about."

"It is entirely for you to decide. Strictly speaking, I suppose you ought to prosecute in the public interest. Most people would say so."

"I daresay they would," said Sir Joseph dryly. "It wouldn't be their money that had gone west. If there's one thing I hate, it's to be swindled. Nobody's ever swindled me and got away with it."

"Well, then, what do you decide?"

"I'll have the brass! Nobody's going to say they got away with two hundred pounds of my money."

Hercule Poirot rose, crossed to the writing table, wrote out a cheque for two hundred pounds, and handed it to the other man.

Sir Joseph said in a weak voice: "Well, I'm damned! Who is this fellow?"

Poirot shook his head.

"If you accept the money, there must be no questions asked."

Sir Joseph folded up the cheque and put it in his pocket.

"That's a pity. But the money's the thing. And what do I owe you, Monsieur Poirot?"

"My fees will not be high. This was, as I said, a very unimportant matter." He paused—and added, "Nowadays nearly all my cases are murder cases. . . ."

Sir Joseph started slightly.

"Must be interesting?" he said.

"Sometimes. Curiously enough, you recall to me one of my early cases in Belguim, many years ago—the chief protagonist was very like you in appearance. He was a wealthy soap manufacturer. He poisoned his wife in order to be free to marry his secretary. . . . Yes—the resemblance is very remarkable. . . ."

A faint sound came from Sir Joseph's lips—they had gone a queer blue colour. All the ruddy hue had faded from his cheeks. His eyes, starting out of his head, stared at Poirot. He slipped down a little in his chair.

Then, with a shaking hand, he fumbled in his pocket. He drew out the cheque and tore it into pieces.

"That's washed out—see? Consider it as your fee."

"Oh, but, Sir Joseph, my fee would not have been as large as that."

"That's all right. You keep it."

"I shall send it to a deserving charity."

"Send it anywhere you like."

Poirot leaned forward. He said: "I think I need hardly point out, Sir Joseph, that in your position you would do well to be exceedingly careful."

Sir Joseph said, his voice almost inaudible: "You needn't worry. I shall be careful all right.

Hercule Poirot left the house. As he went down the steps he said to himself: "So—I was right."

Lady Hoggin said to her husband: "Funny, this tonic tastes quite different. It hasn't got that bitter taste any more. I wonder why?"

Sir Joseph growled: "Chemists. Careless fellows. Make things up differently different times."

Lady Hoggin said doubtfully: "I suppose that must be it."

"Of course it is. What else could it be?"

"Has the man found out anything about Shan Tung?"

"Yes. He got me my money back all right."

"Who was it?"

"He didn't say. Very close fellow, Hercule Poirot. But you needn't worry."

"He's a funny little man, isn't he?"

Sir Joseph gave a slight shiver and threw a sideways glance upwards, as though he felt the invisible presence of Hercule Poirot behind his right shoulder. He had an idea that he would always feel it there.

He said: "He's a clever little devil!"

"Oh!"

Amy Carnaby gazed down incredulously at the cheque for two hundred pounds. She cried: "Emily! *Emily!* Listen to this:

"Dear Miss Carnaby,

Allow me to enclose a contribution to your very deserving fund before it is finally wound up.

                              Yours very truly,
                                Hercule Poirot"

"Amy," said Emily Carnaby, "you've been incredibly lucky. Think where you might be now."

"Wormwood Scrubbs—or is it Holloway?" murmured Amy Carnaby. "But that's all over now—isn't it, Augustus? No more walks to the park with mother or mother's friends and a little pair of scissors."

A faraway wistfulness came into her eyes. She sighed.

"Dear Augustus! It seems a pity. He's so clever. . . . One can teach him anything. . . ."

THE GIRDLE OF HYPPOLITA

ONE THING LEADS to another, as Hercule Poirot is fond of saying without much originality.

He adds that this was never more clearly evidenced than in the case of the stolen Rubens.

He was never much interested in the Rubens. For one thing, Rubens is not a painter he admires, and then the circumstances of the theft were quite ordinary. He took it up to oblige Alexander Simpson, who was by way of being a friend of his, and for a certain private reason of his own not unconnected with the classics!

After the theft, Alexander Simpson sent for Poirot and poured out all his woes. The Rubens was a recent discovery, a hitherto unknown masterpiece, but there was no doubt of its authenticity. It had been placed on display at Simpson's Galleries and it had been stolen in broad daylight. It was at the time when the unemployed were pursuing their tactics of lying down on street crossings and penetrating into the Ritz. A small body of them had entered Simpson's Galleries and lain down with the slogan displayed of "Art is a Luxury. Feed the Hungry." The police had been sent for, everyone had crowded round in eager curiosity, and it was not till the demonstrators had been forcibly removed by the arm of the law that it was noticed that the new Rubens had been neatly cut out of its frame and removed also!

"It was quite a small picture, you see," explained Mr. Simpson. "A man could put it under his arm and walk out while everyone was looking at those miserable idiots of unemployed."

The men in question, it was discovered, had been paid for

their innocent part in the robbery. They were to demonstrate at Simpson's Galleries. But they had known nothing of the reason until afterwards.

Hercule Poirot thought that it was an amusing trick but did not see what he could do about it. The police, he pointed out, could be trusted to deal with a straightforward robbery.

Alexander Simpson said: "Listen to me, Poirot. I know who stole the picture and where it is going."

According to the owner of Simpson's Galleries, it had been stolen by a gang of international crooks on behalf of a certain millionaire who was not above acquiring works of art at a surprisingly low price—and no questions asked! The Rubens, said Simpson, would be smuggled over to France, where it would pass into the millionaire's possession. The English and French police were on the alert; nevertheless, Simpson was of the opinion that they would fail. "And once it has passed into this dirty dog's possession, it's going to be more difficult. Rich men have to be treated with respect. That's where you come in. The situation's going to be delicate. You're the man for that."

Finally, without enthusiasm, Hercule Poirot was induced to accept the task. He agreed to depart for France immediately. He was not very interested in his quest, but because of it he was introduced to the case of the Missing Schoolgirl, which interested him very much indeed.

He first heard of it from Chief Inspector Japp, who dropped in to see him just as Poirot was expressing approval of his valet's packing.

"Ha," said Japp. "Going to France, aren't you?"

Poirot said: "*Mon cher,* you are incredibly well informed at Scotland Yard."

Japp chuckled. He said: "We have our spies! Simpson's got you on to this Rubens business. Doesn't trust us, it seems! Well, that's neither here nor there, but what I want you to do is something quite different. As you're going to Paris anyway, I thought you might as well kill two birds with one stone. Detective Inspector Hearn's over there cooperating with the Frenchies—you know Hearn? Good chap

—but perhaps not very imaginative. I'd like your opinion on the business."

"What is this matter of which you speak?"

"Child's disappeared. It'll be in the papers this evening. Looks as though she's been kidnapped. Daughter of a Canon down at Cranchester. King, her name is; Winnie King."

He proceeded with the story.

Winnie had been on her way to Paris to join that select and high-class establishment for English and American girls —Miss Pope's. Winnie had come up from Cranchester by the early train—had been seen across London by a member of Elder Sisters Limited who undertook such work as seeing girls from one station to another, had been delivered at Victoria to Miss Burshaw, Miss Pope's second in command, and had then, in company with eighteen other girls, left Victoria by the boat train. Nineteen girls had crossed the channel, had passed through the customs at Calais, had got into the Paris train, had lunched in the restaurant car. But when, on the outskirts of Paris, Miss Burshaw had counted heads, it was discovered that only *eighteen* girls could be found!

"Aha," Poirot nodded. "Did the train stop anywhere?"

"It stopped at Amiens, but at that time the girls were in the restaurant car and they all say positively that Winnie was with them then. They lost her, so to speak, on the return journey to their compartments. That is to say, she did not enter her own compartment with the other five girls who were in it. They did not suspect anything was wrong, merely thought she was in one of the two other reserved carriages."

Poirot nodded.

"So she was last seen—when, exactly?"

"About ten minutes after the train left Amiens." Japp coughed modestly. "She was last seen—er—entering the toilette."

Poirot murmured: "Very natural." He went on: "There is nothing else?"

"Yes, one thing." Japp's face was grim. Her hat was found by the side of the line—at a spot approximately fourteen miles from Amiens."

"But no body?"

"No body."

Poirot asked: "What do you yourself think?"

"Difficult to know *what* to think! As there's no sign of her body—she can't have fallen off the train."

"Did the train stop at all after leaving Amiens?"

"No. It slowed up once—for a signal—but it didn't stop, and I doubt if it slowed up enough for anyone to have jumped off without injury. You're thinking that the kid got a panic and tried to run away? It was her first term and she might have been homesick, that's true enough, but all the same she was fifteen and a half—a sensible age—and she'd been in quite good spirits all the journey, chattering away and all that."

Poirot asked: "Was the train searched?"

"Oh, yes, they went right through it before it arrived at the Nord station. The girl wasn't on the train that's quite certain."

Japp added in an exasperated manner: "She just disappeared—into thin air! It doesn't make sense, Monsieur Poirot. It's crazy!"

"What kind of a girl was she?"

"Ordinary normal type as far as I can make out."

"I mean—what did she look like?"

"I've got a snap of her here. She's not exactly a budding beauty."

He proffered the snapshot to Poirot, who studied it in silence.

It represented a lanky girl with her hair in two limp plaits. It was not a posed photograph; the subject had clearly been caught unawares. She was in the act of eating an apple, her lips were parted, showing slightly protruding teeth confined by a dentist's plate. She wore spectacles.

Japp said: "Plain-looking kid—but then they are plain at that age! Was at my dentist's yesterday. Saw a picture in the *Sketch* of Marcia Gaunt, this season's beauty. *I* remember her at fifteen when I was down at the Castle over their burglary business. Spotty, awkward, teeth sticking out, hair all

lank and anyhow. They grow into beauties overnight—I
don't know how they do it! It's like a miracle."

Poirot smiled.

"Women," he said, "are a miraculous sex! What about the
child's family? Have they anything helpful to say?"

Japp shook his head.

"Nothing that's any help. Mother's an invalid. Poor old
Canon King is absolutely bowled over. He swears that the
girl was frightfully keen to go to Paris—had been looking
forward to it. Wanted to study painting and music—that sort
of thing. Miss Pope's girls go in for Art with a capital A. As
you probably know, Miss Pope's is a very well-known establishment. Lots of society girls go there. She's strict—quite a
dragon—and very expensive—and extremely particular
whom she takes."

Poirot sighed.

"I know the type. And Miss Burshaw who took the girls
over from England?"

"Not exactly frantic with brains. Terrified that Miss Pope
will say it's her fault."

Poirot said thoughtfully: "There is no young man in the
case?"

Japp gesticulated towards the snapshot.

"Does she look like it?"

"No, she does not. But notwithstanding her appearance,
she may have a romantic heart. Fifteen is not so young."

"Well," said Japp, "if a romantic heart spirited her off
that train, I'll take to reading lady novelists."

He looked hopefully at Poirot.

"Nothing strikes you—eh?"

Poirot shook his head slowly. He said: "They did not, by
any chance, find her shoes also by the side of the line?"

"Shoes? No. Why shoes?"

Poirot murmured: "Just an idea. . . ."

Hercule Poirot was just going down to his taxi when the
telephone rang. He took off the receiver.

"Yes?"

Japp's voice spoke.

"Glad I've just caught you. It's all off, old man. Found a message at the Yard when I got back. The girl's turned up. At the side of the main road fifteen miles from Amiens. She's dazed and they can't get any coherent story from her. Doctor says she's been doped—however, she's all right. Nothing wrong with her."

Poirot said slowly: "So you have, then, no need of my services?"

"Afraid not! In fact—sorrrry you have been trrrroubled. . . ."

Japp laughed at his own witticism and rang off.

Hercule Poirot did not laugh. He put back the receiver slowly. His face was worried.

Detective Inspector Hearn looked at Poirot curiously.

He said: "I'd no idea you'd be so interested, sir."

Poirot said: "You had word from Chief Inspector Japp that I might consult with you over this matter?"

Hearn nodded.

"He said you were coming over on some other business and that you'd give us a hand with this puzzle. But I didn't expect you, now it's all cleared up. I thought you'd be busy on your own job."

Hercule Poirot said: "My own business can wait. It is this affair here that interests me. You called it a puzzle, and you say it is now ended. But the puzzle is still there, it seems."

"Well, sir, we've got the child back. And she's not hurt. That's the main thing."

"But it does not solve the problem of how you got her back, does it? What does she herself say? A doctor saw her, did he not? What did he say?"

"Said she'd been doped. She was still hazy with it. Apparently, she can't remember anything much after starting off from Cranchester. All later events seem to have been wiped out. Doctor thinks she might just possibly have had slight concussion. There's a bruise on the back of the head. Says that would account for a complete blackout of memory."

Poirot said: "Which is very convenient for—someone!"

Inspector Hearn said in a doubtful voice: "You don't think she is shamming, sir?"

"Do you?"

"No, I'm sure she isn't. She's a nice kid—a bit young for her age."

"No, she is not shamming." Poirot shook his head. "But I would like to know how she got off that train. I want to know who is responsible—and why?"

"As to why, I should say it was an attempt at kidnapping, sir. They meant to hold her to ransom."

"But they didn't!"

"Lost their nerve with the hue and cry—and planted her by the road quick."

Poirot inquired skeptically: "And what ransom were they likely to get from a Canon of Cranchester Cathedral? English Church dignitaries are not millionaires."

Detective Inspector Hearn said cheerfully: "Made a botch of the whole thing, sir, in my opinion."

"Ah, that's your opinion."

Hearn said, his face flushing slightly: "What's yours, sir?"

"I want to know how she was spirited off that train."

The policeman's face clouded over.

"That's a real mystery, that is. One minute she was there, sitting in the dining car, chatting to the other girls. Five minutes later she's vanished—hey presto—like a conjuring trick."

"Precisely, like a conjuring trick! Who else was there in the coach of the train where Miss Pope's reserved compartments were?"

Inspector Hearn nodded.

"That's a good point, sir. That's important. It's particularly important because it was the last coach on the train and as soon as all the people were back from the restaurant car, the doors between the coaches were locked—actually so as to prevent people crowding along to the restaurant car and demanding tea before they'd had time to clear up lunch and get ready. Winnie King came back to the coach with the others—the school had three reserved compartments there."

"And in the other compartment of the coach?"

Hearn pulled out his notebook.

"Miss Jordan and Miss Butters—two middle-aged spinsters going to Switzerland. Nothing wrong with them, highly respectable, well known in Hampshire where they come from. Two French commercial travellers, one from Lyons, one from Paris. Both respectable middle-aged men. A young man, James Elliot, and his wife—flashy piece of goods she was. He's got a bad reputation, suspected by the police of being mixed up in some questionable transactions—but has never touched kidnapping. Anyway, his compartment was searched and there was nothing in his hand luggage to show that he was mixed up in this. Don't see how he *could* have been. Only other person was an American lady, Mrs. Van Suyder, travelling to Paris. Nothing known about her. Looks O.K. That's the lot."

Hercule Poirot said: "And it is quite definite that the train did not stop after it left Amiens?"

"Absolutely. It slowed down once, but not enough to let anybody jump off—not without damaging themselves pretty severely and risk being killed."

Hercule Poirot murmured: "That is what makes the problem so peculiarly interesting. The schoolgirl vanishes into thin air just outside Amiens. She reappears from thin air also just outside Amiens. Where has she been in the meantime?"

Inspector Hearn shook his head.

"It sounds mad, put like that. Oh! By the way, they told me you were asking something about shoes—the girl's shoes. She had her shoes on all right when she was found, but there was a pair of shoes on the line; a signalman found them. Took 'em home with him, as they seemed in good condition. Stout black-laced walking shoes."

"Ah," said Poirot. He looked gratified.

Inspector Hearn said curiously: "I don't get the meaning of the shoes, sir? Do they mean anything?"

"They confirm a theory," said Hercule Poirot. "A theory of how the conjuring trick was done."

Miss Pope's establishment was, like many other establishments of the same kind, situated in Neuilly. Hercule Poirot, staring up at its respectable façade, was suddenly submerged by a flow of girls emerging from its portals.

He counted twenty-five of them, all dressed alike in dark-blue coats and skirts with uncomfortable-looking British hats of dark-blue velour on their heads, round which was tied the distinctive purple and gold of Miss Pope's choice. They were of ages varying from fourteen to eighteen, thick and thin, fair and dark, awkward and graceful. At the end, walking with one of the younger girls, was a grey-haired, fussy-looking woman whom Poirot judged to be Miss Burshaw.

Poirot stood looking after them a minute, then he rang the bell and asked for Miss Pope.

Miss Lavinia Pope was a very different person from her second in command, Miss Burshaw. Miss Pope had personality. Miss Pope was awe-inspiring. Even should Miss Pope unbend graciously to parents, she would still retain that obvious superiority to the rest of the world which is such a powerful asset to a schoolmistress.

Her grey hair was dressed with distinction, her costume was severe but chic. She was competent and omniscient.

The room in which she received Poirot was the room of a woman of culture. It had graceful furniture, flowers, some framed signed photographs of those of Miss Pope's pupils who were of note in the world—many of them in their presentation gowns and feathers. On the walls hung reproductions of the world's artistic masterpieces and some good water-colour sketches. The whole place was clean and polished to the last degree. No speck of dust, one felt, would have the temerity to deposit itself in such a shrine.

Miss Pope received Poirot with the competence of one whose judgment seldom fails.

"Monsieur Hercule Poirot? I know your name, of course. I suppose you have come about this very unfortunate affair of Winnie King. A most distressing incident."

Miss Pope did not look distressed. She took disaster as it should be taken, dealing with it competently and thereby reducing it almost to insignificance.

"Such a thing," said Miss Pope, "has never occurred before."

("And never will again!" her manner seemed to say.)

Hercule Poirot said: "It was the girl's first term here, was it not?"

"It was."

"You had had a preliminary interview with Winnie—and with her parents?"

"Not recently. Two years ago, I was staying near Cranchester—with the Bishop, as a matter of fact——"

(Miss Pope's manner said: "Mark this, please. I am the kind of person who stays with Bishops!")

"While I was there I made the acquaintance of Canon and Mrs. King. Mrs. King, alas, is an invalid. I met Winnie then. A very well-brought-up girl with a decided taste for art. I told Mrs. King that I should be happy to receive her here in a year or two—when her general studies were completed. We specialise here, Monsieur Poirot, in art and music. The girls are taken to the Opera, to the Comédie Française; they attend lectures at the Louvre. The very best masters come here to instruct them in music, singing, and painting. The broader culture—that is our aim."

Miss Pope remembered suddenly that Poirot was not a parent and added abruptly: "What can I do for you, Monsieur Poirot?"

"I would be glad to know what is the present position regarding Winnie?"

"Canon King has come over to Amiens and is taking Winnie back with him. The wisest thing to do after the shock the child has sustained."

She went on: "We do not take delicate girls here. We have no special facilities for looking after invalids. I told the Canon that in my opinion he would do well to take the child home with him."

Hercule Poirot asked bluntly: "What, in your opinion, actually occurred, Miss Pope?"

"I have not the slightest idea, Monsieur Poirot. The whole thing, as reported to me, sounds quite incredible. I really cannot see that the member of my staff who was in charge of the girls was in any way to blame—except that she might, perhaps, have discovered the girl's absence sooner."

Poirot said: "You have received a visit, perhaps, from the police?"

A faint shiver passed over Miss Pope's aristocratic form. She said glacially: "A Monsieur Lefarge of the Préfecture called to see me, to see if I could throw any light upon the situation. Naturally I was unable to do so. He then demanded to inspect Winnie's trunk which had, of course, arrived here with those of the other girls. I told him that that had already been called for by another member of the police. Their departments, I fancy, must overlap. I got a telephone call, shortly afterwards, insisting that I had not turned over all Winnie's possessions to them. I was extremely short with them over that. One must not submit to being bullied by officialdom."

Poirot drew a long breath. He said: "You have a spirited nature. I admire you for it, mademoiselle. I presume that Winnie's trunk had been unpacked on arrival?"

Miss Pope looked a little put out of countenance.

"Routine," she said. "We live strictly by routine. The girls are unpacked for on arrival and their things put away in the way I expect them to be kept. Winnie's things were unpacked with those of the other girls. Naturally, they were afterwards repacked, so that her trunk was handed over exactly as it had arrived."

Poirot said: *"Exactly?"*

He strolled to the wall.

"Surely this is a picture of the famous Cranchester Bridge with the Cathedral showing in the distance."

"You are quite right, Monsieur Poirot. Winnie had evidently painted that to bring me as a surprise. It was in her trunk with a wrapper round it and 'For Miss Pope from Winnie' written on it. Very charming of the child."

"Ah!" said Poirot. "And what do you think of it—as a painting?"

He himself had seen many pictures of Cranchester Bridge. It was a subject that could always be found represented at the Academy each year—sometimes as an oil painting—

sometimes in the water-colour room. He had seen it painted well, painted in a mediocre fashion, painted boringly. But he had never seen it quite as crudely represented as in the present example.

Miss Pope was smiling indulgently.

She said: "One must not discourage one's girls, Monsieur Poirot. Winnie will be stimulated to do better work, of course."

Poirot said thoughtfully: "It would have been more natural, would it not, for her to do a water-colour?"

"Yes. I did not know she was attempting to paint in oils."

"Ah," said Hercule Poirot. "You will permit me, mademoiselle?"

He unhooked the picture and took it to the window. He examined it. Then, looking up, he said: "I am going to ask you, mademoiselle, to give me this picture."

"Well, really, Monsieur Poirot——"

"You cannot pretend that you are very attached to it. The painting is abominable."

"Oh, it has no artistic merit, I agree. But it is a pupil's work and——"

"I assure you, mademoiselle, that it is a most unsuitable picture to have hanging upon your wall."

"I don't know why you should say that, Monsieur Poirot."

"I will prove it to you in a moment."

He took a bottle, a sponge, and some rags from his pocket. He said: "First I am going to tell you a little story, mademoiselle. It has a resemblance to the story of the Ugly Duckling that turned into a Swan."

He was working busily as he talked. The odour of turpentine filled the room.

"You do not perhaps go much to theatrical revues?"

"No, indeed, they seem to me so trivial. . . ."

"Trivial, yes, but sometimes instructive. I have seen a clever revue artist change her personality in the most miraculous way. In one sketch she is a cabaret star, exquisite and glamorous. Ten minutes later, she is an undersized, anaemic child with adenoids, dressed in a gym tunic—ten minutes, later still, she is a ragged gypsy telling fortunes by a caravan."

"Very possible, no doubt, but I do not see——"

"But I am showing you how the conjuring trick was worked on the train. Winnie, the schoolgirl—with her fair plaits, her spectacles, her disfiguring dental plate—goes into the *toilette*. She emerges a quarter of an hour later—to use the words of Detective Inspector Hearn—as 'a flashy piece of goods.' Sheer silk stockings, high-heeled shoes—a mink coat to cover a school uniform, a daring little piece of velvet called a hat perched on her curls—and a face—oh, yes, a face. Rouge, powder, lipstick, mascara? What is the real face of that quick-change *artiste* really like? Probably only the good God knows! But, you, Mademoiselle, you yourself, you have often seen how the awkward schoolgirl changes almost miraculously into the attractive and well-groomed debutante."

Miss Pope gasped.

"Do you mean that Winnie King disguised herself as ——"

"Not Winnie King—no. Winnie was kidnapped on the way across London. Our quick-change *artiste* took her place. Miss Burshaw had never seen Winnie King. How was she to know that the schoolgirl with the lank plaits and the brace on her teeth was not Winnie King at all? So far, so good, but the imposter could not afford actually to arrive here, since you were acquainted with the real Winnie. So, hey presto, Winnie disappears in the *toilette* and merges as wife to a man called Jim Elliot, whose passport includes a wife! The fair plaits, the spectacles, the lisle-thread stockings, the dental plate—all that can go into a small space. But the thick, unglamorous shoes and the hat—that very unyielding British hat—have to be disposed of elsewhere—they go out of the window. Later, the real Winnie is brought across the channel—no one is looking for a sick, half-doped child being brought from England to France—and is quietly deposited from a car by the side of the main road. If she has been doped all along with scopolamine, she will remember very little of what has occurred."

Miss Pope was staring at Poirot. She demanded: "But *why?* What would be the *reason* of such a senseless masquerade?"

Poirot replied gravely: "Winnie's luggage! These people wanted to smuggle something from England into France—something that every customs man was on the lookout for—in fact, stolen goods. But what place is safer than a schoolgirl's trunk? You are well known, Miss Pope; your establishment is justly famous. At the Gare du Nord the trunks of Mesdemoiselles the little *Pensionnaires* are passed *en bloc*. It is the well-known English school of Miss Pope! And then, after the kidnapping, what more natural than to send for and collect the child's luggage—ostensibly from the Préfecture?"

Hercule Poirot smiled.

"But, fortunately, there was the school routine of unpacking trunks on arrival—and a present for you from Winnie—but not the same present that Winnie packed at Cranchester."

He came towards her.

"You have given this picture to me. Observe now, you must admit that it is not suitable for your select school!"

He held out the canvas.

As though by magic, Cranchester Bridge had disappeared. Instead was a classical scene in rich, dim colourings.

Poirot said softly: " 'The Girdle of Hyppolita.' Hyppolita gives her girdle to Hercules—painted by Rubens. A great work of art—*mais tout de même* not quite suitable for your drawing room."

Miss Pope blushed slightly.

"A fine work of art. . . . All the same—as you say—after all, one must consider the susceptibilities of parents. Some of them are inclined to be narrow . . . if you know what I mean. . . ."

It was just as Poirot was leaving the house that the onslaught took place. He was surrounded, hemmed in, overwhelmed by a crowd of girls, thick, thin, dark and fair.

"Mon Dieu!" he murmured. "Here, indeed, is the attack by the Amazons!"

A tall, fair girl was crying out: "A rumor has gone round——"

They surged closer. Hercule Poirot was surrounded. He disappeared in a wave of young, vigorous femininity.

Twenty-five voices arose, pitched in various keys but all uttering the same momentous phrase: "Monsieur Poirot, will you write your name in my autograph book?"

THE MARKET BASING MYSTERY

"AFTER ALL, there's nothing like the country, is there?" said Inspector Japp, breathing in heavily through his nose and out through his mouth in the most approved fashion.

Poirot and I applauded the sentiment heartily. It had been the Scotland Yard inspector's idea that we should all go for the weekend to the little country town of Market Basing. When off duty, Japp was an ardent botanist and discoursed upon minute flowers possessed of unbelievably lengthy Latin names (somewhat strangely pronounced) with an enthusiasm even greater than that he gave to his cases.

"Nobody knows us, and we know nobody," explained Japp. "That's the idea."

This was not to prove quite the case, however, for the local constable happened to have been transferred from a village fifteen miles away where a case of arsenical poisoning had brought him into contact with the Scotland Yard man. However, his delighted recognition of the great man only enhanced Japp's sense of well-being, and as we sat down to breakfast on Sunday morning in the parlor of the village inn, with the sun shining and tendrils of honeysuckle thrusting themselves in at the window, we were all in the best of spirits. The bacon and eggs were excellent, the coffee not so good but passable and boiling hot.

"This is the life," said Japp. "When I retire, I shall have a little place in the country. Far from crime, like this!"

"*Le crime, il est partout*," remarked Poirot, helping himself to a neat square of bread and frowning at a sparrow which had balanced itself impertinently on the window sill.

I quoted lightly:

That rabbit has a pleasant face,
His private life is a disgrace.
I really could not tell to you
The awful things that rabbits do.

Japp, stretching himself backward, said, "I believe I could manage another egg and perhaps a rasher or two of bacon. What do you say, Captain?"

"I'm with you," I returned heartily. "What about you, Poirot?"

Poirot shook his head.

"One must not so replenish the stomach that the brain refuses to function," he remarked.

"I'll risk replenishing the stomach a bit more," laughed Japp. "I take a large size in stomachs; and, by the way, you're getting stout yourself, Monsieur Poirot. Here, miss, eggs and bacon twice."

At that moment, however, an imposing form blocked the doorway. It was Constable Pollard.

"I hope you'll excuse me troubling the inspector, gentlemen, but I'd be glad of his advice."

"I'm on my holiday," said Japp hastily. "No work for me. What is the case?"

"Gentleman up at Leigh House—shot himself—through the head."

"Well, they will do it," said Japp prosaically. "Debt or a woman, I suppose. Sorry I can't help you, Pollard."

"The point is," said the constable, "that he can't have shot himself. Leastways, that's what Dr. Giles says."

Japp put down his cup.

"Can't have shot himself? What do you mean?"

"That's what Dr. Giles says," repeated Pollard. "He says it's plumb impossible. He's puzzled to death, the door being locked on the inside and the window bolted; but he sticks to it that the man couldn't have committed suicide."

That settled it. The further supply of bacon and eggs was waved aside, and a few minutes later we were all walking as fast as we could in the direction of Leigh House, Japp eagerly questioning the constable.

The name of the deceased was Walter Protheroe; he was a man of middle age and something of a recluse. He had come to Market Basing eight years ago and rented Leigh House, a rambling, dilapidated old mansion fast falling into ruin. He lived in a corner of it, his wants attended to by a housekeeper whom he had brought with him. Miss Clegg was her name, and she was a very superior woman and highly thought of in the village. Just lately Mr. Protheroe had had visitors staying with him, a Mr. and Mrs. Parker from London. This morning, unable to get a reply when she went to call her master, and finding the door locked, Miss Clegg became alarmed and telephoned for the police and the doctor. Constable Pollard and Dr. Giles had arrived at the same moment. Their united efforts had succeeded in breaking down the oak door of his bedroom.

Mr. Protheroe was lying on the floor, shot through the head, and the pistol was clasped in his right hand. It looked a clear case of suicide.

After examining the body, however, Dr. Giles became clearly perplexed, and finally he drew the constable aside and communicated his perplexities to him; whereupon Pollard had at once thought of Japp. Leaving the doctor in charge, he had hurried down to the Inn.

By the time the constable's recital was over, we had arrived at Leigh House, a big, desolate house surrounded by an unkempt, weed-ridden garden. The front door was open, and we passed at once into the hall and from there into a small morning room, whence proceeded the sound of voices. Four people were in the room: a somewhat flashily dressed man with a shifty, unpleasant face to whom I took an immediate dislike; a woman of much the same type, though handsome in a coarse fashion; another woman dressed in neat black who stood apart from the rest and whom I took to be the housekeeper; and a tall man dressed in sporting tweeds, with a clever, capable face, and who was clearly in command of the situation.

"Dr. Giles," said the constable, "this is Chief Inspector Japp of Scotland Yard and his two friends."

The doctor greeted us and made us known to Mr. and Mrs. Parker. Then we accompanied him upstairs. Pollard, in obedience to a sign from Japp, remained below, as it were, on guard over the household. The doctor led us upstairs and along a passage. A door was open at the end; splinters hung from the hinges, and the door itself had crashed to the floor inside the room.

We went in. The body was still lying on the floor. Mr. Protheroe had been a man of middle age, bearded, with hair grey at the temples. Japp went and knelt by the body.

"Why couldn't you leave it as you found it?" he grumbled.

The doctor shrugged his shoulders.

"We thought it a clear case of suicide."

"H'm!" said Japp. "Bullet entered the head behind the left ear."

"Exactly," said the doctor. "Clearly impossible for him to have fired it himself. He'd have had to twist his hand right round his head. It couldn't have been done."

"Yet you found the pistol clasped in his hand? Where is it, by the way?"

The doctor nodded to the table.

"But it wasn't clasped in his hand," he said. It was inside the hand, but the fingers weren't closed over it."

"Put there afterward," said Japp; "that's clear enough." He was examining the weapon. "One cartridge fired. We'll test it for fingerprints, but I doubt if we'll find any but yours, Dr. Giles. How long has he been dead?"

"Sometime last night. I can't give the time to an hour or so, as those wonderful doctors in detective stories do. Roughly, he's been dead about twelve hours."

So far, Poirot had not made a move of any kind. He had remained by my side, watching Japp at work and listening to his questions. Only, from time to time, he had sniffed the air very delicately and as if puzzled. I too had sniffed but could detect nothing to arouse interest. The air seemed perfectly fresh and devoid of odor. And yet, from time to time, Poirot continued to sniff it dubiously, as though his keener nose detected something I had missed.

Now, as Japp moved away from the body, Poirot knelt down by it. He took no interest in the wound. I thought at first that he was examining the fingers of the hand that had held the pistol, but in a minute I saw that it was a handkerchief carried in the coat sleeve that interested him. Mr. Protheroe was dressed in a dark-grey lounge suit. Finally Poirot got up from his knees, but his eyes still strayed back to the handkerchief as though puzzled.

Japp called to him to come and help to lift the door. Seizing my opportunity, I too knelt down and, taking the handkerchief from the sleeve, scrutinized it minutely. It was a perfectly plain handkerchief of white cambric; there was no mark or stain on it of any kind. I replaced it, shaking my head and confessing myself baffled.

The others had raised the door. I realized that they were hunting for the key. They looked in vain.

"That settles it," said Japp. "The window's shut and bolted. The murderer left by the door, locking it and taking the key with him. He thought it would be accepted that Protheroe had locked himself in and shot himself and that the absence of the key would not be noticed. You agree, Monsieur Poirot?"

"I agree, yes; but it would have been simpler and better to slip the key back inside the room under the door. Then it would look as though it had fallen from the lock."

"Ah, well, you can't expect everybody to have the bright ideas that you have. You'd have been a holy terror if you'd taken to crime. Any remarks to make, Monsieur Poirot?"

Poirot, it seemed to me, was somewhat at a loss. He looked round the room and remarked mildly and almost apologetically: "He smoked a lot, this monsieur."

True enough, the grate was filled with cigarette stubs, as was an ash tray that stood on a small table near the big arm-chair.

"He must have got through about twenty cigarettes last night," remarked Japp. Stooping down, he examined the contents of the grate carefully, then transferred his attention to the ash tray. "They're all the same kind," he announced, "and smoked by the same man. There's nothing here, Monsieur Poirot."

"I did not suggest that there was," murmured my friend.

"Ha," cried Japp, "what's this?" He pounced on something bright and glittering that lay on the floor near the dead man. "A broken cuff link. I wonder who this belongs to. Dr. Giles, I'd be obliged if you'd go down and send up the housekeeper."

"What about the Parkers? He's very anxious to leave the house—says he's got urgent business in London."

"I daresay. It'll have to get on without him. By the way things are going, it's likely that there'll be some urgent business down here for him to attend to! Send up the housekeeper, and don't let either of the Parkers give you and Pollard the slip. Did any of the household come in here this morning?"

The doctor reflected.

"No, they stood outside in the corridor while Pollard and I came in?"

"Sure of that?"

"Absolutely certain."

The doctor departed on his mission.

"Good man, that," said Japp approvingly. "Some of these sporting doctors are first-class fellows. Well, I wonder who shot this chap. It looks like one of the three in the house. I hardly suspect the housekeeper. She's had eight years to shoot him in if she wanted to. I wonder who these Parkers are? They're not a prepossessing-looking couple."

Miss Clegg appeared at this juncture. She was a thin, gaunt woman with neat grey hair parted in the middle, very staid and calm in manner. Nevertheless, there was an air of efficiency about her which commanded respect. In answer to Japp's questions, she explained that she had been with the dead man for fourteen years. He had been a generous and considerate master. She had never seen Mr. and Mrs. Parker until three days ago, when they arrived unexpectedly to stay. She was of the opinion that they had asked themselves—the master had certainly not seemed pleased to see them. The cuff links which Japp showed her had not belonged to Mr. Protheroe—she was sure of that. Questioned about the pistol, she said that she believed her master had a weapon of that kind. He kept it locked up. She had seen it once some years ago but could not say whether this was the same one. She had heard no shot last night, but that was not surprising, as it was a big, rambling house, and her rooms and those prepared for the Parkers were at the other end of the building. She did not know what time Mr. Protheroe had gone to bed —he was still up when she retired at half-past nine. It was not his habit to go at once to bed when he went to his room. Usually he would sit up half the night, reading and smoking. He was a great smoker.

Then Poirot interposed a question: "Did your Master sleep with his window open or shut, as a rule?"

Miss Clegg considered.

"It was usually open, at any rate at the top."

"Yet now it is closed. Can you explain that?"

"No, unless he felt a draft and shut it."

Japp asked her a few more questions and then dismissed her. Next he interviewed the Parkers separately. Mrs. Parker was inclined to be hysterical and tearful; Mr. Parker was full of bluster and abuse. He denied that the cuff link was his, but as his wife had previously recognized it, this hardly improved matters for him; and as he had also denied ever having been in Protheroe's room, Japp considered that he had sufficient evidence to apply for a warrant.

Leaving Pollard in charge, Japp bustled back to the village and got into telephonic communication with headquarters. Poirot and I strolled back to the inn.

"You're unusually quiet," I said. "Doesn't the case interest you?"

"*Au contraire,* it interests me enormously. But it puzzles me also."

"The motive is obscure," I said thoughtfully, "but I'm certain that Parker's a bad lot. The case against him seems pretty clear but for the lack of motive, and that may come out later."

"Nothing struck you as being especially significant, although overlooked by Japp?"

I looked at him curiously.

"What have you got up your sleeve, Poirot?"

"What did the dead man have up his sleeve?"

"Oh, that handkerchief!"

"Exactly, the handkerchief."

"A sailor carries his handkerchief in his sleeve," I said thoughtfully.

"An excellent point, Hastings, though not the one I had in mind."

"Anything else?"

"Yes, over and over again I go back to the smell of cigarette smoke."

"I didn't smell any," I cried wonderingly.

"No more did I, *cher ami.*"

I looked earnestly at him. It is so difficult to know when Poirot is pulling one's leg, but he seemed thoroughly in earnest and was frowning to himself.

The inquest took place two days later. In the meantime, other evidence had come to light. A tramp had admitted that he had climbed over the wall into the Leigh House garden, where he often slept in a shed that was left unlocked. He declared that at twelve o'clock he had heard two men quarrelling loudly in a room on the first floor. One was demanding a sum of money; the other was angrily refusing. Concealed behind a bush, he had seen the two men as they passed and repassed the lighted window. One he knew well as being Mr. Protheroe, the owner of the house; the other he identified positively as Mr. Parker.

It was clear now that the Parkers had come to Leigh House to blackmail Protheroe, and when later it was discovered that the dead man's real name was Wendover and that he had been a lieutenant in the Navy and had been concerned in the blowing up of the first-class cruiser *Merrythought*, in 1910, the case seemed to be rapidly clearing. It was supposed that Parker, cognizant of the part Wendover had played, had tracked him down and demanded hush money, which the other refused to pay. In the course of the quarrel, Wendover drew his revolver and Parker snatched it from him and shot him, subsequently endeavoring to give it the appearance of suicide.

Parker was committed for trial, reserving his defense. We had attended the police-court proceedings. As we left, Poirot nodded his head.

"It must be so," he murmured to himself. "Yes, it must be so. I will delay no longer."

He went into the post office and wrote off a note, which he dispatched by special messenger. I did not see to whom it was addressed. Then we returned to the inn where we had stayed on that memorable weekend.

Poirot was restless, going to and from the window.

"I await a visitor," he explained. "It cannot be—surely it cannot be that I am mistaken? No, here she is."

To my utter astonishment, in another minute Miss Clegg walked into the room. She was less calm than usual and was breathing hard, as though she had been running. I saw the fear in her eyes as she looked at Poirot.

"Sit down, mademoiselle," he said kindly. "I guessed rightly, did I not?"

For answer she burst into tears.

"Why did you do it?" asked Poirot gently. "Why?"

"I loved him so," she answered. "I was nursemaid to him when he was a little boy. Oh, be merciful to me!"

"I will do all I can. But you understand that I cannot permit an innocent man to hang—even though he is an unpleasing scoundrel."

She sat up and said in a low voice: "Perhaps in the end I could not have, either. Do whatever must be done."

Then, rising, she hurried from the room.

"Did she shoot him?" I asked, utterly bewildered.

Poirot smiled and shook his head.

"He shot himself. Do you remember that he carried his handkerchief in his *right* sleeve? That showed me that he was left-handed. Fearing exposure, after his stormy interview with Mr. Parker, he shot himself. In the morning Miss Clegg came to call him as usual and found him lying dead. As she has just told us, she had known him from a little boy upward and was filled with fury against the Parkers, who had driven him to this shameful death. She regarded them as murderers, and then suddenly she saw a chance of making them suffer for the deed they had inspired. She alone knew that he was left-handed. She changed the pistol to his right hand, closed and bolted the window, dropped the bit of cuff link she had picked up in one of the downstairs rooms, and went out, locking the door and removing the key."

"Poirot," I said in a burst of enthusiasm, "you are magnificent. All that from the one little clue of the handkerchief!"

"And the cigarette smoke. If the window had been closed, and all those cigarettes smoked, the room ought to have been full of stale tobacco. Instead it was perfectly fresh, so I deduced at once that the window must have been open all night, and only closed in the morning, and that gave me a very interesting line of speculation. I could conceive of no circumstances under which a murderer could want to shut the window. It would be to his advantage to leave it open and pretend that the murderer had escaped that way, if the theory of suicide did not go down. Of course, the tramp's evidence, when I heard it, confirmed my suspicions. He could never have overheard that conversation unless the window had been open."

"Splendid!" I said heartily. "Now, what about some tea?"

"Spoken like a true Englishman," said Poirot with a sigh. "I suppose it is not likely that I could obtain here a glass of *sirop?*"

JANE MARPLE   SPINSTER OF ST. MARY MEAD

Everyone who reads detective stories has admired Agatha Christie's boastful little Belgian of the egg-shaped head and the tireless little grey cells. Less dramatic, but no less effective, is her Jane Marple, who captures her prey as inevitably as Hercule Poirot, but without his fanfare. Aunt Jane is a member of an informal Tuesday Night Club, sitting erect in a grandfather's chair, dressed in a black brocade with a cascade of lace down the front of the bodice. Generally she is knitting something soft and fluffy. The other members of the club are a lawyer, a clergyman, a novelist, an artist, and a retired Scotland Yard commissioner. Each week they discuss a problem, a mystery, and propose its solution.

Miss Marple admits that she may not be clever herself, but her long residence in the little village of St. Mary Mead has given her an insight into human nature. One thing she has learned is that people everywhere are very much the same—even murderers—and whenever an opportunity arises, she is likely to prove it.

Short stories about Jane Marple are found in **The Tuesday Club Murders** and in several of Agatha Christie's miscellaneous collections. And this sharp-witted, vinegary little spinster is the central figure also in such outstanding Christie novels as **A Murder Has Been Announced**.

TAPE-MEASURE MURDER

MISS POLITT took hold of the knocker and rapped politely on the cottage door. After a discreet interval she knocked again. The parcel under her left arm shifted a little as she did so, and she readjusted it. Inside the parcel was Mrs. Spenlow's new green winter dress, ready for fitting. From Miss Politt's left hand dangled a bag of black silk, containing a tape measure, a pincushion, and a large, practical pair of scissors.

Miss Politt was tall and gaunt, with a sharp nose, pursed lips, and meagre iron-grey hair. She hesitated before using the knocker for the third time. Glancing down the street, she saw a figure rapidly approaching. Miss Hartnell, jolly, weather-beaten, fifty-five, shouted out in her usual loud bass voice: "Good afternoon, Miss Politt!"

The dressmaker answered: "Good afternoon, Miss Hartnell." Her voice was excessively thin and genteel in its accents. She had started life as a lady's maid. "Excuse me," she went on, "but do you happen to know if by any chance Mrs. Spenlow isn't at home?"

"Not the least idea," said Miss Hartnell.

"It's rather awkward, you see. I was to fit on Mrs. Spenlow's new dress this afternoon. Three-thirty, she said."

Miss Hartnell consulted her wrist watch. "It's a little past the half-hour now."

"Yes. I have knocked three times, but there doesn't seem to be any answer, so I was wondering if perhaps Mrs. Spenlow might have gone out and forgotten. She doesn't forget appointments as a rule, and she wants the dress to wear the day after tomorrow."

Miss Hartnell entered the gate and walked up the path to join Miss Politt outside the door of Laburnam Cottage.

"Why doesn't Gladys answer the door?" she demanded. "Oh, no, of course, it's Thursday—Gladys's day out. I expect Mrs. Spenlow has fallen asleep. I don't expect you've made enough noise with this thing."

Seizing the knocker, she executed a deafening *rat-a-tat-tat* and, in addition, thumped upon the panels of the door. She also called out in a stentorian voice: "What ho, within there!"

There was no response.

Miss Politt murmured: "Oh, I think Mrs. Spenlow must have forgotten and gone out. I'll call round some other time." She began edging away down the path.

"Nonsense," said Miss Hartnell firmly. "She can't have gone out. I'd have met her. I'll just take a look through the windows and see if I can find any signs of life."

She laughed in her usual hearty manner, to indicate that it was a joke, and applied a perfunctory glance to the nearest windowpane—perfunctory because she knew quite well that the front room was seldom used, Mr. and Mrs. Spenlow preferring the small back sitting room.

Perfunctory as it was, though, it succeeded in its object. Miss Hartnell, it is true, saw no signs of life. On the contrary, she saw, through the window, Mrs. Spenlow lying on the hearthrug—dead.

"Of course," said Miss Hartnell, telling the story afterwards, "I managed to keep my head. That Politt creature wouldn't have had the least idea of what to do. 'Got to keep our heads,' I said to her. '*You* stay here and I'll go for Constable Palk.' She said something about not wanting to be left, but I paid no attention at all. One has to be firm with that sort of person. I've always found they enjoy making a fuss. So I was just going off when, at that very moment, Mr. Spenlow came round the corner of the house."

Here Miss Hartnell made a significant pause. It enabled her audience to ask breathlessly: "Tell me, how did he *look?*" Miss Hartnell would then go on: "Frankly, I suspected something at once! He was *far* too calm. He didn't seem surprised in the least. And you may say what you like, it isn't natural for a man to hear that his wife is dead and display no emotion whatever."

Everybody agreed with this statement.

The police agreed with it, too. So suspicious did they consider Mr. Spenlow's detachment that they lost no time in ascertaining how that gentleman was situated as a result of his wife's death. When they discovered that Mrs. Spenlow had been the monied partner, and that her money went to her husband under a will made soon after their marriage, they were more suspicious than ever.

Miss Marple, that sweet-faced (and some said vinegar-tongued) elderly spinster who lived in the house next to the rectory, was interviewed very early—within half an hour of the discovery of the crime. She was approached by Police Constable Palk, importantly thumbing a notebook. "If you don't mind, ma'am, I've a few questions to ask you."

Miss Marple said: "In connection with the murder of Mrs. Spenlow?"

Palk was startled. "May I ask, madam, how you got to know of it?"

"The fish," said Miss Marple.

The reply was perfectly intelligible to Constable Palk. He assumed correctly that the fishmonger's boy had brought it, together with Miss Marple's evening meal.

Miss Marple continued gently: "Lying on the floor in the sitting room, strangled—possibly by a very narrow belt. But whatever it was, it was taken away."

Palk's face was wrathful. "How that young Fred gets to know everything——"

Miss Marple cut him short adroitly. She said: "There's a pin in your tunic."

Constable Palk looked down, startled. He said: "They do say: 'See a pin and pick it up, all the day you'll have good luck.'"

"I hope that will come true. Now what is it you want me to tell you?"

Constable Palk cleared his throat, looked important, and consulted his notebook. "Statement was made to me by Mr. Arthur Spenlow, husband of the deceased. Mr. Spenlow says that at two-thirty, as far as he can say, he was rung up by Miss Marple and asked if he would come over at a quarter past three, as she was anxious to consult him about something. Now, ma'am, is that true?"

"Certainly not," said Miss Marple.

"You did not ring up Mr. Spenlow at two-thirty?"

"Neither at two-thirty nor any other time."

"Ah," said Constable Palk, and sucked his moustache with a good deal of satisfaction.

"What else did Mr. Spenlow say?"

"Mr. Spenlow's statement was that he came over here as requested, leaving his own house at ten minutes past three; that on arrival here he was informed by the maid-servant that Miss Marple was 'not at 'ome.' "

"That part of it is true," said Miss Marple. "He did come here, but I was at a meeting at the Women's Institute."

"Ah," said Constable Palk again.

Miss Marple exclaimed: "Do tell me, Constable, do you suspect Mr. Spenlow?"

"It's not for me to say at this stage, but it looks to me as though somebody, naming no names, had been trying to be artful."

Miss Marple said thoughtfully: "Mr. Spenlow?"

She liked Mr. Spenlow. He was a small, spare man, stiff and conventional in speech, the acme of responsibility. It seemed odd that he should have come to live in the country; he had so clearly lived in towns all his life. To Miss Marple he confided the reason. He said: "I have always intended, ever since I was a small boy, to live in the country someday and have a garden of my own. I have always been very much attached to flowers. My wife, you know, kept a flower shop. That's where I saw her first."

A dry statement, but it opened up a vista of romance. A younger, prettier Mrs. Spenlow, seen against a background of flowers.

Mr. Spenlow, however, really knew nothing about flowers. He had no idea of seeds, of cuttings, of bedding out, of annuals or perennials. He had only a vision—a vision of a small cottage garden thickly planted with sweet-smelling, brightly colored blossoms. He had asked, almost pathetically, for instruction, and had noted down Miss Marple's replies to questions in a little book.

He was a man of quiet method. It was, perhaps, because of this trait that the police were interested in him when his wife was found murdered. With patience and perseverance they learned a good deal about the late Mrs. Spenlow—and soon all St. Mary Mead knew it too.

The late Mrs. Spenlow had begun life as a between-maid in a large house. She had left that position to marry the second gardener, and with him had started a flower shop in London. The shop has prospered. Not so the gardener, who before long had sickened and died.

His widow had carried on the shop and enlarged it in an ambitious way. She had continued to prosper. Then she had sold the business at a handsome price and embarked upon matrimony for the second time—with Mr. Spenlow, a middle-aged jeweler who had inherited a small and struggling business. Not long afterwards, they had sold the business and come down to St. Mary Mead.

Mrs. Spenlow was a well-to-do woman. The profits from her florist's establishment she had invested—"under spirit guidance," as she explained to all and sundry. The spirits had advised her with unexpected acumen.

All her investments had prospered, some in quite a sensational fashion. Instead, however, of this increasing her belief in spiritualism, Mrs. Spenlow basely deserted mediums and sittings and made a brief but wholehearted plunge into an obscure religion with Indian affinities which was based on various forms of deep breathing. When, however, she arrived at St. Mary Mead, she had relapsed into a period of orthodox Church-of-England beliefs. She was a good deal at the Vicarage and attended church services with assiduity. She patronized the village shops, took an interest in the local happenings, and played village bridge.

A humdrum, everyday life. And—suddenly—murder.

Colonel Melchett, the chief constable, had summoned Inspector Slack.

Slack was a positive type of man. When he made up his mind, he was sure. He was quite sure now. "Husband did it, sir," he said.

"You think so?"

"Quite sure of it. You've only got to look at him. Guilty as hell. Never showed a sign of grief or emotion. He came back to the house knowing she was dead."

"Wouldn't he at least have tried to act the part of the distracted husband?"

"Not him, sir. Too pleased with himself. Some gentlemen can't act. Too stiff."

"Any other woman in his life?" Colonel Melchett asked.

"Haven't been able to find any trace of one. Of course, he's the artful kind. He'd cover his tracks. As I see it, he was just fed up with his wife. She'd got the money and, I should say, was a trying woman to live with—always taking up some 'ism' or other. He cold-bloodedly decided to do away with her and live comfortably on his own."

"Yes, that could be the case, I suppose."

"Depend upon it, that was it. Made his plans careful. Pretended to get a phone call——"

Melchett interrupted him: "No call been traced?"

"No, sir. That means either that he lied or that the call was put through from a public telephone booth. The only two public phones in the village are at the station and the post office. Post office it certainly wasn't. Mrs. Blade sees everyone who comes in. Station it might be. Train arrives at two twenty-seven and there's a bit of a bustle then. But the main thing is *he* says it was Miss Marple who called him up, and that certainly isn't true. The call didn't come from her house, and she herself was away at the Institute."

"You're not overlooking the possibility that the husband was deliberately got out of the way—by someone who wanted to murder Mrs. Spenlow?"

"You're thinking of young Ted Gerard, aren't you, sir? I've been working on him—what we're up against there is lack of motive. He doesn't stand to gain anything."

"He's an undesirable character, though. Quite a pretty little spot of embezzlement to his credit."

"I'm not saying he isn't a wrong 'un. Still, he did go to his boss and own up to that embezzlement. And his employers weren't wise to it."

"And Oxford Grouper," said Melchett.

"Yes, sir. Became a convert and went off to do the straight thing and own up to having pinched money. I'm not saying, mind you, that it mayn't have been astuteness—he may have thought he was suspected and decided to gamble on honest repentance."

"You have a skeptical mind, Slack," said Colonel Melchett. "By the way, have you talked to Miss Marple at all?"

"What's *she* got to do with it, sir?"

"Oh, nothing. But she hears things, you know. Why don't you go and have a chat with her? She's a very sharp old lady."

Slack changed the subject. "One thing I've been meaning to ask you, sir: That domestic-service job where the deceased started her career—Sir Robert Abercrombie's place. That's where that jewel robbery was—emeralds—worth a packet. Never got them. I've been looking it up—must have happened when the Spenlow woman was there, though she'd have been quite a girl at the time. Don't think she was mixed up in it, do you, sir? Spenlow, you know, was one of those little tuppenny-ha'penny jewelers—just the chap for a fence."

Melchett shook his head. "Don't think there's anything in that. She didn't even know Spenlow at the time. I remember the case. Opinion in police circles was that a son of the house was mixed up in it—Jim Abercrombie—awful young waster. Had a pile of debts, and just after the robbery they were all paid off—some rich woman, so they said, but I don't know— old Abercrombie hedged a bit about the case—tried to call the police off."

"It was just an idea, sir," said Slack.

Miss Marple received Inspector Slack with gratification, especially when she heard that he had been sent by Colonel Melchett.

"Now, really, that is very kind of Colonel Melchett. I didn't know he remembered me."

"He remembers you, all right. Told me that what you

didn't know of what goes on in St. Mary Mead isn't worth knowing."

"Too kind of him, but really I don't know anything at all. About this murder, I mean."

"You know what the talk about it is."

"Of, course—but it wouldn't do, would it, to repeat just idle talk?"

Slack said, with an attempt at geniality: "This isn't an official conversation, you know. It's in confidence, so to speak."

"You mean you really want to know what people are saying? Whether there's any truth in it or not?"

"That's the idea."

"Well, of course, there's been a great deal of talk and speculation. And there are really two distinct camps, if you understand me. To begin with, there are the people who think that the husband did it. A husband or a wife is, in a way, the natural person to suspect, don't you think so?"

"Maybe," said the inspector cautiously.

"Such close quarters, you know. Then, so often, the money angle. I hear that it was Mrs. Spenlow who had the money and therefore Mr. Spenlow does benefit by her death. In this wicked world I'm afraid the most uncharitable assumptions are often justified."

"He comes into a tidy sum, all right."

"Just so. It would seem quite plausible, wouldn't it, for him to strangle her, leave the house by the back, come across the fields to my house, ask for me and pretend he'd had a telephone call from me, then go back and find his wife murdered in his absence—hoping, of course, that the crime would be put down to some tramp or burglar."

The inspector nodded. "What with the money angle—and if they'd been on bad terms lately——"

But Miss Marple interrupted him: "Oh, but they hadn't."

"You know that for a fact?"

"Everyone would have known if they'd quarreled! The maid, Gladys Brent—she'd have soon spread it round the village."

The inspector said feebly, "She mightn't have known," and received a pitying smile in reply.

Miss Marple went on: "And then there's the other school of thought. Ted Gerard. A good-looking young man. I'm afraid, you know, that good looks are inclined to influence one more than they should. Our last curate but one—quite a magical effect! All the girls came to church—evening service as well as morning. And many older women became unusually active in parish work—and the slippers and scarves that were made for him! Quite embarrassing for the poor young man.

"But, let me see, where was I? Oh, yes, this young man, Ted Gerard. Of course, there has been talk about him. He's come down to see her so often. Though Mrs. Spenlow told me herself that he was a member of what I think they call the *Oxford* Group. A religious movement. They are quite sincere and very earnest, I believe, and Mrs. Spenlow was impressed by it all."

Miss Marple took a breath and went on: "And I'm sure there was no reason to believe that there was anything more in it than that, but you know what people are. Quite a lot of people are convinced that Mrs. Spenlow was infatuated with the young man and that she'd lent him quite a lot of money. And it's perfectly true that he was actually seen at the station that day. In the train—the two twenty-seven down train. But of course it would be quite easy, wouldn't it, to slip out of the other side of the train and go through the cutting and over the fence and round by the hedge and never come out of the station entrance at all? So that he need not have been seen going to the cottage. And of course people do think that what Mrs. Spenlow was wearing was rather peculiar."

"Peculiar?"

"A kimono. Not a dress." Miss Marple blushed. "That sort of thing, you know, is, perhaps, rather suggestive to some people."

"You think it was suggestive?"

"Oh, no, *I* don't think so. I think it was perfectly natural."

"You think it was natural?"

"Under the circumstances, yes." Miss Marple's glance was cool and reflective.

Inspector Slack said: "It might give us another motive for the husband. Jealousy."

"Oh, no, Mr. Spenlow would never be jealous. He's not the sort of man who notices things. If his wife had gone away and left a note on the pincushion, it would be the first he'd know of anything of that kind."

Inspector Slack was puzzled by the intent way she was looking at him. He had an idea that all her conversation was intended to hint at something he didn't understand. She said now, with some emphasis: "Didn't *you* find any clues, Inspector—on the spot?"

"People don't leave fingerprints and cigarette ash nowadays, Miss Marple."

"But this, I think," she suggested, "was an old-fashioned crime——"

Slack said sharply: "Now what do you mean by that?"

Miss Marple remarked slowly: "I think, you know, that Constable Palk could help you. He was the first person on the—on the 'scene of the crime,' as they say."

Mr. Spenlow was sitting in a deck chair. He looked bewildered. He said, in his thin, precise voice: "I may, of course, be imagining what occurred. My hearing is not as good as it was. But I distinctly think I heard a small boy call after me, 'Yah, who's a Crippen?' It—it conveyed the impression to me that he was of the opinion that I had—had killed my dear wife."

Miss Marple, gently snipping off a dead rose head, said: "That was the impression he meant to convey, no doubt."

"But what could possibly have put such an idea into a child's head?"

Miss Marple coughed. "Listening, no doubt, to the opinions of his elders."

"You—you really mean that other people think that also?"

"Quite half the people in St. Mary Mead."

"But—my dear lady—what can possibly have given rise to such an idea? I was sincerely attached to my wife. She did not, alas, take to living in the country as much as I had hoped she would do, but perfect agreement on every subject is an impossible ideal. I assure you I feel her loss very keenly."

"Probably. But if you will excuse my saying so, you don't sound as though you do."

Mr. Spenlow drew his meagre frame up to its full height. "My dear lady, many years ago I read of a certain Chinese philosopher who, when his dearly loved wife was taken from him, continued calmly to beat a gong in the street—a customary Chinese pastime, I presume—exactly as usual. The people of the city were much impressed by his fortitude."

"But," said Miss Marple, "the people of St. Mary Mead react rather differently. Chinese philosophy does not appeal to them."

"But you understand?"

Miss Marple nodded. "My Uncle Henry," she explained, "was a man of unusual self-control. His motto was 'Never display emotion.' He, too, was very fond of flowers."

"I was thinking," said Mr. Spenlow with something like eagerness, "that I might, perhaps, have a pergola on the west side of the cottage. Pink roses and, perhaps, wisteria. And there is a white starry flower, whose name for the moment escapes me——"

In the tone in which she spoke to her grandnephew, aged three, Miss Marple said: "I have a very nice catalogue here, with pictures. Perhaps you would like to look through it—I have to go up to the village."

Leaving Mr. Spenlow sitting happily in the garden with his catalogue, Miss Marple went up to her room, hastily rolled up a dress in a piece of brown paper, and leaving the house, walked briskly up to the post office. Miss Politt, the dressmaker, lived in rooms over the post office.

But Miss Marple did not at once go through the door and up the stairs. It was just two-thirty, and, a minute late, the Much Benham bus drew up outside the post-office door. It was one of the events of the day in St. Mary Mead. The post-mistress hurried out with parcels, parcels connected with the shop side of her business, for the post office also dealt in sweets, cheap books, and children's toys.

For some four minutes Miss Marple was alone in the post office.

Not till the postmistress returned to her post did Miss Marple go upstairs and explain to Miss Politt that she wanted her old grey crepe altered and made more fashionable if that were possible. Miss Politt promised to see what she could do.

The chief constable was rather astonished when Miss Marple's name was brought to him. She came in with many apologies. "So sorry—so very sorry to disturb you. You are so busy, I know, but then you have always been so very kind, Colonel Melchett, and I felt I would rather come to you instead of to Inspector Slack. For one thing, you know, I should hate Constable Palk to get into any trouble. Strictly speaking, I suppose he shouldn't have touched anything at all."

Colonel Melchett was slightly bewildered. He said: "Palk? That's the St. Mary Mead constable, isn't it? What has he been doing?"

"He picked up a pin, you know. It was in his tunic. And it occurred to me at the time that it was quite probable he had actually picked it up in Mrs. Spenlow's house."

"Quite, quite. But, after all, you know, what's a pin? Matter of fact he did pick the pin up just by Mrs. Spenlow's body.

"Came and told Slack about it yesterday—you put him up to that, I gather? Oughtn't to have touched anything, of course, but, as I said, what's a pin? It was only a common pin. Sort of thing any woman might use."

"Oh, no, Colonel Melchett, that's where you're wrong. To a man's eye, perhaps, it looked like an ordinary pin, but it wasn't. It was a special pin, a very thin pin, the kind you buy by the box, the kind used mostly by dressmakers."

Melchett stared at her, a faint light of comprehension breaking in on him. Miss Marple nodded her head several times eagerly.

"Yes, of course. It seems to me so obvious. She was in her

kimono because she was going to try on her new dress, and
she went into the front room, and Miss Politt just said something about measurements and put the tape measure round
her neck—and then all she'd have to do was to cross it and
pull—quite easy, so I've heard. And then of course she'd go
outside and pull the door to and stand there knocking as
though she'd just arrived. But the pin shows she'd *already
been in the house.*"

"And it was Miss Politt who telephoned to Spenlow?"

"Yes. From the post office at two-thirty—just when the
bus comes and the post office would be empty."

Colonel Melchett said: "But my dear Miss Marple, why?
In heaven's name, why? You can't have a murder without a
motive."

"Well, I think, you know, Colonel Melchett, from all I've
heard, that the crime dates from a long time back. It reminds
me, you know, of my two cousins, Antony and Gordon.
Whatever Antony did always went right for him, and with
poor Gordon it was just the other way about: race horses
went lame, and stocks went down, and property depreciated.
. . . As I see it, the two women were in it together."

"In what?"

"The robbery. Long ago. Very valuable emeralds, so I've
heard. The lady's maid and the tweeny. Because one thing
hasn't been explained—how, when the tweeny married the
gardner, did they have enough money to set up a flower shop?

"The answer is, it was her share of the—the swag, I think
is the right expression. Everything she did turned out well.
Money made money. But the other one, the lady's maid,
must have been unlucky. She came down to being just a village dressmaker. Then they met again. Quite all right at first,
I expect, until Mr. Ted Gerard came on the scene.

"Mrs. Spenlow, you see, was already suffering from con-
science and was inclined to be emotionally religious. This
young man no doubt urged her to 'face up' and to 'come
clean' and I daresay she was strung up to do so. But Miss
Politt didn't see it that way. All she saw was that she might
go to prison for a robbery she had committed years ago. So
she made up her mind to put a stop to it all. I'm afraid, you

know, that she was always rather a wicked woman. I don't believe she'd have turned a hair if that nice, stupid Mr. Spenlow had been hanged."

Colonel Melchett said slowly: "We can—er—verify your theory—up to a point. The identity of the Politt woman with the lady's maid at the Abercrombies', but——"

Miss Marple reassured him.

"It will be all quite easy. She's the kind of woman who will break down at once when she's taxed with the truth. And then, you see, I've got her tape measure. I—er—abstracted it yesterday when I was trying on. When she misses it and thinks the police have got it—well, she's quite an ignorant woman and she'll think it will prove the case against her in some way."

She smiled at him encouragingly. "You'll have no trouble, I can assure you." It was the tone in which his favorite aunt had once assured him that he could not fail to pass his entrance examination into Sandhurst.

And he had passed.

THE BLUE GERANIUM

"WHEN I WAS DOWN HERE last year——" said Sir Henry Clithering, and stopped.

His hostess, Mrs. Bantry, looked at him curiously.

The ex-Commissioner of Scotland Yard was staying with old friends of his, Colonel and Mrs. Bantry, who lived near St. Mary Mead.

Mrs. Bantry, pen in hand, had just asked his advice as to who should be invited to make a sixth guest at dinner that evening.

"Yes," said Mrs. Bantry encouragingly. "When you were here last year?"

"Tell me," said Sir Henry, "do you know a Miss Marple?"

Mrs. Bantry was surprised. It was the last thing she had expected.

"Know Miss Marple? Who doesn't! The typical old maid of fiction. Quite a dear, but hopelessly behind the times. Do you mean you would like me to ask *her* to dinner?"

"You are surprised?"

"A little, I must confess. I should hardly have thought you —but perhaps there's an explanation?"

"The explanation is simple enough. When I was down here last year we got into the habit of discussing unsolved mysteries—there were five or six of us—Raymond West, the novelist, started it. We each supplied a story to which we knew the answer, but nobody else did. It was supposed to be an exercise in the deductive faculties—to see who could get nearest the truth."

"Well?"

"Like in the old story—we hardly realized that Miss Marple was playing; but we were very polite about it—

didn't want to hurt the old dear's feelings. And now comes the cream of the jest. The old lady outdid us every time!"

"What?"

"I assure you—straight to the truth like a homing pigeon."

"But how extraordinary! Why, dear old Miss Marple has hardly ever been out of St. Mary Mead."

"Ah! But according to her, that has given her unlimited opportunities of observing human nature—under the microscope, as it were."

"I suppose there's something in that," conceded Mrs. Bantry. "One would at least know the petty side of people. But I don't think we have any really exciting criminals in our midst. I think we must try her with Arthur's ghost story after dinner. I'd be thankful if she'd find a solution to that."

"I didn't know that Arthur believed in ghosts."

"Oh, he doesn't. That's what worries him so. And it happened to a friend of his, George Pritchard—a most prosaic person. It's really rather tragic for poor George. Either this extraordinary story is true—or else——"

"Or else what?"

Mrs. Bantry did not answer. After a minute or two she said irrelevantly, "You know, I like George—everyone does. One can't believe that he—but people do do such extraordinary things."

Sir Henry nodded. He knew, better than Mrs. Bantry, the extraordinary things that people did.

So it came about that evening that Mrs. Bantry looked around her dinner table (shivering a little as she did so, because the dining room, like most English dining rooms, was extremely cold) and fixed her gaze on the very upright old lady sitting on her husband's right. Miss Marple wore black lace mittens; an old lace fichu was draped round her shoulders and another piece of lace surmounted her white hair. She was talking animatedly to the elderly doctor, Dr. Lloyd, about the workhouse and the suspected shortcomings of the district nurse.

Mrs. Bantry marvelled anew. She even wondered whether Sir Henry had been making an elaborate joke—but there seemed no point in that. Incredible that what he had said could really be true.

Her glance went on and rested affectionately on her red-faced, broad-shouldered husband as he sat talking horses to Jane Helier, the beautiful and popular actress. Jane, more beautiful (if that were possible) off the stage than on, opened enormous blue eyes and murmured at discreet intervals: "Really?" "Oh fancy!" "How extraordinary!" She knew nothing whatever about horses and cared less.

"Arthur," said Mrs. Bantry, "you're boring poor Jane to distraction. Leave horses alone and tell her your ghost story instead. You know . . . George Pritchard."

"Eh, Dolly? Oh, but I don't know——"

"Sir Henry wants to hear it too. I was telling him something about it this morning. It would be interesting to hear what everyone has to say about it."

"Oh, do!" said Jane. "I love ghost stories."

"Well——" Colonel Bantry hesitated. "I've never believed much in the supernatural. But this——

"I don't think any of you know George Pritchard. He's one of the best. His wife—well, she's dead now, poor woman. I'll just say this much: she didn't give George any too easy a time when she was alive. She was one of those semi-invalids—I believe she really had something wrong with her, but whatever it was she played it for all it was worth. She was capricious, exacting, unreasonable. She complained from morning to night. George was expected to wait on her hand and foot, and every thing he did was always wrong and he got cursed for it. Most men, I'm fully convinced, would have hit her over the head with a hatchet long ago. Eh, Dolly, isn't that so?"

"She was a dreadful woman," said Mrs. Bantry with conviction. "If George Pritchard had brained her with a hatchet, and there had been any woman on the jury, he would have been triumphantly acquitted."

"I don't quite know how this business started. George was rather vague about it. I gather Mrs. Pritchard had always had a weakness for fortunetellers, palmists, clairvoyants—anything of that sort. George didn't mind. If she found amusement in it, well and good. But he refused to go into rhapsodies himself, and that was another grievance.

"A succession of hospital nurses was always passing through the house, Mrs. Pritchard usually becoming dissatisfied with them after a few weeks. One young nurse had been very keen on this fortunetelling stunt, and for a time Mrs. Pritchard had been extremely fond of her. Then she suddenly fell out with her and insisted on her going. She had back another nurse who had been with her previously—an older woman, experienced and tactful in dealing with a neurotic patient. Nurse Copling according to George, was a very good sort—a sensible woman to talk to. She put up with Mrs. Pritchard's tantrums and nerve-storms with complete indifference.

"Mrs. Pritchard always lunched upstairs, and it was usual at lunch time for George and the nurse to come to some arrangement for the afternoon. Strictly speaking, the nurse went off from two to four, but 'to oblige,' as the phrase goes, she would sometimes take her time off after tea if George wanted to be free for the afternoon. On this occasion she mentioned that she was going to see a sister at Golders Green and might be a little late returning. George's face fell, for he had arranged to play a round of golf. Nurse Copling, however, reassured him.

" 'We'll neither of us be missed, Mr. Pritchard.' A twinkle came into her eye. 'Mrs. Pritchard's going to have more exciting company than ours.'

" 'Who's that?'

" 'Wait a minute.' Nurse Copling's eye twinkled more than ever. 'Let me get it right. *Zarida, Psychic Reader of the Future.*'

" 'Oh, Lord!' groaned George. 'That's a new one, isn't it?'

" 'Quite new. I believe my predecessor, Nurse Carstairs, sent her along. Mrs. Pritchard hasn't seen her yet. She made me write, fixing an appointment for this afternoon.'

" 'Well, at any rate, I shall get my golf,' said George, and he went off with the kindliest feelings toward Zarida, the Reader of the Future.

"On his return to the house, he found Mrs. Pritchard in a

state of great agitation. She was, as usual, lying on her invalid couch, and she had a bottle of smelling salts in her hand which she sniffed at frequent intervals.

" 'George,' she exclaimed. 'What did I tell you about this house? The moment I came into it, *I felt* there was something wrong! Didn't I tell you so at the time?'

"Repressing his desire to reply, 'You always do,' George said, 'No, can't say I remember it.'

" 'You never do remember anything that has to do with me. Men are all extraordinarily callous—but I really believe that you are more insensitive than most.'

" 'Oh, come now, Mary dear, that's not fair.'

" 'Well, as I was telling you, this woman *knew* at once! She—she actually blenched—if you know what I mean—as she came in at that door, and she said, "There is evil here—evil and danger. I feel it." '

"Very unwisely, George laughed.

" 'Well, you have had your money's worth this afternoon.'

"His wife closed her eyes and took a long sniff from her smelling bottle.

" 'How you hate me! You would jeer and laugh if I were dying.'

"George protested and after a minute or two she went on.

" 'You may laugh, but I shall tell you the whole thing. This house is definitely dangerous to me—the woman said so.'

"George's formerly kind feeling toward Zarida underwent a change. He knew his wife was perfectly capable of insisting on moving to a new house if the caprice got hold of her.

" 'What else did she say?' he asked.

" 'She couldn't tell me very much. She was so upset. One thing she did say. I had some violets in a glass. She pointed at them and cried out. 'Take those away. No blue flowers—never have blue flowers. *Blue flowers are fatal to you—remember that.*'

" 'And you know,' added Mrs. Pritchard, 'I always have told you that blue as a color is repellent to me. I feel a natural instinctive sort of warning against it.'

"George was much too wise to remark that he had never heard her say so before. Instead, he asked what the mysterious Zarida was like. Mrs. Pritchard entered with gusto upon a description.

" 'Black hair in coiled knobs over her ears—her eyes were half closed—great black rims round them—she had a black veil over her mouth and chin—she spoke in a kind of singing voice with a marked foreign accent—Spanish, I think——'

" 'In fact, all the usual stock in trade,' said George cheerfully.

"His wife immediately closed her eyes.

" 'I feel extremely ill,' she said. 'Ring for nurse. Unkindness upsets me, as you know only too well.'

"It was two days later that Nurse Copling came to George with a grave face.

" 'Will you come to Mrs. Pritchard, please? She has had a letter which upsets her greatly.'

"He found his wife with the letter in her hand. She held it out to him.

" 'Read it,' she said.

"George read it. It was on heavily scented paper, and the writing was big and black.

" '*I have seen the Future. Be warned before it is too late. Beware of the full moon. The Blue Primrose means Warning; the Blue Hollyhock means Danger; the Blue Geranium means Death. . . .*'

"Just about to burst out laughing, George caught Nurse Copling's eye. She made a quick warning gesture. He said rather awkwardly, 'The woman's probably trying to frighten you, Mary. Anyway, there aren't such things as blue primroses and blue geraniums.'

"But Mrs. Pritchard began to cry and say her days were numbered. Nurse Copling came out with George upon the landing.

" 'Of all the silly tomfoolery,' he burst out.

" 'I suppose it is.'

"Something in the nurse's tone struck him, and he stared at her in amazement.

" 'Surely, nurse, you don't believe——'

" 'No, no, Mr. Pritchard. I don't believe in reading the future—that's nonsense. What puzzles me is the *meaning* of this. Fortunetellers are usually out for what they can get. But this woman seems to be frightening Mrs. Pritchard with no advantage to herself. I can't see the point. There's another thing——'

" 'Yes?'

" 'Mrs. Pritchard says that something about Zarida was faintly familiar to her.'

" 'Well?'

" 'Well, I don't like it, Mr. Pritchard, that's all.'

" 'I didn't know you were so superstitious, nurse.'

" 'I'm not superstitious; but I know when a thing is fishy.'

"It was about four days after this that the first incident happened. To explain it to you, I shall have to describe Mrs. Pritchard's room——"

"You'd better let me do that," interrupted Mrs. Bantry. "It was papered with one of these new wallpapers where you apply clumps of flowers to make a kind of herbaceous border. The effect is almost like being in a garden—though, of course, the flowers are all wrong; I mean they simply couldn't be in bloom all at the same time——"

"Don't let a passion for horticultural accuracy run away with you, Dolly," said her husband. "We all know you're an enthusiastic gardener."

"Well, it *is* absurd," protested Mrs. Bantry. "To have bluebells and daffodils and lupins and hollyhocks and Michaelmas daisies all grouped into a tangle together."

"Most unscientific," said Colonel Bantry. "But to proceed with the story. . . . Among these massed flowers were primroses—clumps of yellow and pink primroses. Well, one morning Mrs. Pritchard rang her bell violently and the household came running—thought she was *in extremis*. But not at all. She was terribly excited and pointing to the wallpaper; and there, sure enough, was *one blue primrose* in the midst of the others . . ."

"Oh," said Miss Helier, "how creepy!"

"The question was: hadn't the blue primrose always been

there? That was George's suggestion and the nurse's. But Mrs. Pritchard wouldn't have it. She had never noticed it till that very morning and the night before had been full moon. She was very upset about it."

"I met George Pritchard that same day and he told me about it," said Mrs. Bantry. "I went to see Mrs. Pritchard and did my best to ridicule the whole thing, but without success. I came away really concerned, and I remember I met Jean Instow and told her about it. Jean is a queer girl. She said, 'So she's really upset about it?' I told her that I thought the woman was perfectly capable of dying of fright, that she was really abnormally superstitious.

"I remember Jean rather startled me with what she said next. She said, 'Well, that might be all for the best, mightn't it?' And she said it so coolly, in so matter-of-fact a tone that I was really—well, shocked. Of course, I know it's done nowadays—to be brutal and outspoken; but I never get used to it. Jean smiled at me rather oddly and said, 'You don't like my saying that—but it's true. What use is Mrs. Pritchard's life to her? None at all; and it's hell for George Pritchard. To have his wife frightened out of existence would be the best thing that could happen to him.' I said, 'George is most awfully good to her always.' And she said, 'Yes, he deserves a reward, poor dear. He's a very attractive person, George Pritchard. The last nurse thought so—the pretty one —what was her name? Carstairs. That was the cause of the row between her and Mrs. P.'

"Now I didn't like hearing Jean say that. Of course, one had *wondered*——"

"Yes, dear," said Miss Marple placidly. "One always does. Is Miss Instow a pretty girl? I suppose she plays golf?"

"Yes. She's good at all games. And she's attractive-looking, very fair, with a healthy skin and nice steady blue eyes. Of course, we always have felt that she and George Pritchard—I mean if things had been different—they are so well suited to one another."

"And they were friends?" asked Miss Marple.

"Oh, yes. Great friends."

"Do you think, Dolly," said Colonel Bantry plaintively, "that I might be allowed to go on with my story?"

"Arthur," said Mrs. Bantry resignedly, "wants to get back to his ghosts."

"I had the rest of the story from George himself," went on the colonel. "There's no doubt that Mrs. Pritchard got the wind up badly toward the end of the next month. She marked off on a calendar the day when the moon would be full, and on that night she had both the nurse and then George into her room and made them study the wallpaper carefully. There were pink hollyhocks and red ones, but there were no blue ones. Then when George left the room she locked the door——"

"And in the morning there was a large blue hollyhock," said Miss Helier joyfully.

"Quite right," said Colonel Bantry. "Or, at any rate, nearly right. One flower of a hollyhock just above her head had turned blue. It staggered George; and of course the more it staggered him the more he refused to take the thing seriously. He insisted that the whole thing was some kind of practical joke. He ignored the evidence of the locked door and the fact that Mrs. Pritchard discovered the change before anyone—even Nurse Copling—was admitted into her bedroom.

"As I say, it staggered George, and it made him unreasonable. His wife wanted to leave the house, and he wouldn't let her. He was inclined to believe in the supernatural for the first time, but he wasn't going to admit it. He usually gave in to his wife, but this time he just wouldn't. Mary was not to make a fool of herself, he said. The whole thing was the most infernal nonsense.

"And so the next month sped away. Mrs. Pritchard made less protest than one would have imagined. I think she was superstitious enough to believe that she couldn't escape her fate. She repeated again and again, 'The blue primrose—warning. The blue hollyhock—danger. The blue geranium—*death*.' And she would lie there looking at the clump of pinky-red geraniums nearest her bed.

"The whole business was pretty nervy. Even the nurse

caught the infection. She came to George two days before full moon and begged him to take Mrs. Pritchard away. George was angry.

"If all the flowers on that damned wall turned into blue devils it couldn't kill anyone!' he shouted.

" 'It might. Shock has killed people before.'

" 'Nonsense,' said George.

"George has always been a shade pigheaded. You can't drive him. I believe he had a secret idea that his wife worked the changes herself and that it was all some morbid hysterical plan of hers.

"Well, the fatal night came. Mrs. Pritchard locked her door as usual. She was very calm—in almost an exalted state of mind. The nurse was worried by her state and wanted to give her a stimulant—an injection of strychnine—but Mrs. Pritchard refused. In a way, I believe, she was enjoying herself. George said she was."

"I think that's quite possible," said Mrs. Bantry. "There must have been a strange sort of glamor about the whole thing."

"There was no violent ringing of a bell the next morning. Mrs. Pritchard usually woke about eight. When, at eight-thirty, there was no sign from her, nurse rapped loudly on the door. Getting no reply, she fetched George and insisted on the door being broken open. They did so with the help of a chisel.

"One look at the still figure on the bed was enough for Nurse Copling. She sent George to telephone for the doctor, but it was too late. Mrs. Pritchard, the doctor said, must have been dead at least eight hours. Her smelling salts lay by her hand on the bed, *and on the wall beside her one of the pinky-red geraniums was a bright deep blue*."

"Horrible," said Miss Heiler with a shiver.

Sir Henry was frowning.

"No additional details?"

Colonel Bantry shook his head, but Mrs. Bantry spoke quickly.

"The gas."

"What about the gas?" asked Sir Henry.

"When the doctor arrived there was a slight smell of gas, and sure enough he found the gas ring in the fireplace very slightly turned on; but so little that it couldn't have mattered."

"Did Mr. Pritchard and the nurse not notice it when they first went in?"

"The nurse said she did notice a slight smell. George said he didn't notice gas, but something made him feel queer; but he put that down to shock—and probably it was. At any rate, there was no question of gas poisoning. The smell was scarcely noticeable."

"And that's the end of the story?"

"No, it isn't. One way and another, there was a lot of talk. The servants, you see, had overheard things—had heard, for instance, Mrs. Pritchard telling her husband that he hated her and would jeer if she were dying. And also more recent remarks. She said one day, apropos of his refusing to leave the house, 'Very well, when I am dead, I hope everyone will realize that you have killed me.' And as ill luck would have it, he had been mixing some weed killer for the garden paths the very day before. One of the younger servants had seen him and had afterward observed his taking up a glass of hot milk to his wife.

"The talk spread and grew. The doctor had given a certificate—I don't know exactly in what terms—shock, syncope, heart failure, probably some medical term meaning nothing much. However, the poor lady had not been a month in her grave before the exhumation order was applied for and granted."

"And the result of the autopsy was nil, I remember," said Sir Henry gravely.

"The whole thing is really very curious," said Mrs. Bantry. "That fortuneteller, for instance—Zardia. At the address where she was supposed to be, no one had ever heard of any such person!"

"She appeared once—out of the blue," said her husband, "and then utterly vanished."

"And what is more," continued Mrs. Bantry, "little Nurse Carstairs, who was supposed to have recommended her, had never even heard of her."

"It's a mysterious story," said Dr. Lloyd. "One can make guesses; but to guess——"

He shook his head.

"Has Mr. Pritchard married Miss Instow?" asked Miss Marple in her gentle voice.

"Now why do you ask that?" inquired Sir Henry.

Miss Marple opened gentle blue eyes.

"It seems to me so important," she said. "Have they married?"

Colonel Bantry shook his head.

"We—well, we expected something of the kind—but it's eighteen months now. I don't believe they even see much of each other."

"That is important," said Miss Marple. "Very important."

"Then you think the same as I do," said Mrs. Bantry.

"Now, Dolly," said her husband. "It's unjustifiable—what you're going to say. You can't go about accusing people."

"Don't be so—so manly, Arthur. Men are always afraid to say *anything*. Anyway, this is all between ourselves. It's just a wild fantastic idea of mine that possibly—only *possibly*—Jean Instow disguised herself as a fortuneteller. Mind you, she may have done it for a joke. I don't for a minute think she meant any harm; but if she did do it, and if Mrs. Pritchard was foolish enough to die of fright—well, that's what Miss Marple meant, wasn't it?"

"No, dear, not quite," said Miss Marple. "You see, if I were going to kill anyone—which of course, I wouldn't dream of doing for a minute, because it would be very wicked, and besides, I don't like killing—not even wasps, though I know it has to be, and I'm sure the gardener does it as humanely as possible. Let me see, what was I saying?"

"If you wished to kill anyone," prompted Sir Henry.

"Oh yes. Well, if I did, I shouldn't be at all satisfied to trust to *fright*. I know one reads of people dying of it, but it seems a very uncertain sort of thing, and the most nervous people are far more brave than one really thinks they are.

I should like something definite and certain, and make a thoroughly good plan about it."

"Miss Marple," said Sir Henry, "you frighten me. I hope you will never wish to remove me."

Miss Marple looked at him reproachfully.

"I thought I had made it clear that I would never contemplate such wickedness," she said. "No, I was trying to put myself in the place of—er—a certain person."

"Do you mean George Pritchard?" asked Colonel Bantry. "I'll never believe it of George—though, mind you, even the nurse believes it. I went and saw her about a month afterward, at the time of the exhumation. She didn't know how it was done—in fact, she wouldn't say anything at all—but it was clear enough that she believed George to be in some way responsible for his wife's death."

"Well," said Dr. Lloyd, "perhaps she wasn't so far wrong. And mind you, a nurse often *knows*. She's got no proof—but she *knows*."

Sir Henry leaned forward.

"Come now, Miss Marple," he said persuasively. "You're lost in a daydream. Won't you tell us all about it?"

Miss Marple started and turned pink.

"I beg your pardon," she said. "I was just thinking about our district nurse. A most difficult problem."

"More difficult than the problem of a blue geranium?"

"It really depends on the primroses," said Miss Marple. "I mean, Mrs. Bantry said they were yellow and pink. If it was a pink primrose that turned blue, of course, that fits in perfectly. But if it happened to be a yellow one——"

"It was a pink one," said Mrs. Bantry.

She stared. They all stared at Miss Marple.

"Then that seems to settle it," said Miss Marple. She shook her head regretfully. "And the wasp season and everything. And, of course, the gas."

"It reminds you, I suppose, of countless village tragedies?" said Sir Henry.

"Not tragedies," said Miss Marple. "And certainly nothing criminal. But it does remind me a little of the trouble we are having with the district nurse. After all, nurses are human beings, and what with having to be so correct in the behavior and wearing those uncomfortable collars and being so thrown with the family—well, can you wonder that things happen?"

A glimmer of light broke upon Sir Henry.

"You mean Nurse Carstairs?"

"Oh, no. Not Nurse Carstairs. Nurse *Copling*. You see, she had been there before, and very much thrown with Mr. Pritchard, who you say is an attractive man. I daresay she thought, poor thing—well, we needn't go into that. I don't suppose she knew about Miss Instow, and of course afterward, when she found out, it turned her against him and she tried to do all the harm she could. Of course, the letter really gave her away, didn't it?"

"What letter?"

"Well, she wrote to the fortuneteller at Mrs. Pritchard's request, and the fortuneteller came, apparently in answer to the letter. But later it was discovered that there never had been such a person at that address. So that shows that Nurse Copling was in it. She only pretended to write—so what could be more likely than that *she* was the fortuneteller herself?"

"I never saw the point about the letter," said Sir Henry.

"Rather a bold step to take," said Miss Marple, "because Mrs. Pritchard might have recognized her in spite of the disguise—though, of course, if she had, the nurse could have said it was a joke."

"What did you mean," said Sir Henry, "when you said that if you were a certain person you would not have trusted to fright?"

"One couldn't be *sure* that way," said Miss Marple. "No, I think that the warnings and the blue flowers were, if I may use a military term"—she laughed self-consciously—"just *camouflage*."

"And the real thing?"

"I know," said Miss Marple apologetically, "that I've got wasps on the brain. Poor things, destroyed in the thousands —and usually on such a beautiful summer's day. But I remember thinking, when I saw the gardener shaking up the cyanide of potassium in a bottle with water, how like smelling salts it looked. And if it were put in a smelling-salt bottle and substituted for the real one—well, the poor lady was in the habit of using her smelling salts. Indeed, you said they were found by her hand. Then, of course, while Mr. Pritchard went to telephone to the doctor, the nurse would change it for the real bottle, and she'd just turn on the gas a little bit to mask any smell of almonds and in case anyone felt queer, and I always have heard that cyanide leaves no trace if you wait long enough. But, of course, I may be wrong, and it may have been something entirely different in the bottle; but that doesn't really matter, does it?"

Jane Helier leaned forward and said, "But the blue geranium and the other flowers?"

"Nurses always have litmus paper, don't they?" said Miss Marple, "for—well, for testing. Not a very pleasant subject. We won't dwell on it. I have done a little nursing myself." She grew delicately pink. "Blue turns red with acids, and red turns blue with alkalies. So easy to paste some red litmus over a ready flower—near the bed, of course. And then, when the poor lady used her smelling salts, the strong ammonia fumes would turn it blue. Really most ingenious. Of course, the geranium wasn't blue when they first broke into the room—nobody noticed it till afterward. When nurse changed the bottles, she held the Sal Ammoniac against the wallpaper for a minute, I expect."

"You might have been there, Miss Marple," said Sir Henry.

"What worries me," said Miss Marple, "is poor Mr. Pritchard and that nice girl, Miss Instow. Probably both suspecting each other and keeping apart—and life so very short."

She shook her head.

"You needn't worry," said Sir Henry. "As a matter of fact, I have something up my sleeve. A nurse has been arrested on a charge of murdering an elderly patient who had left her a legacy. It was done with cyanide of potassium substituted for smelling salts. Nurse Copling trying the same trick again. Miss Instow and Mr. Pritchard need have no doubts."

"Now isn't that nice?" cried Miss Marple. "I don't mean about the new murder, of course. That's very sad, and shows how much wickedness there is in the world, and that if once you give way—which reminds me I *must* finish my little conversation with Dr. Lloyd about the village nurse."

THE FOUR SUSPECTS

THE CONVERSATION HOVERED round undiscovered and unpunished crimes. Everyone in turn vouchsafed his opinion: Colonel Bantry; his plump, amiable wife; Jane Helier; Dr. Lloyd; and even old Miss Marple. The one person who did not speak was the one best fitted, in most people's opinion, to do so. Sir Henry Clithering, ex-Commissioner of Scotland Yard, sat silent, twisting his mustache—or rather stroking it—and half smiling, as if some inward thought amused him.

"Sir Henry," said Mrs. Bantry at last. "If you don't say something I shall scream. Are there a lot of crimes that go unpunished or are there not?"

"You're thinking of newspaper headlines, Mrs. Bantry. *SCOTLAND YARD AT FAULT AGAIN*. And a list of unsolved mysteries to follow."

"Which really, I suppose, form a very small percentage of the whole?" said Dr. Lloyd.

"Yes, that is so. The hundreds of crimes that are solved and the perpetrators who are punished are seldom heralded and sung. But that isn't quite the point at issue, is it? When you talk of *undiscovered* crimes and *unsolved* crimes, you are talking of two different things. In the first category come all the crimes that Scotland Yard never hears about, the crimes that no one even knows have been committed."

"But I suppose there aren't very many of those?" said Mrs. Bantry.

"Aren't there?"

"Sir Henry! You don't mean there *are?*"

"I should think," said Miss Marple thoughtfully, "that there must be quite a very large number."

The charming old lady, with her old-world unruffled air, made her statement in a tone of the utmost placidity.

"My dear Miss Marple," said Colonel Bantry.

"Of course," said Miss Marple, "a lot of people are stupid. And stupid people get found out, whatever they do. But there are quite a number of people who aren't stupid, and one shudders to think of what they might accomplish unless they had very strongly rooted principles."

"Yes," said Sir Henry, "there are a lot of people who aren't stupid. How often does some crime come to light simply by reason of a bit of unmitigated bungling, and each time one asks oneself the question: If this hadn't been bungled, would anyone ever have known?"

"But that's very serious, Clithering," said Colonel Bantry. "Very serious, indeed."

"Is it?"

"What do you mean? Of course it's serious!"

"You say crime goes unpunished. But does it? Unpunished by the law perhaps; but cause and effect works outside the law. To say that every crime brings its own punishment is by way of being a platitude, and yet in my opinion nothing can be truer."

"Perhaps, perhaps," said Colonel Bantry. "But that doesn't alter the seriousness—the—er—seriousness——"

He paused, rather at a loss.

Sir Henry Clithering smiled.

"Ninety-nine people out of a hundred are doubtless of your way of thinking," he said. "But you know, it isn't really guilt that is important—it's innocence. That's the thing that nobody will realize."

"I don't understand," said Jane Helier.

"I do," said Miss Marple. "When Mrs. Trent found half a crown missing from her bag, the person it affected most was the daily woman, Mrs. Arthur. Of course the Trents thought it was her, but being kindly people and knowing she had a large family and a husband who drinks, well—they naturally didn't want to go to extremes. But they felt differently towards her, and they didn't leave her in charge of the house when they went away, which made a great difference to her; and other people began to get a feeling about her too. And then it suddenly came out that it was the governess. Mrs. Trent saw her through a door reflected in a mirror. The purest chance—though I prefer to call it Providence. And that, I think, is what Sir Henry means. Most people would be only interested in who took the money, and it turned out to be the most unlikely person—just like in detective stories! But the real person it was life and death to was poor Mrs. Arthur, who had done nothing. That's what you mean, isn't it, Sir Henry?"

"Yes, Miss Marple, you've hit on my meaning exactly. Your charwoman person was lucky in the instance you relate. Her innocence was finally proved. But some people may go through a lifetime crushed by the weight of a suspicion that is really unjustified."

"Are you thinking of some particular instance, Sir Henry?" asked Mrs. Bantry shrewdly.

"As a matter of fact, Mrs. Bantry, I am. A very curious case. A case where we believe murder to have been committed, but with no possible chance of ever proving it."

"Poison, I suppose," breathed Jane. "Something untraceable."

Dr. Lloyd moved restlessly and Sir Henry shook his head.

"No, dear lady. *Not* the secret arrow poison of the South American Indians! I wish it *were* something of that kind. We have to deal with something much more prosaic—so prosaic, in fact, that there is no hope of bringing the deed home to its perpetrator. An old gentleman who fell downstairs and broke his neck—one of those regrettable accidents which happen every day."

"But what happened really?"

"Who can say?" Sir Henry shrugged his shoulders. "A push from behind? A piece of string tied across the top of the stairs and carefully removed afterwards? That we shall never know."

"But you do think that it—well, that it wasn't an accident? Why?" asked the doctor.

"That's rather a long story, but—well, yes, we're pretty sure. As I said, there's no chance of being able to bring the deed home to anyone—the evidence would be too flimsy. But there's the other aspect of the case—the one I was speaking about. You see, there were four people who might have done the trick. One's guilty—*but the other three are innocent.* And unless the truth is found out, those three are going to remain under the terrible shadow of doubt."

"I think," said Mrs. Bantry, "that you'd better tell us your long story."

"I needn't make it so very long after all," said Sir Henry. "I can at any rate condense the beginning. That deals with a German secret society—the *Schwartze Hand*—something after the lines of the Camorra or what is most people's idea of the Camorra. A scheme of blackmail and terrorization. The thing started quite suddenly after the war and spread to an amazing extent. Numberless people were victimized by it. The authorities were not successful in coping with it, for its secrets were jealously guarded, and it was almost impossible to find anyone who could be induced to betray them.

"Nothing much was ever known about it in England, but in Germany it was having a most paralyzing effect. It was finally broken up and dispersed through the efforts of one man, a Dr. Rosen, who had at one time been very prominent in Secret Service work. He became a member, penetrated its inmost circle, and was, as I say, instrumental in bringing about its downfall.

"But he was, in consequence, a marked man, and it was deemed wise that he should leave Germany—at any rate for a time. He came to England, and we had letters about him from the police in Berlin. He came and had a personal interview with me. His point of view was both dispassionate and resigned. He had no doubts of what the future held for him.

" 'They will get me, Sir Henry,' he said. 'Not a doubt of it.' He was a big man with a fine head and a very deep voice, with only a slight guttural intonation to tell of his nationality. 'That is a foregone conclusion. It does not matter. I am prepared. I faced the risk when I undertook this business. I have done what I set out to do. The organization can never be put together again. But there are many members of it at liberty and they will take the only revenge they can—my life. It is simply a question of time; but I am anxious that that time should be as long as possible. You see, I am collecting and editing some very interesting material—the result of my life's work. I should like, if possible, to be able to complete my task.'

"He spoke very simply, with a certain grandeur which I could not but admire. I told him we would take all precautions, but he waved my words aside.

" 'Some day, sooner or later, they will get me,' he repeated. 'When that day comes, do not distress yourself. You will, I have no doubt, have done all that is possible.'

"He then proceeded to outline his plans, which were simple enough. He proposed to take a small cottage in the country where he could live quietly and go on with his work. In the end he selected a village in Somerset—King's Gnaton, which was seven miles from a railway station and singularly untouched by civilization. He bought a charming cottage, had various improvements and alterations made, and settled down most contentedly. His household consisted of his niece, Greta, a secretary, and Gertrude, an old German servant who had served him faithfully for nearly forty years, and a handy man and gardener who was a native of King's Gnaton.

"The four suspects," said Dr. Lloyd softly.

"Exactly. The four suspects. There is not much more to tell. Life went on peacefully at King's Gnaton for five months and then the blow fell. Dr. Rosen fell down the stairs one morning and was found dead about half an hour later. At the time the accident must have taken place, Gertrude was in her kitchen with the door closed and heard nothing—so *she* says. Fraülein Greta was in the garden planting bulbs—so *she* says. The gardener, Dobbs, was in the small potting shed having his elevenses—so *he* says; and the secretary was out for a walk, and once more there is only his own word for it. No one had an alibi; no one can corroborate anyone else's story.

But one thing *is* certain. No one from outside could have done it, for a stranger in the little village of King's Gnaton would be noticed without fail. Both the back and the front doors were locked, all the members of the household having their own keys. So you see, it narrows down to those four. And yet each one seems to be above suspicion. Greta, his own brother's child. Gertrude, with forty years of faithful service. Dobbs, who has never been out of King's Gnaton. And Charles Templeton, the secretary—"

"Yes," said Colonel Bantry, "what about him? He seems the suspicious person to my mind. What do you know about him?"

"It is what I knew about him that put him completely out of court—at any rate at the time," said Sir Henry gravely. "You see, Charles Templeton was one of my own men."

"Oh!" said Colonel Bantry, considerably taken aback.

"Yes. I wanted to have someone on the spot, and at the same time I didn't want to cause talk in the village. Rosen really needed a secretary. I put Templeton on the job. He's a gentleman, he speaks German fluently, and he's altogether a very able fellow."

"But, then, which do you suspect?" asked Mrs. Bantry in a bewildered tone. "They all seem so—well, impossible."

"Yes, so it appears. But you can look at the thing from another angle. Fräulein Greta was his niece and a very lovely girl, but the war has shown us time and again that brother can turn against sister, or father against son, and so on, and the loveliest and gentlest of young girls did some of the most amazing things. The same thing applies to Gertrude, and who knows what other forces might be at work in her case. A quarrel, perhaps, with her master, a growing resentment all the more lasting became of the long faithful years behind her. Elderly women of that class can be amazingly bitter sometimes. And Dobbs? Was he above suspicion merely because he had no connection with the family? Money will do much. In some way Dobbs might have been approached and bought.

"For one thing seems certain: some message or some order must have come from outside. Otherwise why five months'

THE FOUR SUSPECTS 109

immunity? No, the agents of the society must have been at work. Not yet sure of Rosen's perfidy, they delayed till the betrayal had been traced to him beyond any possible doubt. And then, all doubts set aside, they must have sent their message to the spy within the gates—the message that said 'Kill.' "

"How nasty!" said Jane Helier.

"But how did the message come? That was the point I tried to elucidate—the one hope of solving my problem. One of those four people must have been communicated with in some way. There would be no delay—I knew that—as soon as the command came it would be carried out. That was a characteristic of the *Schwartze Hand*.

"I went into the question, went into it in a way that will probably strike you as being ridiculously meticulous. Who had come to the cottage that morning? I eliminated nobody. Here is the list."

He took an envelope from his pocket and selected a paper from its contents.

"*The butcher,* bringing some neck of mutton. Investigated and found correct.

"*The grocer's assistant,* bringing a packet of corn flour, two pounds of sugar, a pound of butter, and a pound of coffee. Also investigated and found correct.

"*The postman,* bringing two circulars for Fraülein Rosen, a local letter for Gertrude, three letters for Dr. Rosen, one with a foreign stamp, and two letters for Mr. Templeton, one also with a foreign stamp."

Sir Henry paused and then took a sheaf of documents from the envelope.

"It may interest you to see these for yourself. They were handed to me by the various people concerned, or collected from the wastepaper basket. I need hardly say they've been tested by experts for invisible ink, and so forth."

Everyone crowded round to look. The circulars were respectively from a nurseryman and from a prominent London fur establishment. The two bills addressed to Dr. Rosen were a local one for seeds for the garden and one from a London stationery firm. The letters addressed to him ran as follows:

My Dear Rosen—Just back from Dr. Helmuth Spath's. I saw Edgar Jackson the other day. He and Amos Perry have just come back from Tsingtau. In all Honesty I can't say I envy them the trip. Let me have news of you soon. As I said before: beware of certain person. You know who I mean, though you don't agree.—Yours, Georgina.

"Mr. Templeton's mail consisted of this bill, which, as you see, is an account rendered from his tailor, and a letter from a friend in Germany," went on Sir Henry. "The latter, unfortunately, he tore up while out on his walk. Finally we have the letter received by Gertrude."

Dear Mrs. Swartz—We're hoping as how you be able to come the social on friday evening. the vicar says has he hopes you will—one and all being welcome. The resipy for the ham was very good, and I thanks you for it. Hoping as this finds you well and that we shall see you friday i remain— Yours faithfully, Emma Greene.

Dr. Lloyd smiled a little over this and so did Mrs. Bantry.

"I think the last letter can be put out of court," said Dr. Lloyd.

"I thought the same," said Sir Henry, "but I took the precaution of verifying that there was a Mrs. Greene and a church social. One can't be too careful, you know."

"That's what our friend Miss Marple always says," reminded Dr. Lloyd, smiling. "You're lost in a daydream, Miss Marple. What are you thinking about?"

Miss Marple gave a start.

"So stupid of me," she said. "I was just wondering why the word Honesty in Dr. Rosen's letter was spelled with a capital H."

Mrs. Bantry picked it up.

"So it is," she said. *"Oh!"*

"Yes, dear," said Miss Marple. "I thought you'd notice!"

"There's a definite warning in that letter," said Colonel Bantry. "That's the first thing caught my attention. I notice more than you'd think. Yes, a definite warning—against whom?"

"There's rather a curious point about that letter," said Sir Henry. "According to Temple, Dr. Rosen opened the letter at breakfast and tossed it across to him saying he didn't know who the fellow was from Adam."

"But it wasn't a fellow," said Jane Helier. "It was signed 'Georgina.' "

"It's difficult to say which it is," said Dr. Lloyd. "It might be Georgey; but it certainly looks more like Georgina. Only it strikes me that the writing is a man's."

"You know, that's interesting," said Colonel Bantry. "His tossing it across the table like that and pretending he knew nothing about it. Wanted to watch somebody's face? Whose face? The girl's or the man's?"

"Or even the cook's?" suggested Mrs. Bantry. "She might have been in the room bringing in the breakfast. But what I don't see is . . ."

She frowned over the letter. Miss Marple drew closer to her. Miss Marple's finger went out and touched the sheet of paper. They murmured together.

"But why did the secretary tear up the other letter?" asked Jane Helier suddenly. "It seems—oh! I don't know—it seems queer. Why should he have letters from Germany? Although, of course, if he's above suspicion, as you say——"

"But Sir Henry didn't say that," interrupted Miss Marple, looking up quickly from her murmured conference with Mrs. Bantry. "He said *four* suspects. So that shows he includes Mr. Templeton. I'm right, am I not, Sir Henry?"

"Yes, Miss Marple. I have learned one thing through bitter experience. Never say to yourself that *anyone* is above suspicion. I gave you reasons just now why three of these people might be guilty, unlikely as it seemed. I did not at that time apply the same process to Charles Templeton. But I came to it by pursuing the rule I have just mentioned. And I was forced to recognize this: that every army and every navy and every police force has a certain number of traitors within its ranks, much as we hate to admit the idea.

And I examined dispassionately the case against Charles Templeton.

"I asked myself very much the same questions Miss Helier has just asked. Why should he, alone of all the house, not be able to produce the letter he had received—a letter, moreover, with a German stamp on it. Why should he have letters from Germany?

"The last question was an innocent one, and I actually put it to him. His reply was simple enough. His mother's sister was married to a German. The letter had been from a German girl cousin. So I learned something I did not know before—that Charles Templeton had relations with people in Germany. And that put him definitely on the list of suspects. He is my own man—a lad I have always liked and trusted; but in common justice and fairness I must admit that he heads that list.

"But there it is—I do not know! I do not *know*. . . . And in all probability I never shall know. It is not a question of punishing a murderer. It is a question that to me seems a hundred times more important. It is the blighting, perhaps, of an honorable man's whole career . . . because of suspicion—a suspicion that I dare not disregard."

Miss Marple coughed and said gently, "Then, Sir Henry, if I understand you rightly, it is young Mr. Templeton who is so much on your mind?"

"Yes, in a sense. It should, in theory, be the same for all four, but that is not actually the case. Dobbs, for instance —suspicion may attach to him in my mind, but it will not actually affect his career. Nobody in the village has ever had any idea that old Dr. Rosen's death was anything but an accident. Gertrude is slightly more affected. It must make, for instance, a difference in Fraülein Rosen's attitude toward her. But that, possibly, is not of great importance to her.

"As for Greta Rosen—well, here we come to the crux of the matter. Greta is a very pretty girl and Charles Templeton is a good-looking young man, and for five months they were thrown together with no outside distractions. The inevitable happened. They fell in love—even if they did not come to the point of admitting the fact in words.

"And then the catastrophe happens. It is three months ago now, and a day or two after I returned, Greta Rosen came to see me. She had sold the cottage and was returning to Germany, having finally settled her uncle's affairs. She came to me personally, although she knew I had retired, because it was really about a personal matter she wanted to see me. She beat about the bush a little, then at last it all came out. What did I think? That letter with the German stamp—she had worried about it and worried about it—the one Charles had torn up. Was it all right? Surely it *must* be all right. Of course she believed his story, but—oh, if she only *knew!* If she only knew—for certain.

"You see? The same feeling: the wish to trust—but the horrible lurking suspicion, thrust resolutely to the back of the mind, but persisting nevertheless. I spoke to her with absolute frankness and asked her to do the same. I asked her whether she had been on the point of caring for Charles, and he for her.

" 'I think so,' she said. 'Oh, yes, I know it was so. We were so happy. Every day passed so contentedly. We knew—we both knew. There was no hurry—there was all the time in the world. Some day he would tell me he loved me, and I should tell him that I, too—ah, but you can guess. And now it is all changed. A black cloud has come between us—when we meet we do not know what to say. . . . We are each saying to ourselves, "If I were *sure!*" That is why, Sir Henry, I beg of you to say to me, "You may be sure, whoever killed your uncle, it was not Charles Templeton." Say it to me! Oh, say it to me, I beg you!'

"And damn it all," cried Sir Henry, bringing down his fist with a bang on the table, "I couldn't say it to her. They'll drift farther and farther apart, those two—with suspicion like a ghost between them—a ghost that can't be laid."

He leaned back in his chair, his face looking tired and grey. He shook his head once or twice despondently.

"And there's nothing more can be done, unless"—he sat up straight again and a tiny whimsical smile crossed his face —"unless Miss Marple can help us. Can't you, Miss Marple? I've a feeling that letter might be in your line; you know—

the one about the church social. Doesn't it remind you of something or someone that makes everything perfectly plain? Can't you do something to help two helpless young people who want to be happy?"

Behind the whimsicality there was something earnest in his appeal. He had come to think very highly of the mental powers of this frail old-fashioned maiden lady. He looked across at her with something like hope in his eyes.

Miss Marple coughed and smoothed her lace.

"It does remind me a little of Annie Poultney," she admitted. "Of course, the letter is perfectly plain—both to Mrs. Bantry and myself. I don't mean the church social letter, but the other one. You living so much in London and not being a gardener, Sir Henry, you would not have been likely to notice."

"Eh?" said Sir Henry. "Notice what?"

Mrs. Bantry reached out a hand and selected a circular. She opened it and read aloud with gusto:

"Dr. Helmuth Spath. Pure lilac, a wonderfully fine flower, carried on exceptionally long and stiff stem. Splendid for cutting and garden decoration. A novelty of striking beauty.

"Edgar Jackson. Beautifully shaped chrysanthemumlike flower of a distinct brick-red color.

"Amos Perry. Brilliant red, highly decorative.

"Tsingtau. Brilliant orange-red, showy garden plant and lasting cut flower.

"Honesty——"

"With a capital H, you remember," murmured Miss Marple.

"Honesty. Rose and white shades, enormous, perfect-shaped flower."

Mrs. Bantry flung down the circular and said with immense explosive force: *"Dahlias!"*

"And their initial letters spell *'death,'*" explained Miss Marple.

"But the letter came to Dr. Rosen himself," objected Sir Henry.

"That was the clever part of it," said Miss Marple. "That and the warning in it. What would he do, getting a letter from someone he didn't know, full of names he didn't know. Why, of course, toss it over to his secretary."

"Then, after all——"

"*Oh, no!*" said Miss Marple. "*Not* the secretary. Why, that's what makes it so perfectly clear that it *wasn't* him. He'd never have let that letter be found! And, equally, he'd never have destroyed a letter to himself with a German stamp on it. Really, his innocence is—if you'll allow me to use the word—just *shining*."

"Then who——"

"Well, it seems almost certain—as certain as anything can be in this world. There was another person at the breakfast table and she would—quite naturally under the circumstances—put out her hand for the letter and read it. And that would be that. You remember that she got a gardening circular by the same post——"

"Greta Rosen," said Sir Henry, slowly. "Then her visit to me——"

"Gentlemen never see through these things," said Miss Marple. "And I'm afraid they often think we old women are—well, cats, to see things the way we do. But there it is. One does know a great deal about one's own sex, unfortunately. I've no doubt there was a barrier between them. The young man felt a sudden inexplicable repulsion. He suspected, purely through instinct, and couldn't hide the suspicion. And I really think that the girl's visit to you was just pure *spite*. She was safe enough really; but she just went out of her way to fix your suspicions definitely on poor Mr. Templeton. You weren't nearly so suspicious of him until after her visit."

"I'm sure it was nothing she said——" began Sir Henry.

"Gentlemen," said Miss Marple calmly, "never see through these things."

"And that girl——" He stopped. "She commits a cold-blooded murder and gets off scot-free!"

"Oh, no, Sir Henry," said Miss Marple. "Not scot-free. Neither you nor I believe that. Remember what you said not long ago. No, Greta Rosen will not escape punishment. To begin with, she must be in with a very queer set of people—

blackmailers and terrorists—associates who will do her no good and will probably bring her to a miserable end. As you say, one mustn't waste thoughts on the guilty—it's the innocent who matter. There's that poor old Gertrude, for instance—the one who reminded me of Annie Poultney. Poor Annie Poultney. Fifty years of faithful service and then suspected of making away with Miss Lamb's will, though nothing could be proved. Almost broke the poor creature's faithful heart; and then after she was dead it came to light in the secret drawer of the tea caddy, where old Miss Lamb had put it herself for safety. But too late for poor Annie.

"That's what worries me so about that poor old German woman. When one is old, one becomes embittered very easily. I feel much sorrier for her than for Mr. Templeton, who is young and good-looking and probably a favorite with the ladies. You will write to her, won't you, Sir Henry, and just tell her that her innocence is established beyond doubt? Her dear old master dead, and she no doubt brooding and feeling herself suspected of . . ."

"I will write, Miss Marple," said Sir Henry. He looked at her curiously. "You know, I shall never quite understand you. Your outlook is always different from what I expect."

"My outlook, I am afraid, is a very petty one," said Miss Marple humbly. "I hardly ever go out of St. Mary Mead."

"And yet you have solved what may be called an international mystery," said Sir Henry. "For you *have* solved it. I am convinced of that."

Miss Marple blushed, then bridled a bit.

"I was, I think, well educated for the standard of my day. My sister and I had a German governess—a fraülein. A very sentimental creature. She taught us the language of flowers —a forgotten study nowadays, but most charming. A yellow tulip, for instance, means 'Hopeless Love,' while a China aster means 'I Die of Jealousy at Your Feet.' That letter was signed Georgina, which I seem to remember is Dahlia in German, and that of course made the whole thing perfectly clear. I wish I could remember the meaning of Dahlia, but, alas, that eludes me. My memory is not what it was."

"At any rate, it didn't mean 'death.' "

"No, indeed. Horrible, is it not? There are very sad things in the world."

"There are," said Mrs. Bantry with a sigh. "It's lucky one has flowers and one's friends."

"She puts us last, you observe," said Dr. Lloyd.

"A man used to send me purple orchids every night to the theater," said Jane dreamily.

" 'I Await Your Favors'—that's what orchids mean," said Miss Marple brightly.

Sir Henry gave a peculiar sort of cough and turned his head away.

Miss Marple gave a sudden exclamation.

"I've remembered! Dahlias mean 'treachery and misrepresentation.' "

"Wonderful," said Sir Henry. "Absolutely wonderful." And he sighed.

HARLEY QUIN   THE INVISIBLE

One of the most fantastic of all fictional detectives is Harley
Quin. He first appeared late one cold New Year's Eve, a tall,
slender figure seeking shelter from the icy blasts while his car
was being repaired outside Royston Manor, where a house party
was in progress. Curiously, as he stood in the doorway, the light
from the stained glass above seemed to dress him in every color
of the rainbow; and later, as he sat talking with his host, the fire-
light threw a bar of shadow across his face like a mask. Moreover, this Harley Quin, like his prototype, sometimes seems to
be strangely invisible; yet he has the uncanny power of showing
you what you have already seen with your own eyes, of making
clear to you what you have heard with your own ears. In a moment of crisis it is Harley Quin who speaks the cue. Watch
then for the flash of lightning and the thunder!

The strange chronicle of Harley Quin is comprised in **The
Mysterious Mr. Quin**, published as a single volume. It is also
included in the omnibus, **Triple Threat.**

THE FACE OF HELEN

MR. SATTERTHWAITE was at the opera and sat alone in his big box on the first tier. Outside the door was a printed card bearing his name. An appreciator and a connoisseur of all the arts, Mr. Satterthwaite was especially fond of good music and was a regular subscriber to Covent Garden every year, reserving a box for Tuesdays and Fridays throughout the season.

But it was not often that he sat in it alone. He was a gregarious little gentleman, and he liked filling his box with the elite of the great world to which he belonged and also with the aristocracy of the artistic world, in which he was equally at home. He was alone tonight because a countess had disappointed him. The Countess, besides being a beautiful and celebrated woman, was also a good mother. Her children had been attacked by that common and distressing disease, the mumps, and the Countess remained at home in tearful confabulation with exquisitely starched nurses. Her husband, who had supplied her with the aforementioned children and a title, but who was otherwise a complete nonentity, had seized at the chance to escape. Nothing bored him more than music.

So Mr. Satterthwaite sat alone. *Cavalleria Rusticana* and *Pagliacci* were being given that night, and, since the first had never appealed to him, he arrived just after the curtain went down on Santuzza's death agony, in time to glance round the house with a practised eye before everyone streamed out, bent on paying visits or fighting for coffee or lemonade. Mr. Satterthwaite adjusted his opera glasses, looked round the house, marked down his prey, and sallied forth with a well mapped out plan of campaign ahead of him, a plan, however, which he did not put into execution, for just outside his box he cannoned into a tall, dark man and recognised him with a pleasurable thrill of excitement.

"Mr. Quin," cried Mr. Satterthwaite.

He seized his friend warmly by the hand, clutching him as though he feared any minute to see him vanish into thin air.

"You must share my box," said Mr. Satterthwaite determinedly. "You are not with a party?"

"No, I am sitting by myself in the stalls," responded Mr. Quin with a smile.

"Then that is settled," said Mr. Satterthwaite with a sigh of relief.

His manner was almost comic, had there been anyone to observe it.

"You are very kind," said Mr. Quin.

"Not at all. It is a pleasure. I didn't know you were fond of music?"

"There are reasons why I am attracted to *Pagliacci*."

"Ah! Of course," said Mr. Satterthwaite, nodding sapiently, though, if put to it, he would have found it hard to explain just why he had used that expression. "Of course, you would be."

They went back to the box at the first summons of the bell, and, leaning over the front of it, they watched the people returning to the stalls.

"That's a beautiful head," observed Mr. Satterthwaite suddenly.

He indicated with his glasses a spot immediately beneath them in the stalls circle. A girl sat there whose face they could not see—only the pure gold of her hair that fitted with the closeness of a cap till it merged into the white neck.

"A Greek head," said Mr. Satterthwaite reverently. "Pure Greek." He sighed happily. "It's a remarkable thing when you come to think of it—how very few people have hair that *fits* them. It's more noticeable now that everyone is shingled."

"You are so observant," said Mr. Quin.

"I see things," admitted Mr. Satterthwaite. "I do see things. For instance, I picked out that head at once. We must have a look at her face sooner or later. But it won't match, I'm sure. That would be a chance in a thousand."

Almost as the words left his lips, the lights flickered and went down, the sharp rap of the conductor's baton was heard, and the opera began. A new tenor, said to be a second Caruso, was singing that night. He had been referred to by the newspapers as a Jugo-Slav, a Czech, an Albanian, a Magyar, and a Bulgarian, with a beautiful impartiality. He had given an extraordinary concert at the Albert Hall, a programme of the folk songs of his native hills, with a specially tuned orchestra. They were in strange half tones, and the would-be musical had pronounced them "too marvellous." Real musicians had reserved judgement, realising that the ear had to be specially trained and attuned before any criticism was possible. It was quite a relief to some people to find this evening that Yoaschbim could sing in ordinary Italian with all the traditional sobs and quivers.

The curtain went down on the first act, and applause burst out vociferously. Mr. Satterthwaite turned to Mr. Quin. He realised that the latter was waiting for him to pronounce judgement, and plumed himself a little. After all, he *knew*. As a critic he was well-nigh infallible.

Very slowly he nodded his head.

"It is the real thing," he said.

"You think so?"

"As fine a voice as Caruso's. People will not recognise that it is so at first, for his technique is not yet perfect. There are ragged edges, a lack of certainty in the attack. But the voice is there—magnificent."

"I went to his concert at the Albert Hall," said Mr. Quin.

"Did you? I could not go."

"He made a wonderful hit with a shepherd's song."

"I read about it," said Mr. Satterthwaite. "The refrain ends each time with a high note—a kind of cry. A note midway between A and B flat. Very curious."

Yoaschbim had taken three calls, bowing and smiling. The

lights went up and the people began to file out. Mr. Satterthwaite leaned over to watch the girl with the golden head.
She rose, adjusted her scarf, and turned.

Mr. Satterthwaite caught his breath. There were, he knew,
such faces in the world—faces that made history——

The girl moved to the gangway, her companion, a young
man, beside her. And Mr. Satterthwaite noticed how every
man in the vicinity looked—and continued to look covertly.

"Beauty!" said Mr. Satterthwaite to himself. "There is
such a thing. Not charm, nor attraction, nor magnetism,
nor any of the things we talk about so glibly—just sheer
beauty. The shape of a face, the line of an eyebrow, the
curve of a jaw." He quoted softly under his breath: *The
face that launched a thousand ships.*" And for the first time
he realised the meaning of those words.

He glanced across at Mr. Quin, who was watching him in
what seemed such perfect comprehension that Mr. Satterthwaite felt there was no need for words.

"I've always wondered," he said simply, "what such
women were really like."

"You mean?"

"The Helens, the Cleopatras, the Mary Stuarts."

Mr. Quin nodded thoughtfully.

"If we go out," he suggested, "we may—see."

They went out together, and their quest was successful.
The pair they were in search of were seated on a lounge
halfway up the staircase. For the first time, Mr. Satterthwaite
noted the girl's companion, a dark young man, not handsome, but with a suggestion of restless fire about him. A face
full of strange angles; jutting cheekbones, a forceful, slightly
crooked jaw, deep-set eyes that were curiously light under
the dark, overhanging brows.

"An interesting face," said Mr. Satterthwaite to himself.
"A real face. It means something."

The young man was leaning forward talking earnestly.
The girl was listening. Neither of them belonged to Mr. Sat-
terthwaite's world. He took them to be of the "arty" class.
The girl wore a rather shapeless garment of cheap green silk.
Her shoes were of soiled white satin. The young man wore

his evening clothes with an air of being uncomfortable in them.

The two men passed and repassed several times. The fourth time they did so, the couple had been joined by a third —a fair young man with a suggestion of the clerk about him. With his coming a certain tension had set in. The newcomer was fidgetting with his tie and seemed ill at ease; the girl's beautiful face was turned gravely up towards him, and her companion was scowling furiously.

"The usual story," said Mr. Quin very softly as they passed.

"Yes," said Mr. Satterthwaite with a sigh. "It's inevitable, I suppose. The snarling of two dogs over a bone. It always has been, it always will be. And yet, one could wish for something different. Beauty——" He stopped. Beauty, to Mr. Satterthwaite, meant something very wonderful. He found it difficult to speak of it. He looked at Mr. Quin, who nodded his head gravely in understanding.

They went back to their seats for the second act.

At the close of the performance, Mr. Satterthwaite turned eagerly to his friend.

"It is a wet night. My car is here. You must allow me to drive you—er—somewhere."

The last word was Mr. Satterthwaite's delicacy coming into play. "To drive you home" would, he felt, have savoured of curiosity. Mr. Quin had always been singularly reticent. It was extraordinary how little Mr. Satterthwaite knew about him.

"But perhaps," continued the little man, "you have your own car waiting?"

"No," said Mr. Quin. "I have no car waiting."

"Then——"

But Mr. Quin shook his head.

"You are most kind," he said, "but I prefer to go my own way. Besides," he said with a rather curious smile, "if anything should—happen, it will be for you to act. Good night, and thank you. Once again we have seen the drama together."

He had gone so quickly that Mr. Satterthwaite had no

time to protest, but he was left with a faint uneasiness stirring in his mind. To what drama did Mr. Quin refer? *Pagliacci* or another?

Masters, Mr. Satterthwaite's chauffeur, was in the habit of waiting in a side street. His master disliked the long delay while the cars drew up in turn before the opera house. Now, as on previous occasions, he walked rapidly round the corner and along the street towards where he knew he should find Masters awaiting him. Just in front of him were a girl and a man, and even as he recognized them another man joined them.

It all broke out in a minute. A man's voice, angrily uplifted. Another man's voice in injured protest. And then the scuffle. Blows, angry breathing, more blows, the form of a policeman appearing majestically from nowhere—and in another minute Mr. Satterthwaite was beside the girl where she shrank back against the wall.

"Allow me," he said. "You must not stay here."

He took her by the arm and marshalled her swiftly down the street. Once she looked back.

"Oughtn't I——?" she began uncertainly.

Mr. Satterthwaite shook his head.

"It would be very unpleasant for you to be mixed up in it. You would probably be asked to go along to the police station with them. I am sure neither of your—friends would wish that."

He stopped.

"This is my car. If you will allow me to do so, I shall have much pleasure in driving you home."

The girl looked at him searchingly. The staid respectability of Mr. Satterthwaite impressed her favourably. She bent her head.

"Thank you," she said, and got into the car, the door of which Masters was holding open.

In reply to a question from Mr. Satterthwaite, she gave an address in Chelsea, and he got in beside her.

The girl was upset and not in the mood for talking, and Mr. Satterthwaite was too tactful to intrude upon her

thoughts. Presently, however, she turned to him and spoke
of her own accord.

"I wish," she said pettishly, "people wouldn't be so silly."

"It is a nuisance," agreed Mr. Satterthwaite.

His matter-of-fact manner put her at her ease, and she
went on as though feeling the need of confiding in someone.

"It wasn't as though—I mean, well, it was like this. Mr.
Eastney and I have been friends for a long time—ever since
I came to London. He's taken no end of trouble about my
voice, and got me some very good introductions, and he's
been more kind to me than I can say. He's absolutely music
mad. It was very good of him to take me tonight. I'm sure
he can't really afford it. And then Mr. Burns came up and
spoke to us—quite nicely, I'm sure, and Phil, Mr. Eastney,
got sulky about it. I don't know why he should. It's a free
country, I'm sure. And Mr. Burns is always pleasant and
good-tempered. Then just as we were walking to the Tube,
he came up and joined us, and he hadn't so much as said
two words before Philip flew out at him like a madman. And
—oh! I don't like it."

"Don't you?" asked Mr. Satterthwaite very softly.

She blushed, but very little. There was none of the conscious siren about her. A certain measure of pleasurable excitement in being fought for there must be—that was only
nature—but Mr. Satterthwaite decided that a worried per-
plexity lay uppermost, and he had the clue to it in another
moment when she observed inconsequently. "I do hope he
hasn't hurt him."

"Now which is 'him'?" thought Mr. Satterthwaite, smiling
to himself in the darkness.

He backed his own judgement and said: "You hope Mr.—
er—Eastney hasn't hurt Mr. Burns?"

She nodded.

"Yes, that's what I said. It seems so dreadful. I wish I
knew."

The car was drawing up.

"Are you on the telephone?" he asked.

"Yes."

"If you like, I will find out exactly what has happened and then telephone to you."

The girl's face brightened.

"Oh! That would be very kind of you. Are you sure it's not too much bother?"

"Not in the least."

She thanked him again and gave him her telephone number, adding with a touch of shyness: "My name is Gillian West."

As he was driven through the night, bound on his errand, a curious smile came to Mr. Satterthwaite's lips.

He thought: "So that is all it is—'The shape of a face, the curve of a jaw!'"

But he fulfilled his promise.

The following Sunday afternoon, Mr. Satterthwaite went to Kew Gardens to admire the rhododendrons. Very long ago (incredibly long ago, it seemed to Mr. Satterthwaite) he had driven down to Kew Gardens with a certain young lady to see the bluebells. Mr. Satterthwaite had arranged very carefully beforehand in his own mind exactly what he was going to say and the precise words he would use in asking the young lady for her hand in marriage. He was just conning them over in his mind, and responding to her raptures about the bluebells a little absent-mindedly, when the shock came. The young lady stopped exclaiming at the bluebells and suddenly confided in Mr. Satterthwaite (as a true friend) her love for another. Mr. Satterthwaite put away the little set speech he had prepared and hastily rummaged for sympathy and friendship in the bottom drawer of his mind.

Such was Mr. Satterthwaite's romance—a rather tepid early Victorian one, but it had left him with a romantic attachment to Kew Gardens, and he would often go there to see the bluebells, or, if he had been abroad later than usual, the rhododendrons, and would sigh to himself, and feel rather sentimental, and really enjoy himself very much indeed in an old-fashioned, romantic way.

This particular afternoon he was strolling back past the teahouses when he recognised a couple sitting at one of the small tables on the grass. They were Gillian West and the fair young man, and at that same moment they recognised him. He saw the girl flush and speak eagerly to her companion. In another minute he was shaking hands with them both in his correct, rather prim fashion, and had accepted the shy invitation proffered him to have tea with them.

"I can't tell you, sir," said Mr. Burns, "how grateful I am to you for looking after Gillian the other night. She told me all about it."

"Yes, indeed," said the girl. "It was ever so kind of you."

Mr. Satterthwaite felt pleased and interested in the pair. Their naïveté and sincerity touched him. Also, it was to him a peep into a world with which he was not well acquainted. These people were of a class unknown to him.

In his little dried-up way, Mr. Satterthwaite could be very sympathetic. Very soon he was hearing all about his new friends. He noted that Mr. Burns had become Charlie, and he was not unprepared for the statement that the two were engaged.

"As a matter of fact," said Mr. Burns with refreshing candour, "it just happened this afternoon, didn't it, Gil?"

Burns was a clerk in a shipping firm. He was making a fair salary, had a little money of his own, and the two proposed to be married quite soon.

Mr. Satterthwaite listened, and nodded, and congratulated.

"An ordinary young man," he thought to himself, "a very ordinary young man. Nice, straightforward young chap, plenty to say for himself, good opinion of himself without being conceited, nice-looking without being unduly handsome. Nothing remarkable about him and will never set the Thames on fire. And the girl loves him."

Aloud he said, "And Mr. Eastney——"

He purposely broke off, but he had said enough to produce an effect for which he was not unprepared. Charlie Burns's face darkened, and Gillian looked troubled. More than troubled, he thought. She looked afraid.

"I don't like it," she said in a low voice. Her words were addressed to Mr. Satterthwaite, as though she knew by instinct that he would understand a feeling incomprehensible to her lover. "You see—he's done a lot for me. He's encouraged me to take up singing, and—and helped me with it. But I've known all the time that my voice wasn't really good—not first-class. Of course, I've had engagements——"

She stopped.

"You've had a bit of trouble, too," said Burns. "A girl wants someone to look after her. Gillian's had a lot of unpleasantness, Mr. Satterthwaite. Altogether she's had a lot of unpleasantness. She's a good-looker, as you can see, and—well, that often leads to trouble for a girl."

Between them, Mr. Satterthwaite became enlightened as to various happenings which were vaguely classed by Burns under the heading of "unpleasantness." The young man who had shot himself, the extraordinary conduct of the Bank Manager (who was a married man!), the violent stranger (who must have been balmy!), the wild behaviour of the elderly artist. A trail of violence and tragedy that Gillian West had left in her wake, recited in the commonplace tones of Charles Burns. "And it's my opinion," he ended, "that this fellow Eastney is a bit cracked. Gillian would have had trouble with him if I hadn't turned up to look after her."

His laugh sounded a little fatuous to Mr. Satterthwaite, and no responsive smile came to the girl's face. She was looking earnestly at Mr. Satterthwaite.

"Phil's all right," she said slowly. "He cares for me, I know, and I care for him like a friend—but—but not anything more. I don't know how he'll take the news about Charlie, I'm sure. He—I'm so afraid he'll be——"

She stopped, inarticulate in face of the dangers she vaguely sensed.

"If I can help you in any way," said Mr. Satterthwaite warmly, "pray command me."

He fancied Charlie Burns looked vaguely resentful, but Gillian said at once: "Thank you."

Mr. Satterthwaite left his new friends after having promised to take tea with Gillian on the following Thursday.

When Thursday came, Mr. Satterthwaite felt a little thrill of pleasurable anticipation. He thought: "I'm an old man—

but not too old to be thrilled by a face. A face——" Then he shook his head with a sense of foreboding.

Gillian was alone. Charlie Burns was to come in later. She looked much happier, Mr. Satterthwaite thought, as though a load had been lifted from her mind. Indeed, she frankly admitted as much.

"I dreaded telling Phil about Charlie. It was silly of me. I ought to have known Phil better. He was upset, of course, but no one could have been sweeter. Really sweet he was. Look what he sent me this morning—a wedding present. Isn't it magnificent?"

It was indeed rather magnificent for a young man in Philip Eastney's circumstances. A wireless set of the latest type.

"We both love music so much, you see," explained the girl. "Phil said that when I was listening to a concert on this, I should always think of him a little. And I'm sure I shall. Because we have been such friends."

"You must be proud of your friend," said Mr. Satterthwaite gently. "He seems to have taken the blow like a true sportsman."

Gillian nodded. He saw the quick tears come into her eyes.

"He asked me to do one thing for him. Tonight is the anniversary of the day we first met. He asked me if I would stay at home quietly this evening and listen to the wireless programme—not go out with Charlie anywhere. I said of course I would, and that I was very touched, and that I would think of him with a lot of gratitude and affection."

Mr. Satterthwaite nodded, but he was puzzled. He was seldom at fault in his delineation of character, and he would have judged Philip Eastney quite incapable of such a sentimental request. The young man must be of a more banal order than he supposed. Gillian evidently thought the idea quite in keeping with her rejected lover's character. Mr. Satterthwaite was a little—just a little—disappointed. He was sentimental himself, and knew it, but he expected better things of the rest of the world. Besides, sentiment belonged to his age. It had no part to play in the modern world.

He asked Gillian to sing and she complied. He told her her voice was charming, but he knew quite well in his own mind that it was distinctly second-class. Any success that could have come to her in the profession she had adopted would have been won by her face, not her voice.

He was not particularly anxious to see young Burns again, so presently he rose to go. It was at that moment that his attention was attracted by an ornament on the mantelpiece which stood out among the other rather gimcrack objects like a jewel on a dust heap.

It was a curving beaker of thin green glass, long-stemmed and graceful, and poised on the edge of it was what looked like a gigantic soap bubble, a ball of iridescent glass. Gillian noticed his absorption.

"That's an extra wedding present from Phil. It's rather pretty, I think. He works in a sort of glass factory."

"It is a beautiful thing," said Mr. Satterthwaite reverently. "The glass blowers of Murano might have been proud of that."

He went away with his interest in Philip Eastney strangely stimulated. An extraordinarily interesting young man. And yet the girl with the wonderful face preferred Charlie Burns. What a strange and inscrutable universe!

It had just occurred to Mr. Satterthwaite that, owing to the remarkable beauty of Gillian West, his evening with Mr. Quin had somehow missed fire. As a rule, every meeting with that mysterious individual had resulted in some strange and unforeseen happening. It was with the hope of perhaps running against the man of mystery that Mr. Satterthwaite bent his steps towards the Arlecchino Restaurant where once, in the days gone by, he had met Mr. Quin and which Mr. Quin had said he often frequented.

Mr. Satterthwaite went from room to room at the Arlecchino, looking hopefully about him, but there was no sign of Mr. Quin's dark, smiling face. There was, however, somebody else. Sitting at a small table alone was Philip Eastney

The place was crowded and Mr. Satterthwaite took his seat opposite the young man. He felt a sudden strange sense of exultation, as though he were caught up and made part of a shimmering pattern of events. He was in this thing—whatever it was. He knew now what Mr. Quin had meant that evening at the opera. There was a drama going on, and in it was a part, an important part, for Mr. Satterthwaite. He must not fail to take his cue and speak his lines.

He sat down opposite Philip Eastney with the sense of accomplishing the inevitable. It was easy enough to get into conversation. Eastney seemed anxious to talk. Mr. Satterthwaite was, as always, an encouraging and sympathetic listener. They talked of the war, of explosives, of poison gases. Eastney had a lot to say about these last, for during the greater part of the war he had been engaged in their manufacture. Mr. Satterthwaite found him really interesting.

There was one gas, Eastney said, that had never been tried. The Armistice had come too soon. Great things had been hoped for it. One whiff of it was deadly. He warmed to animation as he spoke.

Having broken the ice, Mr. Satterthwaite gently turned the conversation to music. Eastney's thin face lit up. He spoke with the passion and abandon of the real music lover. They discussed Yoaschbim, and the young man was enthusiastic. Both he and Mr. Satterthwaite agreed that nothing on earth could surpass a really fine tenor voice. Eastney as a boy had heard Caruso, and he had never forgotten it.

"Do you know that he could sing to a wine glass and shatter it?" he demanded.

"I always thought that was a fable," said Mr. Satterthwaite, smiling.

"No, it's gospel truth, I believe. The thing's quite possible. It's a question of resonance."

He went off into technical details. His face was flushed and his eyes shone. The subject seemed to fascinate him, and Mr. Satterthwaite noted that he seemed to have a thorough grasp of what he was talking about. The older man realised that he was talking to an exceptional brain, a brain that might almost be described as that of a genius. Brilliant, erratic, undecided as yet as to the true channel to give it outlet, but undoubtedly genius.

And he thought of Charlie Burns and wondered at Gillian West.

It was with quite a start that he realised how late it was getting, and he called for his bill. Eastney looked slightly apologetic.

"I'm ashamed of myself—running on so," he said. "But it was a lucky chance sent you along here tonight. I—I needed someone to talk to this evening."

He ended his speech with a curious little laugh. His eyes were still blazing with some subdued excitement. Yet there was something tragic about him.

"It has been quite a pleasure," said Mr. Satterthwaite. "Our conversation has been most interesting and instructive to me."

He then made his funny, courteous little bow and passed out of the restaurant. The night was a warm one and as he walked slowly down the street a very odd fancy came to him. He had the feeling that he was not alone—that someone was walking by his side. In vain he told himself that the idea was a delusion—it persisted. Someone was walking beside him down that dark, quiet street, someone whom he could not see. He wondered what it was that brought the figure of Mr. Quin so clearly before his mind. He felt exactly as though Mr. Quin were there walking beside him, and yet he had only to use his eyes to assure himself that it was not so, that he was alone.

But the thought of Mr. Quin persisted, and with it came something else—a need, an urgency of some kind, an oppressive foreboding of calamity. There was something he must do—and do quickly. There was something very wrong, and it lay in his hands to put it right.

So strong was the feeling that Mr. Satterthwaite forebore to fight against it. Instead, he shut his eyes and tried to bring that mental image of Mr. Quin nearer. If he could only have asked Mr. Quin—but even as the thought flashed through his mind he knew it was wrong. It was never any use asking Mr. Quin anything. "The threads are all in your hands"—that was the kind of thing Mr. Quin would say.

The threads. Threads of what? He analysed his own feeling and impressions carefully. That presentiment of danger, now. Whom did it threaten?

At once a picture rose up before his eyes, the picture of Gillian West sitting alone listening to the wireless.

Mr. Satterthwaite flung a penny to a passing newspaper boy and snatched at a paper. He turned at once to the London Radio programme. Yoaschbim was broadcasting tonight, he noted with interest. He was singing "Salve Dimora," from *Faust,* and afterwards a selection of his folk songs—"The Shepherd's Song," "The Fish," "The Little Deer," etc.

Mr. Satterthwaite crumpled the paper together. The knowledge of what Gillian was listening to seemed to make the picture of her clearer. Sitting there alone——

An odd request, that, of Philip Eastney's. Not like the man, not like him at all. There was no sentimentality in Eastney. He was a man of violent feeling, a dangerous man, perhaps——

Again his thoughts brought up with a jerk. *A dangerous man*—that meant something. *"The threads are all in your hands."* That meeting with Philip Eastney tonight—rather odd. A lucky chance, Eastney had said. Was it chance? Or was it part of that interwoven design of which Mr. Satterthwaite had once or twice been conscious this evening?

He cast his mind back. There must be *something* in Eastney's conversation, some clue there. There must, or else why this strange feeling of urgency? What had he talked about? Singing, war work, Caruso.

Caruso—Mr. Satterthwaite's thoughts went off at a tangent. Yoaschbim's voice was very nearly equal to that of Caruso. Gillian would be sitting listening to it now as it rang out true and powerful, echoing round the room, setting glasses ringing——

He caught his breath. Glasses ringing! Caruso, singing to a wine glass and the wine glass breaking. Yoaschbim singing in the London studio and in a room over a mile away the crash and tinkle of glass—not a wine glass, a thin, green, glass beaker. A crystal soap bubble falling, a soap bubble that perhaps was not empty——

It was at that moment that Mr. Satterthwaite, as judged by passers-by, suddenly went mad. He tore open the newspaper once more, took a brief glance at the wireless announcements, and then began to run for his life down the quiet street. At the end of it he found a crawling taxi, and, jumping into it, he yelled an address to the driver and the information that it was life or death to get there quickly. The driver, judging him mentally afflicted but rich, did his utmost.

Mr. Satterthwaite lay back, his head a jumble of fragmentary thoughts, forgotten bits of science learned at school, phrases used by Eastney that night. Resonance—natural periods—if the period of the force coincides with the natural period—there was something about a suspension bridge, soldiers marching over it and the swing of their stride being the same as the period of the bridge. Eastney had studied the subject. Eastney knew. And Eastney was a genius.

At ten forty-five Yoaschbim was to broadcast. It was that now. Yes, but the *Faust* had to come first. It was "The Shepherd's Song," with the great shout after the refrain, that would—that would—do what?

His mind went whirling round again. Tones, overtones, halftones. He didn't know much about these things—but Eastney knew. Pray heaven he would be in time!

The taxi stopped. Mr. Satterthwaite flung himself out and raced up the stone stairs to a second floor like a young athlete. The door of the flat was ajar. He pushed it open and the great tenor voice welcomed him. The words of "The Shepherd's Song" were familiar to him in a less unconventional setting.

Shepherd, see thy horse's flowing mane——

He was in time then. He burst open the sitting-room door. Gillian was sitting there in a tall chair by the fireplace.

Barya Mischa's daughter is to wed today:
To the wedding I must haste away.

She must have thought him mad. He clutched at her,
crying out something incomprehensible, and half pulled,
half dragged her out till they stood upon the stairway.

To the wedding I must haste away——
    Ya-ha!

A wonderful high note, full-throated, powerful, hit full
in the middle, a note any singer might be proud of. And with
it another sound—the faint tinkle of broken glass.

A stray cat darted past them and in through the flat door.
Gillian made a movement, but Mr. Satterthwaite held her
back, speaking incoherently.

"No, no—it's deadly: no smell, nothing to warn you. A
mere whiff, and it's all over. Nobody knows quite how
deadly it would be. It's unlike anything that's ever been
tried before."

He was repeating the things that Philip Eastney had
told him over the table at dinner.

Gillian stared at him uncomprehendingly.

Philip Eastney drew out his watch and looked at it. It
was just half-past eleven. For the last three quarters of an
hour he had been pacing up and down the Embankment.
He looked out over the Thames and then turned—to look
into the face of his dinner companion.

"That's odd," he said, and laughed. "We seem fated to
run into each other tonight."

"If you call it Fate," said Mr. Satterthwaite.

Philip Eastney looked at him more attentively and his
own expression changed.

"Yes?" he said quietly.

Mr. Satterthwaite went straight to the point.

"I have just come from Miss West's flat."

"Yes?"

The same voice, with the same deadly quiet.

"We have—taken a dead cat out of it."

There was silence, then Eastney said: "Who are you?"

Mr. Satterthwaite spoke for some time. He recited the whole history of events.

"So you see, I was in time," he ended up. He paused and added quite gently: "Have you anything to—say?"

He expected something, some outburst, some wild justification. But nothing came.

"No," said Philip Eastney quietly, and turned on his heel and walked away.

Mr. Satterthwaite looked after him till his figure was swallowed up in the gloom. In spite of himself, he had a strange fellow feeling for Eastney, the feeling of an artist for another artist, of a sentimentalist for a real lover, of a plain man for a genius.

At last he roused himself with a start and began to walk in the same direction as Eastney. A fog was beginning to come up. Presently he met a policeman, who looked at him suspiciously.

"Did you hear a kind of splash just now?" asked the policeman.

"No," said Mr. Satterthwaite.

The policeman was peering out over the river.

"Another of these suicides, I expect," he grunted disconsolately. "They will do it."

"I suppose," said Mr. Satterthwaite, "that they have their reasons."

"Money, mostly," said the policeman. "Sometimes it's a woman," he said as he prepared to move away. "It's not always their fault, but some women cause a lot of trouble."

"Some women," agreed Mr. Satterthwaite softly.

When the policeman had gone on, he sat down on a seat with the fog coming up all around him, and thought about Helen of Troy, and wondered if she were a nice, ordinary woman, blessed or cursed with a wonderful face.

THE BIRD WITH THE BROKEN WING

MR. SATTERTHWAITE looked out of the window. It was raining steadily. He shivered. Very few country houses, he reflected, were really properly heated. It cheered him to think that in a few hours' time he would be speeding toward London. Once one had passed sixty years of age, London was really much the best place.

He was feeling a little old and pathetic. Most of the members of the house party were so young. Four of them had just gone off into the library to do table turning. They had invited him to accompany them, but he had declined. He failed to derive any amusement from the ouija board or planchette, with the monotonous counting of the letters of the alphabet and the usual meaningless jumble of letters that resulted.

Yes, London was the best place for him. He was glad that he had declined Madge Keeley's invitation when she had rung up to invite him over to Laidell half an hour ago. An adorable young person, certainly, but London was best.

Mr. Satterthwaite shivered again and remembered that the fire in the library was usually a good one. He opened the door and adventured cautiously into the darkened room.

"If I'm not in the way——"

"Was that N or M? We shall have to count again. No, of course not, Mr. Satterthwaite. Do you know, the most exciting things have been happening. The spirit says her name is Ada Spiers and John here is going to marry someone called Gladys Bun almost immediately."

Mr. Satterthwaite sat down in a big easy chair in front of the fire. His eyelids drooped over his eyes and he dozed.

From time to time he returned to consciousness, hearing fragments of speech.

"It can't be P A B Z L—not unless he's a Russian. John you're shoving. I *saw* you. I believe it's a new spirit come."

Another interval of dozing. Then a name jerked him wide awake.

"Q U I N. Is that right?" "Yes, it's rapped once for Yes." "Quin. Have you a message for someone here? Yes. For me? For John? For Sarah? For Evelyn? No—but there's no one else. Oh! It's for Mr. Satterthwaite, perhaps? It says "Yes." Mr. Satterthwaite, it's a message for you."

"What does it say?"

Mr. Satterthwaite was broad awake now, sitting taut and erect in his chair, his eyes shining.

The table rocked and one of the girls counted.

"L A I—it can't be—that doesn't make sense. No word begins L A I."

"Go on," said Mr. Satterthwaite, and the command in his voice was so sharp that he was obeyed without question.

"L A I D E L—and another L—Oh! That seems to be all."

"Go on."

"Tell us some more, please."

A pause.

"There doesn't seem to be any more. The table's gone quite dead. How silly."

"No," said Mr. Satterthwaite thoughtfully. "I don't think it's silly."

He rose and left the room. He went straight to the telephone. Presently he was through.

"Can I speak to Miss Keeley? Is that you, Madge, my dear? I want to change my mind, if I may, and accept your kind invitation. It is not so urgent as I thought that I should get back to town. Yes—yes—I will arrive in time for dinner."

He hung up the receiver, a strange flush on his withered cheeks. Mr. Quin—the mysterious Mr. Harley Quin. Mr. Satterthwaite counted over on his fingers the times he had been brought into contact with that man of mystery. Where Mr. Quin was concerned—*things happened!* What had happened or was going to happen—at Laidell?

Whatever it was, there was work for him, Mr. Satterthwaite, to do. In some ways or other, he would have an active part to play. He was sure of that.

Laidell was a large house. Its owner, David Keeley, was one of those quiet men with indeterminate personalities who seem to count as part of the furniture. Their inconspicuousness has nothing to do with brain power—David Keeley was a most brilliant mathematician and had written a book totally incomprehensible to ninety-nine hundredths of humanity. But, like so many men of brilliant intellect, he radiated no bodily vigour or magnetism. It was a standing joke that David Keeley was a real "invisible man." Footmen passed him by with the vegetables, and guests forgot to say how do you do or good-bye.

His daughter Madge was very different. A fine upstanding young woman, bursting with energy and life. Thorough, healthy and normal, and extremely pretty.

It was she who received Mr. Satterthwaite when he arrived.

"How nice of you to come—after all."

"Very delightful of you to let me change my mind. Madge, my dear, your'e looking very well."

"Oh! I'm always well."

"Yes, I know. But it's more than that. You look—well, blooming is the word I have in mind. Has anything happened, my dear? Anything—well—special?"

She laughed—blushed a little.

"It's too bad, Mr. Satterthwaite. You always guess things."

He took her hand.

"So it's that, is it? Mr. Right has come along?"

It was an old-fashioned term, but Madge did not object to it. She rather liked Mr. Satterthwaite's old-fashioned ways.

"I suppose so—yes. But nobody's supposed to know. It's a secret. But I don't really mind your knowing, Mr. Satterthwaite. You're always so nice and sympathetic."

Mr. Satterthwaite thoroughly enjoyed romance at second hand. He was sentimental and Victorian.

"I mustn't ask who the lucky man is? Well, then all I can

say is that I hope he is worthy of the honour you are conferring on him."

Rather a duck, old Mr. Satterthwaite, thought Madge.

"Oh! We shall get on awfully well together, I think," she said. "You see, we like doing the same things, and that's so awfully important, isn't it? We've really got a lot in common —and we know all about each other and all that. It's really been coming on for a long time. That gives one such a nice safe feeling, doesn't it?"

"Undoubtedly," said Mr. Satterthwaite. "But in my experience one can never really know all about anyone else. That is part of the interest and charm of life."

"Oh! I'll risk it," said Madge, laughing, and they went up to dress for dinner.

Mr. Satterthwaite was late. He had not brought a valet, and having his things unpacked for him by a stranger always flurried him a little. He came down to find everyone assembled, and in the modern style Madge merely said: "Oh! Here's Mr. Satterthwaite. I'm starving. Let's go in."

She led the way with a tall grey-haired woman—a woman of striking personality. She had a very clear, rather incisive, voice, and her face was clear-cut and rather beautiful.

"How d'you do, Satterthwaite," said Mr. Keeley.

Mr. Satterthwaite jumped.

"How do you do," he said. "I'm afraid I didn't see you."

"Nobody does," said Mr. Keeley sadly.

They went in. The table was a low oval of mahogany. Mr. Satterthwaite was placed between his young hostess and a short dark girl—a very hearty girl with a loud voice and a ringing determined laugh that expressed more the determination to be cheerful at all costs than any real mirth. Her name seemed to be Doris and she was the type of young woman Mr. Satterthwaite most disliked. She had, he considered, no artistic justification for existence.

On Madge's other side was a man of about thirty whose likeness to the grey-haired woman proclaimed them mother and son.

Next to him——

Mr. Satterthwaite caught his breath.

He didn't know what it was exactly. It was not beauty. It was something else—something much more elusive and intangible than beauty.

She was listening to Mr. Keeley's rather ponderous dinnertable conversation, her head bent a little sideways. She was there, it seemed to Mr. Satterthwaite—and yet she was not there! She was, somehow, a great deal less substantial than anyone else seated round the oval table. Something in the droop of her body sideways was beautiful—was more than beautiful. She looked up—her eyes met Mr. Satterthwaite's for the moment across the table—and the word he wanted leapt to his mind.

Enchantment—that was it. She had the quality of enchantment. She might have been one of those creatures who are only half human—one of the Hidden People from the Hollow Hills. She made everyone else look rather too real.

But at the same time, in a queer way, she stirred his pity. It was as though semihumanity handicapped her. He sought for a phrase and found it.

"A bird with a broken wing," said Mr. Satterthwaite.

Satisfied, he turned his mind back to the subject of Girl Guides and hoped that the girl Doris had not noticed his abstraction. When she turned to the man on the other side of her—a man Mr. Satterthwaite had hardly noticed—he himself turned to Madge.

"Who is the lady sitting next to your father?" he asked in a low voice.

"Mrs. Graham? Oh, no, you mean Mabelle. Don't you know her? Mabelle Annesley. She was a Clydesley—one of the ill-fated Clydesleys."

He started. The ill-fated Clydesleys. He remembered. A brother had shot himself, a sister had been drowned, another had perished in an earthquake. A queer doomed family. This girl must be the youngest of them.

His thoughts were recalled suddenly. Madge's hand touched his under the table. Everyone else was talking. She gave a faint inclination of her head to her left.

"That's him," she murmured ungrammatically.

Mr. Satterthwaite nodded quickly in comprehension. So this young Graham was the man of Madge's choice. Well, she could hardly have done better as far as appearances went—and Mr. Satterthwaite was a shrewd observer. A pleasant, likeable, rather matter-of-fact young fellow. They'd make a nice pair—no nonsense about either of them— good, healthy, sociable young folk.

Laidell was run on old-fashioned lines. The ladies left the dining room first. Mr. Satterthwaite moved up to Graham and began to talk to him. His estimate of the young man was confirmed, yet there was something that struck him as being not quite true to type. Roger Graham was distrait, his mind seemed far away, his hand shook as he replaced the glass on the table.

"He's got something on his mind," thought Mr. Satterthwaite acutely. "Not nearly as important as he thinks it is, I daresay. All the same, I wonder what it is."

Mr. Satterthwaite was in the habit of swallowing a couple of digestive pastilles after meals. Having neglected to bring them down with him, he went up to his room to fetch them.

On his way down to the drawing room, he passed along the long corridor on the ground floor. About halfway along it was a room known as the terrace room. As Mr. Satterthwaite looked through the open doorway in passing, he stopped short.

Moonlight was streaming into the room. The latticed panes gave it a queer rhythmic pattern. A figure was sitting on the low window sill, drooping a little sideways and softly twanging the strings of a ukulele—not in a jazz rhythm, but in a far older rhythm, the beat of fairy horses riding on fairy hills.

Mr. Satterthwaite stood fascinated. She wore a dress of dull dark-blue chiffon, ruched and pleated so that it looked like the feathers of a bird. She bent over the instrument, crooning to it.

He came into the room—slowly, step by step. He was close to her when she looked up and saw him. She didn't start, he noticed, or seem surprised.

"I hope I'm not intruding," he began.

"Please—sit down."

He sat near her on a polished oak chair. She hummed softly under her breath.

"There's a lot of magic about tonight," she said. "Don't you think so?"

Yes, there was a lot of magic about.

"They wanted me to fetch my uke," she explained. "And as I passed here, I thought it would be so lovely to be alone here—in the dark and the moon."

"Then I——" Mr. Satterthwaite half rose, but she stopped him.

"Don't go. You—you fit in, somehow. It's queer, but you do."

He sat down again.

"It's been a queer sort of evening," she said. "I was out in the woods late this afternoon, and I met a man—such a strange sort of man—tall and dark, like a lost soul. The sun was setting, and the light of it through the trees made him look like a kind of Harlequin."

"Ah!" Mr. Satterthwaite leaned forward—his interest quickened.

"I wanted to speak to him—he—he looked so like somebody I know. But I lost him in the trees."

"I think I know him," said Mr. Satterthwaite.

"Do you? He is—interesting, isn't he?"

"Yes, he is interesting."

There was a pause. Mr. Satterwaite was perplexed. There was something, he felt, that he ought to do—and he didn't know what it was. But surely—surely, it had to do with this girl. He said rather clumsily: "Sometimes—when one is unhappy—one wants to get away——"

"Yes. That's true." She broke off suddenly. "Oh! I see what you mean. But you're wrong. It's just the other way round. I wanted to be alone because I'm happy."

"Happy?"

"Terribly happy."

She spoke quite quietly, but Mr. Satterthwaite had a sudden sense of shock. What this strange girl meant by being happy wasn't the same as Madge Keeley would have meant, by the same words. Happiness, for Mabelle Annesley, meant some kind of intense and vivid ecstasy—something that was not only human but more than human. He shrank back a little.

"I—didn't know," he said clumsily.

"Of course you couldn't. And it's not—the actual thing—I'm not happy yet—but I'm going to be." She leaned forward. "Do you know what it's like to stand in a wood—a big wood with dark shadows and trees very close all round you—a wood you might never get out of—and then, suddenly—just in front of you, you see the country of your dreams—shining and beautiful—you've only got to step out from the trees and the darkness and you've found it?"

"So many things look beautiful," said Mr. Satterthwaite, "before we've reached them. Some of the ugliest things in the world look the most beautiful."

There was a step on the floor. Mr. Satterthwaite turned his head. A fair man with a stupid, rather wooden, face stood there. He was the man Mr. Satterthwaite had hardly noticed at the dinner table.

"They're waiting for you, Mabelle," he said.

She got up; the expression had gone out of her face; her voice was flat and calm.

"I'm coming, Gerard," she said. "I've been talking to Mr. Satterthwaite."

She went out of the room, Mr. Satterthwaithe following. He turned his head over his shoulder as he went and caught the expression on her husband's face, a hungry, despairing look.

"Enchantment," thought Mr. Satterthwaite. "He feels it right enough. Poor fellow—poor fellow."

The drawing room was well lighted. Madge and Doris Coles were vociferous in reproaches.

"Mabelle, you little beast—you've been ages."

She sat on a low stool, tuned the ukulele, and sang. They all joined in.

"Is it possible," thought Mr. Satterthwaite, "that so many idiotic songs could have been written about My Baby?"

But he had to admit that the syncopated wailing tunes

were stirring. Though, of course, they weren't a patch on the old-fashioned waltz.

The air got very smoky. The syncopated rhythm went on.

"No conversation," thought Mr. Satterthwaite. "No good music. No *peace*." He wished the world had not become definitely so noisy.

Suddenly Mabelle Annesley broke off, smiling across the room at him, and began to sing a song of Grieg's.

"My swan—my fair one——"

It was a favourite of Mr. Satterthwaite's. He liked the note of ingenuous surprise at the end.

"Wert only a swan then? A swan then?"

After that, the party broke up. Madge offered drinks, while her father picked up the discarded ukulele and began twanging it absent-mindedly. The party exchanged good nights, drifted nearer and nearer to the door. Everyone talked at once. Gerard Annesley slipped away unostentatiously, leaving the others.

Outside the drawing-room door, Mr. Satterthwaite bade Mrs. Graham a ceremonious good night. There were two staircases, one close at hand, the other at the end of a long corridor. It was by the latter that Mr. Satterthwaite reached his room. Mrs. Graham and her son passed up the stairs near at hand where the quiet Gerard Annesley had already preceded them.

"You'd better get your ukulele, Mabelle," said Madge. "You'll forget it in the morning if you don't. You've got to make such an early start."

"Come on, Mr. Satterthwaite," said Doris Coles, seizing him boisterously by one arm. "Early to bed—et cetera."

Madge took him by the other arm and all three ran down the corridor to peals of Doris's laughter. They paused at the end to wait for David Keeley, who was following at a much more sedate pace, turning out electric lights as he came. The four of them went upstairs together.

Mr. Satterthwaite was just preparing to descend to the dining room for breakfast on the following morning when there was a light tap on the door and Madge Keeley entered. Her face was dead white and she was shivering all over.

"Oh! Mr. Satterthwaite."

"My dear child, what's happened?" He took her hand.

"Mabelle—Mabelle Annesley——"

"Yes?"

What had happened? What? Something terrible—he knew that. Madge could hardly get the words out.

"She—she hanged herself last night. On the back of her door. Oh! It's too horrible." She broke down—sobbing.

Hanged herself. Impossible. Incomprehensible!

He said a few soothing old-fashioned words to Madge and hurried downstairs. He found David Keeley looking perplexed and incompetent.

"I've telephoned to the police, Satterthwaite. Apparently that's got to be done. So the doctor said. He's just finished examining the—the— Good Lord, it's a beastly business. She must have been desperately unhappy—to do it that way. Queer that song last night. Swan Song, eh? She looked rather like a swan—a black swan."

Yes.

"Swan Song," repeated Keeley. "Shows it was in her mind, eh?"

"It would seem so—yes, certainly, it would seem so."

He hesitated, then asked if he might see—if, that is——

His host comprehended the stammering request.

"If you want to—I'd forgotten you have a *penchant* for human tragedies."

He led the way up the broad staircase. Mr. Satterthwaite followed him. At the head of the stairs was the room occupied by Roger Graham, and opposite it, on the other side of the passage, his mother's room. The latter door was ajar and a faint wisp of smoke floated through it.

A momentary surprise invaded Mr. Satterthwaite's mind. He had not judged Mrs. Graham to be a woman who smoked so early in the day. Indeed, he had had the idea that she did not smoke at all.

They went along the passage to the end door but one.

David Keeley entered the room and Mr. Satterthwaite followed him.

The room was not a very large one and showed signs of a man's occupation. A door in the wall led into a second room. A bit of cut rope still dangled from a hook high up on the door. On the bed——

Mr. Satterthwaite stood for a minute looking down on the heap of huddled chiffon. He noticed that it was ruched and pleated like the plumage of a bird. At the face, after one glance, he did not look again.

He glanced from the door with its dangling rope to the communicating door through which they had come.

"Was that open?"

"Yes. At least the maid says so."

"Annesley slept in there? Didn't he hear anything?"

"He says—nothing."

"Almost incredible," murmured Mr. Satterthwaite. He looked back at the form on the bed.

"Where is he?"

"Annesley? He's downstairs with the doctor."

They went downstairs to find an inspector of police had arrived. Mr. Satterthwaite was agreeably surprised to recognise in him an old acquaintance, Inspector Winkfield. The inspector went upstairs with the doctor and a few minutes later a request came that all members of the house party should assemble in the drawing room.

The blinds had been drawn and the whole room had a funereal aspect. Doris Coles looked frightened and subdued. Every now and then she dabbed her eyes with a handkerchief. Madge was resolute and alert, her feelings fully under control by now. Mrs. Graham was composed, as always, her face grave and impassive. The tragedy seemed to have affected her son more keenly than anyone. He looked a positive wreck this morning. David Keeley, as usual, had subsided into the background.

The bereaved husband sat alone, a little apart from the others. There was a queer dazed look about him, as though he could hardly realise what had taken place.

Mr. Satterthwaite, outwardly composed, was inwardly seething with the importance of a duty shortly to be performed.

Inspector Winkfield, followed by Dr. Morris, came in and shut the door behind him. He cleared his throat and spoke.

"This is a very sad occurrence—very sad, I'm sure. It's necessary, under the circumstances, that I should ask everybody a few questions. You'll not object, I'm sure. I'll begin with Mr. Annesley. You'll forgive my asking, sir, but had your good lady ever threatened to take her life?"

Mr. Satterthwaite opened his lips impulsively, then closed them again. There was plenty of time. Better not speak too soon.

"I—no, I don't think so."

His voice was so hesitating, so peculiar, that everyone shot a covert glance at him.

"You're not sure, sir?"

"Yes—I'm—quite sure. She didn't."

"Ah! Were you aware that she was unhappy in any way?"

"No, I—no, I wasn't."

"She said nothing to you? About feeling depressed, for instance?"

"I—no, nothing."

Whatever the inspector thought, he said nothing. Instead, he proceeded to his next point.

"Will you describe to me briefly the events of last night?"

"We—all went up to bed. I fell asleep immediately and heard nothing. The housemaid's scream aroused me this morning. I rushed into the adjoining room and found my wife—and found her——"

His voice broke. The inspector nodded.

"Yes, yes, that's quite enough. We needn't go into that. When did you last see your wife the night before?"

"I—downstairs."

"Downstairs?"

"Yes, we all left the drawing room together. I went straight up, leaving the others talking in the hall."

"And did you see your wife again? Didn't she say good night when she came up to bed?"

"I was asleep when she came up."

"But she only followed you a few minutes later. That's right, isn't it, sir?" He looked at David Keeley, who nodded.

"She hadn't come up half an hour later."

Annesley spoke stubbornly. The inspector's eyes strayed gently to Mrs. Graham.

"She didn't stay in your room talking, madam?"

Did Mr. Satterthwaite fancy it, or was there a slight pause before Mrs. Graham said, with her customary quiet decision of manner: "No, I went straight into my room and closed the door. I heard nothing."

"And you say, sir"—the inspector had shifted his attention back to Annesley—"that you slept and heard nothing. The communicating door was open, was it not?"

"I—I believe so. But my wife would have entered her room by the other door from the corridor."

"Even so, sir, there would have been certain sounds—a choking noise, a drumming of heels on the door——"

"No."

It was Mr. Satterthwaite who spoke, impetuously, unable to stop himself. Every eye turned toward him in surprise. He himself became nervous, stammered, and turned pink.

"I—I beg your pardon, Inspector. But I must speak. You are on the wrong tack—the wrong tack altogether. Mrs. Annesley did not kill herself—I am sure of it. She was murdered."

There was a dead silence; then Inspector Winkfield said quietly: "What leads you to say that, sir?"

"I—it is a feeling. A very strong feeling."

"But I think, sir, there must be more than that to it. There must be some particular reason."

Well, of course, there *was* a particular reason. There was the mysterious message from Mr. Quin. But you couldn't tell a police inspector that. Mr. Satterthwaite cast about desperately and found something.

"Last night—when we were talking together, she said she

was very happy. Very happy—just that. That wasn't like a woman thinking of committing suicide."

He was triumphant. He added: "She went back to the drawing room to fetch her ukulele, so that she wouldn't forget it in the morning. That didn't look like suicide either."

"No," admitted the inspector. "No, perhaps it didn't." He turned to David Keeley. "Did she take the ukulele upstairs with her?"

The mathematician tried to remember.

"I think—yes, she did. She went upstairs carrying it in her hand. I remember seeing it just as she turned the corner of the staircase before I turned off the light down here."

"Oh!" cried Madge. "But it's here now."

She pointed dramatically to where the ukulele lay on a table.

"That's curious," said the inspector. He stepped swiftly across and rang the bell.

A brief order sent the butler in search of the housemaid, whose business it was to do the rooms in the morning. She came and was quite positive in her answer. The ukulele had been there first thing that morning when she had dusted.

Inspector Winkfield dismissed her and then said curtly: "I would like to speak to Mr. Satterthwaite in private, please. Everyone else may go. But no one is to leave the house."

Mr. Satterthwaite twittered into speech as soon as the door had closed behind the others.

"I—I am sure, Inspector, that you have the case excellently in hand. Excellently. I just felt that—having, as I say, a very strong feeling——"

The inspector arrested further speech with an upraised hand.

"You're quite right, Mr. Satterthwaite. The lady was murdered."

"You knew it?" Mr. Satterthwaite was chagrined.

"There were certain things that puzzled Dr. Morris." He looked across at the doctor, who had remained, and the doctor assented to his statement with a nod of the head. "We made a thorough examination. The rope that was round her neck wasn't the rope that she was strangled with—

it was something much thinner that did the job, something more like a wire. It had cut right into the flesh. The mark of the rope was super-imposed on it. She was strangled and then hung up on that door afterward to make it look like suicide."

"But who——?"

"Yes," said the inspector. "Who? That's the question. What about the husband sleeping next door, who never said good night to his wife and who heard nothing? I should say we hadn't far to look. Must find out what terms they were on. That's where you can be useful to us, Mr. Satterthwaite. You've the *ongtray* here, and you can get the hang of things in a way we can't. Find out what relations there were between the two."

"I hardly like——" began Mr. Satterthwaite, stiffening.

"It won't be the first murder mystery you've helped us with. I remember the case of Mrs. Strangeways. You've got a *flair* for that sort of thing, sir. An absolute *flair*."

Yes, it was true—he *had* a *flair*. He said quietly: "I will do my best, Inspector."

Had Gerard Annesley killed his wife? Had he? Mr. Satterthwaite recalled that look of misery last night. He loved her—and he was suffering. Suffering will drive a man to strange deeds.

But there was something else—some other factor. Mabelle had spoken of herself as coming out of a wood—she was looking forward to happiness—not a quiet, rational happiness—but a happiness that was irrational—a wild ecstasy——

If Gerard Annesley had spoken the truth, Mabelle had not come to her room till at least half an hour later than he had done. Yet David Keeley had seen her going up those stairs. There were two other rooms occupied in that wing. There was Mrs. Graham's and there was her son's.

Her son's. But he and Madge——

Surely Madge would have guessed. But Madge wasn't the guessing kind. All the same, no smoke without fire——

Smoke!

Ah! he remembered. *A wisp of smoke curling out through Mrs. Graham's bedroom door.*

He acted on impulse. Straight up the stairs he went and into her room. It was empty. He closed the door behind him and locked it.

He went across to the grate. A heap of charred fragments. Very gingerly he raked them over with his finger. His luck was in. In the very centre were some unburned fragments—fragments of letters.

Very disjointed fragments, but they told him something of value.

"Life can be wonderful, Roger darling. I never knew ——" "all my life has been a dream till I met you, Roger ——" "——Gerard knows, I think—I am sorry, but what can I do. Nothing is real to me but you, Roger. We shall be together soon. What are you going to tell him at Laidell, Roger? You write strangely—but I am not afraid——"

Very carefully, Mr. Satterthwaite put the fragments into an envelope from the writing table. He went to the door, unlocked it, and opened it to find himself face to face with Mrs. Graham.

It was an awkward moment, and Mr. Satterthwaite was momentarily out of countenance. He did what was, perhaps, the best thing—attacked the situation with simplicity.

"I have been searching your room, Mrs. Graham. I have found something—a packet of letters imperfectly burned."

A wave of alarm passed over her face. It was gone in a flash, but it had been there.

"Letters from Mrs. Annesley to your son."

She hesitated for a minute, then said quietly: "That is so. I thought they would be better burned."

"For what reason?"

"My son is engaged to be married. These letters—if they had been brought into publicity through the poor girl's suicide—might have caused much pain and trouble."

"Your son could burn his own letters."

She had no answer ready for that. Mr. Satterthwaite pursued his advantage.

"You found these letters in his room, brought them into your room, and burned them. Why? You were afraid, Mrs. Graham."

"I am not in the habit of being afraid, Mr. Satterthwaite."

"No—but this was a desperate case."

"Desperate?"

"Your son might have been in danger of arrest—for murder."

"Murder!"

He saw her face go white; he went on quickly: "You heard Mrs. Annesley go into your son's room last night. Had he told her of his engagement? No, I see he hadn't. He told her then. They quarrelled, and he——"

"That's a lie!"

They had been so absorbed in their duel of words that they had not heard approaching footsteps. Roger Graham had come up behind them, unperceived by either.

"It's all right, Mother. Don't—worry. Come into my room, Mr. Satterthwaite."

Mr. Satterthwaite followed him into his room. Mrs. Graham had turned away and did not attempt to follow them. Roger Graham shut the door.

"Listen, Mr. Satterthwaite. You think I killed Mabelle. You think I strangled her—here—and took her along and hung her up on that door—later—when everyone was asleep?"

Mr. Satterthwaite stared at him. Then he said, surprisingly: "No, I do not think so."

"Thank God for that. I couldn't have killed Mabelle. I—I loved her. Or didn't I? I don't know. It's a tangle that I can't explain. I'm fond of Madge—I always have been. And she's such a good sort. We suit each other. But Mabelle was different. It was—I can't explain it—a sort of enchantment. I was, I think, afraid of her."

Mr. Satterthwaite nodded.

"It was madness—a kind of bewildering ecstasy. But it was impossible. It wouldn't have worked. That sort of thing—doesn't last. I know what it means now to have a spell cast over you."

"Yes, it must have been like that," said Mr. Satterthwaite thoughtfully.

"I—I wanted to get out of it all. I was going to tell Mabelle —last night."

"But you didn't?"

"No, I didn't," said Graham slowly. "I swear to you, Mr. Satterthwaite, that I never saw her after I said good night downstairs."

"I believe you," said Mr. Satterthwaite.

He got up. It was not Roger Graham who had killed Mabelle Annesley. He could have fled from her, but he could not have killed her. He had been afraid of her, afraid of that wild, intangible, fairylike quality of hers. He had known enchantment—and turned his back on it. He had gone for the safe, sensible thing that he had known "would work" and had relinquished the intangible dream that might lead him he knew not where.

He was a sensible young man, and, as such, uninteresting to Mr. Satterthwaite, who was an artist and a connoisseur in life.

He left Roger Graham in his room and went downstairs. The drawing room was empty. Mabelle's ukulele lay on a stool by the window. He took it up and twanged it absent-mindedly. He knew nothing of the instrument, but his ear told him that it was abominably out of tune. He turned a key experimentally.

Doris Coles came into the room. She looked at him reproachfully.

"Poor Mabelle's uke," she said.

Her clear condemnation made Mr. Satterthwaite feel obstinate.

"Tune it for me," he said, and added, "if you can."

"Of course I can," said Doris, wounded at the suggestion of incompetence in any direction.

She took it from him, twanged a string, turned a key briskly—and the string snapped.

"Well, I never. Oh! I see—but how extraordinary. It's the wrong string—a size too big. It's an A string. How stupid to put that on. Of course it snaps when you try to tune it up. How stupid people are."

"Yes," said Mr. Satterthwaite. "They are—even when they try to be clever."

His tone was so odd that she stared at him. He took the ukulele from her and removed the broken string. He went out of the room holding it in his hand. In the library he found David Keeley.

"Here," he said.

He held out the string. Keeley took it.

"What's this?"

"A broken ukulele string." He paused and then went on: *"What did you do with the other one?"*

"The other one?"

"The one you strangled her with. You were very clever, weren't you? It was done very quickly—just in that moment we were all laughing and talking in the hall.

"Mabelle came back into this room for her ukulele. You had taken the string off as you fiddled with it just before. You caught her round the throat with it and strangled her. Then you came out and locked the door and joined us. Later, in the dead of night, you came down and—and disposed of the body by hanging it on the door of her room. And you put another string on the ukulele—*but it was the wrong string.* That's why you were stupid."

There was a pause.

"But why did you do it?" said Mr. Satterthwaite. "In God's name, *why?"*

Mr. Keeley laughed, a funny giggling little laugh that made Mr. Satterthwaite feel rather sick.

"It was so very simple," he said. "That's why! And then— nobody even noticed me. Nobody ever noticed what I was doing. I thought—I thought I'd have the laugh on them."

And again he gave that furtive little giggle and looked at Mr. Satterthwaite with mad eyes.

Mr. Satterthwaite was glad that at that moment Inspector Winkfield came into the room.

It was twenty-four hours later, on his way to London, that Mr. Satterthwaite awoke from a doze to find a tall, dark man sitting opposite to him in the railway carriage. He was not altogether surprised.

"My dear Mr. Quin!"

"Yes—I am here."

Mr. Satterthwaite said slowly: "I can hardly face you. I am ashamed. I failed."

"Are you so sure of that?"

"I did not save her."

"But you discovered the truth?"

"Yes, that is true. One or other of those young men might have been accused—might even have been found guilty. So, at any rate, I saved a man's life. But she—she—that strange, enchanting creature——" His voice broke off.

Mr. Quin looked at him.

"Is death the greatest evil that can happen to anyone?"

"I—well—perhaps——No."

Mr. Satterthwaite remembered—Madge and Roger Graham—Mabelle's face in the moonlight—its serene unearthly happiness——

"No," he admitted. "No—perhaps death is not the greatest evil."

He remembered the ruffled blue chiffon of her dress that had seemed to him like the plumage of a bird, a bird with a broken wing.

When he looked up, he found himself alone. Mr. Quin was no longer there. But he had left something behind.

On the seat was a roughly carved bird fashioned out of some dim blue stone. It had, possibly, no great artistic merit. But it had something else.

It had the vague quality of enchantment.

So said Mr. Satterthwaite—and Mr. Satterthwaite was a connoisseur.

MR. PARKER PYNE   PERSONAL CONSULTANT

Mr. Parker Pyne (Christopher Parker Pyne, to give him his full name) is the family counsellor type of detective, with a knack of smoothing out one's personal problems while you wait, when he isn't engaged in a more orthodox and professional crime hunt.

For thirty-five years Mr. Parker Pyne sat in a government office, compiling statistics, and now that he has retired he is making use of his experience in a novel fashion. Unhappiness, he asserts, can be classified under five main heads—no more, no less. As a doctor diagnoses a patient's malady, he analyses his clients' unhappiness—and applies the remedy.

The two Parker Pyne stories that follow are taken from the miscellaneous collection entitled **The Regatta Mystery.** An even dozen additional exploits are included in **Mr. Parker Pyne: Detective.**

THE REGATTA MYSTERY

MR. ISAAC POINTZ removed a cigar from his lips and said approvingly: "Pretty little place."

Having thus set the seal of his approval upon Dartmouth harbor, he replaced the cigar and looked about him with the air of a man pleased with himself, his appearance, his surroundings, and life generally.

As regards the first of these, Mr. Isaac Pointz was a man of fifty-eight, in good health and condition, with perhaps a slight tendency to liver. He was not exactly stout, but comfortable-looking, and a yachting costume, which he wore at the moment, is not the most kindly of attires for a middle-aged man with a tendency to *embonpoint*. Mr. Pointz was very well turned out—correct to every crease and button—his dark and slightly oriental face beaming out under the peak of his yachting cap. As regards his surroundings, these may have been taken to mean his companions—his partner Mr. Leo Stein; Sir George and Lady Marroway; an American business acquaintance, Mr. Samuel Leathern, and his schoolgirl daughter Eve; Mrs. Rustington; and Evan Llewellyn.

The party had just come ashore from Mr. Pointz's yacht—the *Merrimaid*. In the morning they had watched the yacht racing, and they had now come ashore to join for a while in the fun of the fair—coconut shies, fat ladies, the human spider, and the merry-go-round. It is hardly to be doubted that these delights were relished most by Eve Leathern. When Mr. Pointz finally suggested that it was time to adjourn to the Royal George for dinner, hers was the only dissentient voice.

"Oh, Mr. Pointz—I did so want to have my fortune told by the real gypsy in the caravan."

Mr. Pointz had doubts of the essential realness of the gypsy in question but he gave indulgent assent.

"Eve's just crazy about the fair," said her father apologetically. "But don't you pay any attention if you want to be getting along."

"Plenty of time," said Mr. Pointz benignantly. "Let the little lady enjoy herself. I'll take you on at darts, Leo."

"Twenty-five and over wins a prize," chanted the man in charge of the darts in a high nasal voice.

"Bet you a fiver my total score beats yours," said Pointz.

"Done," said Stein with alacrity.

The two men were soon wholeheartedly engaged in their battle.

Lady Marroway murmured to Evan Llewellyn: "Eve is not the only child in the party."

Llewellyn smiled assent but somewhat absently.

He had been absent-minded all that day. Once or twice his answers had been wide of the point.

Pamela Marroway drew away from him and said to her husband: "That young man has something on his mind."

Sir George murmured: "Or someone?"

And his glance swept quickly over Janet Rustington.

Lady Marroway frowned a little. She was a tall woman exquisitely groomed. The scarlet of her fingernails was matched by the dark-red coral studs in her ears. Her eyes were dark and watchful. Sir George affected a careless "hearty English gentleman" manner—but his bright-blue eyes held the same watchful look as his wife's.

Isaac Pointz and Leo Stein were Hatton Garden diamond merchants. Sir George and Lady Marroway came from a different world—the world of Antibes and Juan les Pins—of golf at St.-Jean-de-Luz—of bathing from the rocks at Madeira in the winter.

In outward seeming they were as the lilies that toiled not, neither did they spin. But perhaps this was not quite true. There are divers ways of toiling and also of spinning.

"Here's the kid back again," said Evan Llewellyn to Mrs. Rustington.

He was a dark young man—there was a faintly hungry wolfish look about him which some women found attractive.

It was difficult to say whether Mrs. Rustington found him so. She did not wear her heart on her sleeve. She had married young—and the marriage had ended in disaster in less than a year. Since that time it was difficult to know what Janet Rustington thought of anyone or anything—her manner was always the same—charming but completely aloof.

Eve Leathern came dancing up to them, her lank fair hair bobbing excitedly. She was fifteen—an awkward child—but full of vitality.

"I'm going to be married by the time I'm seventeen," she exclaimed breathlessly. "To a very rich man, and we're going to have six children, and Tuesdays and Thursdays are my lucky days, and I ought always to wear green or blue, and an emerald is my lucky stone, and——"

"Why, pet, I think we ought to be getting along," said her father.

Mr. Leathern was a tall, fair, dyspeptic-looking man with a somewhat mournful expression.

Mr. Pointz and Mr. Stein were turning away from the darts. Mr. Pointz was chuckling and Mr. Stein was looking somewhat rueful.

"It's all a matter of luck," he was saying.

Mr. Pointz slapped his pocket cheerfully.

"Took a fiver off you all right. Skill, my boy, skill. My old dad was a first-class dart player. Well, folks, let's be getting along. Had your fortune told, Eve? Did they tell you to beware of a dark man?"

"A dark woman," corrected Eve. "She's got a cast in her eye and she'll be real mean to me if I give her a chance. And I'm to be married by the time I'm seventeen . . ."

She ran on happily as the party steered its way to the Royal George.

Dinner had been ordered before hand by the forethought of Mr. Pointz, and a bowing waiter led them upstairs and into a private room on the first floor. Here a round table was ready laid. The big, bulging bow window opened on the harbor square and was open. The noise of the fair came up to them, and the raucous squeal of three roundabouts, each blaring a different tune.

"Best shut that if we're to hear ourselves speak," observed Mr. Pointz dryly, and suited the action to the word.

They took their seats round the table and Mr. Pointz beamed affectionately at his guests. He felt he was doing them well and he liked to do people well. His eye rested on one after another. Lady Marroway—fine woman—not quite the goods, of course, he knew that—he was perfectly well aware that what he had called all his life the *crème de la crème* would have very little to do with the Marroways—but then the *crème de la crème* were supremely unaware of his own existence. Anyway, Lady Marroway was a smart-looking woman—and he didn't mind if she *did* rook him a bit at bridge. Didn't enjoy it quite so much from Sir George. Fishy eye the fellow had. Brazenly on the make. But he wouldn't make too much out of Isaac Pointz. He'd see to that all right.

Old Leathern wasn't a bad fellow—long-winded, of course, like most Americans—fond of telling endless long stories. And he had that disconcerting habit of requiring precise information. What was the population of Dartmouth? In what year had the Naval College been built? And so on. Expected his host to be a kind of walking Baedeker. Eve was a nice cheery kid—he enjoyed chaffing her. Voice rather like a corn crake, but she had all her wits about her. A bright kid.

Young Llewellyn—he seemed a bit quiet. Looked as though he had something on his mind. Hard up, probably. These writing fellows usually were. Looked as though he might be keen on Janet Rustington. A nice woman—attractive and clever, too. But she didn't ram her writing down your throat. High-brow sort of stuff she wrote, but you'd never think it to hear her talk. And old Leo! *He* wasn't getting younger or thinner. And blissfully unaware that his partner was at that moment thinking precisely the same thing about him, Mr. Pointz corrected Mr. Leathern as to pilchards being connected with Devon and not Cornwall and prepared to enjoy his dinner.

"Mr. Pointz," said Eve when plates of hot mackerel had been set before them and the waiters had left the room.

"Yes, young lady."

"Have you got that big diamond with you right now? The one you showed us last night and said you always took about with you?"

Mr. Pointz chuckled.

"That's right. My mascot, I call it. Yes, I've got it with me all right."

"I think that's awfully dangerous. Somebody might get it away from you in the crowd at the fair."

"Not they," said Mr. Pointz. "I'll take good care of that."

"But they *might*," insisted Eve. "You've got gangsters in England as well as we have, haven't you?"

"They won't get the Morning Star," said Mr. Pointz. "To begin with, it's in a special inner pocket. And anyway—old Pointz knows what he's about. Nobody's going to steal the Morning Star."

Eve laughed.

"Uh-huh—bet I could steal it!"

"I bet you couldn't," Mr. Pointz twinkled back at her.

"Well, I bet I could. I was thinking about it last night in bed—after you'd handed it round the table for us all to look at. I thought of a real cute way to steal it."

"And what's that?"

Eve put her head on one side, her fair hair wagged excitedly. "I'm not telling you—now. What do you bet I couldn't?"

Memories of Mr. Pointz' youth rose in his mind.

"Half a dozen pairs of gloves," he said.

"Gloves," cried Eve disgustedly. "Who wears gloves?"

"Well—do you wear silk stockings?"

"Do I not? My best pair laddered this morning."

"Very well, then. Half a dozen pairs of the finest silk stockings——"

"Oo-er," said Eve blissfully. "And what about you?"

"Well, I need a new tobacco pouch."

"Right. That's a deal. Not that you'll get your tobacco pouch. Now I'll tell you what you've got to do. You must hand it round like you did last night——"

She broke off as two waiters entered to remove the plates.

When they were starting on the next course of chicken, Mr. Pointz said: "Remember this, young woman, if this is to represent a real theft, I should send for the police and you'd be searched."

"That's quite O.K. by me. You needn't be quite so life-like as to bring the police into it. But Lady Marroway or Mrs. Rustington can do all the searching you like."

"Well, that's that then," said Mr. Pointz. "What are you setting up to be? A first-class jewel thief?"

"I might take to it as a career—if it really paid."

"If you got away with the Morning Star, it would pay you. Even after recutting, that stone would be worth over thirty thousand pounds."

"My!" said Eve, impressed. "What's that in dollars?"

Lady Marroway uttered an exclamation.

"And you carry such a stone about with you?" she said reproachfully. "Thirty thousand pounds." Her darkened eyelashes quivered.

Mrs. Rustington said softly: "It's a lot of money. . . . And then there's the fascination of the stone itself. . . . It's beautiful."

"Just a piece of carbon," said Evan Llewellyn.

"I've always understood it's the 'fence' that's the difficulty in jewel robberies," said Sir George. "He takes the lion's share—eh, what?"

"Come on," said Eve excitedly. "Let's start. Take the diamond out and say what you said last night."

Mr. Leathern said in his deep, melancholy voice, "I do apologize for my offspring. She gets kinder worked up——"

"That'll do, Pops," said Eve. "Now then, Mr. Pointz——"

Smiling, Mr. Pointz fumbled in an inner pocket. He drew something out. It lay on the palm of his hand, blinking in the light.

A diamond. . . .

Rather stiffly, Mr. Pointz repeated as far as he could remember his speech of the previous evening on the *Merrimaid*.

"Perhaps you ladies and gentlemen would like to have a look at this? It's an unusually beautiful stone. I call it the Morning Star, and it's by way of being my mascot—goes about with me anywhere. Like to see it?"

He handed it to Lady Marroway, who took it, exclaimed at its beauty, and passed it to Mr. Leathern, who said, "Pretty good—yes, pretty good," in a somewhat artificial manner and, in his turn, passed it to Llewellyn.

The waiters coming in at that moment, there was a slight hitch in the proceedings. When they had gone again, Evan said, "Very fine stone," and passed it to Leo Stein, who did not trouble to make any comment but handed it quickly on to Eve.

"How perfectly lovely," cried Eve in a high, affected voice.

"Oh!" She gave a cry of consternation as it slipped from her hand. "I've dropped it."

She pushed back her chair and got down to grope under the table. Sir George, at her right, bent also. A glass got swept off the table in the confusion. Stein, Llewellyn, and Mrs. Rustington all helped in the search. Finally Lady Marroway joined in.

Only Mr. Pointz took no part in the proceedings. He remained in his seat sipping his wine and smiling sardonically.

"Oh, dear," said Eve, still in her artificial manner. "How dreadful! Where *can* it have rolled to? I can't find it anywhere."

One by one the assistant searchers rose to their feet.

"It's disappeared all right, Pointz," said Sir George, smiling.

"Very nicely done," said Mr. Pointz, nodding approval. "You'd make a very good actress, Eve. Now the question is, have you hidden it somewhere or have you got it on you?"

"Search me," said Eve dramatically.

Mr. Pointz's eye sought out a large screen in the corner of the room.

He nodded towards it and then looked at Lady Marroway and Mrs. Rustington.

"If you ladies will be so good——"

"Why, certainly," said Lady Marroway, smiling.

The two women rose.

Lady Marroway said, "Don't be afraid, Mr. Pointz. We'll vet her properly."

The three went behind the screen.

The room was hot. Evan Llewellyn flung open the window. A news vender was passing. Evan threw down a coin and the man threw up a paper.

Llewellyn unfolded it.

"Hungarian situation's none too good," he said.

"That the local rag?" asked Sir George. "There's a horse I'm interested in ought to have run at Haldon today—Natty Boy."

"Leo," said Mr. Pointz. "Lock the door. We don't want those waiters popping in and out till this business is over."

"Natty Boy won three to one," said Evan.

"Rotten odds," said Sir George.

"Mostly Regatta news," said Evan, glancing over the sheet.

The three young women came out from the screen.

"Not a sign of it," said Janet Rustington.

"You can take it from me she hasn't got it on her," said Lady Marroway.

Mr. Pointz thought he would be quite ready to take it from her. There was a grim tone in her voice and he felt no doubt that the search had been thorough.

"Say, Eve, you haven't swallowed it?" asked Mr. Leathern anxiously. "Because maybe that wouldn't be too good for you."

"I'd have seen her do that," said Leo Stein quietly. "I was watching her. She didn't put anything in her mouth."

"I couldn't swallow a great thing all points like that," said Eve. She put her hands on her hips and looked at Mr. Pointz. "What about it, big boy?" she asked.

"You stand over there where you are and don't move," said that gentleman.

Among them, the men stripped the table and turned it upside down. Mr. Pointz examined every inch of it. Then he transferred his attention to the chair on which Eve had been sitting and those on either side of her.

The thoroughness of the search left nothing to be desired. The other four men joined in and the women also. Eve Leathern stood by the wall near the screen and laughed with intense enjoyment.

Five minutes later Mr. Pointz rose with a slight groan from his knees and dusted his trousers sadly. His pristine freshness was somewhat impaired.

"Eve," he said. "I take off my hat to you. You're the finest thing in jewel thieves I've ever come across. What you've done with that stone beats me. As far as I can see, it must be in the room, as it isn't on you. I give you best."

"Are the stockings mine?" demanded Eve.

"They're yours, young lady."

"Eve, my child, where *can* you have hidden it?" demanded Mrs. Rustington curiously.

Eve pranced forward.

"I'll show you. You'll all be just mad with yourselves."

She went across to the side table, where the things from the dinner table had been roughly stacked. She picked up her little black evening bag——

"Right under your eyes. Right . . ."

Her voice, gay and triumphant, trailed off suddenly.

"Oh," she said. *"Oh. . . ."*

"What's the matter, honey?" said her father.

Eve whispered: "It's gone . . . it's *gone*. . . ."

"What's all this?" asked Pointz, coming forward.

Eve turned to him impetuously.

"It was like this. This pochette of mine has a big paste stone in the middle of the clasp. It fell out last night, and just when you were showing that diamond round I noticed that it was much the same size. And so I thought in the night what a good idea for a robbery it would be to wedge your diamond into the gap with a bit of plasticine. I felt sure nobody would ever spot it. That's what I did tonight.

First I dropped it—then went down after it with the bag in my hand, stuck it into the gap with a bit of plasticine which I had handy, put my bag on the table, and went on pretending to look for the diamond. I thought it would be like the Purloined Letter—you know—lying there in full view under all your noses—and just looking like a common bit of rhinestone. And it was a good plan—none of you *did* notice."

"I wonder," said Mr. Stein.

"What did you say?"

Mr. Pointz took the bag, looked at the empty hole with a fragment of plasticine still adhering to it, and said slowly: "It may have fallen out. We'd better look again."

The search was repeated, but this time it was a curiously silent business. An atmosphere of tension pervaded the room.

Finally everyone in turn gave it up. They stood looking at each other.

"It's not in this room," said Stein.

"And nobody's left the room," said Sir George significantly.

There was a moment's pause. Eve burst into tears.

Her father patted her on the shoulder.

"There, there," he said awkwardly.

Sir George turned to Leo Stein.

"Mr. Stein," he said. "Just now you murmured something under your breath. When I asked you to repeat it, you said it was nothing. But as a matter of fact I heard what you said. Miss Eve had just said that none of us noticed the place where she had put the diamond. The words you murmured were: 'I wonder.' What we have to face is the probability that one person *did* notice—that that person is in this room now. I suggest that the only fair and honorable thing is for every one present to submit to a search. The diamond cannot have left the room."

When Sir George played the part of the old English gentleman, none could play it better. His voice rang with sincerity and indignation.

"Bit unpleasant, all this," said Mr. Pointz unhappily.

"It's all my fault," sobbed Eve. "I didn't mean——"

"Buck up, kiddo," said Mr. Stein kindly. "Nobody's blaming you."

Mr. Leathern said in his slow, pedantic manner, "Why, certainly, I think that Sir George's suggestion will meet with the fullest approval from all of us. It does from me."

"I agree," said Evan Llewellyn.

Mrs. Rustington looked at Lady Marroway, who nodded a brief assent. The two of them went back behind the screen and the sobbing Eve accompanied them.

A waiter knocked on the door and was told to go away.

Five minutes later eight people looked at each other incredulously.

The Morning Star had vanished into space. . . .

Mr. Parker Pyne looked thoughtfully at the dark, agitated face of the young man opposite him.

"Of course," he said. "You're Welsh, Mr. Llewellyn."

"What's that got to do with it?"

Mr. Parker Pyne waved a large, well-cared-for hand.

"Nothing at all, I admit. I am interested in the classification of emotional reactions as exemplified by certain racial types. That is all. Let us return to the consideration of your particular problem."

"I don't really know why I came to you," said Evan Llewellyn. His hands twitched nervously, and his dark face had a haggard look. He did not look at Mr. Parker Pyne and that gentleman's scrutiny seemed to make him uncomfortable. "I don't know why I came to you," he repeated. "But where the hell *can* I go? And what the hell can I *do?* It's the powerlessness of not being able to do anything at all that gets me. . . . I saw your advertisement and I remember that a chap had once spoken of you and said that you got results. . . . And—well—I came! I suppose I was a fool. It's the sort of position nobody can do anything about."

"Not at all," said Mr. Parker Pyne. "I am the proper person to come to. I am a specialist in unhappiness. This business has obviously caused you a good deal of pain. You are sure the facts are exactly as you have told me?"

"I don't think I've left out anything. Pointz brought out the diamond and passed it around—that wretched American child stuck it on her ridiculous bag, and when we came to look at the bag, the diamond was gone. It wasn't on anyone—old Pointz himself even was searched—he suggested it himself—and I'll swear it was nowhere in that room! *And nobody left the room*——"

"No waiters, for instance?" suggested Mr. Parker Pyne. Llewellyn shook his head.

"They went out before the girl began messing about with the diamond, and afterwards Pointz locked the door so as to keep them out. No, it lies between one of us."

"It would certainly seem so," said Mr. Parker Pyne thoughtfully.

"That damned evening paper," said Evan Llewellyn bitterly. "I saw it come into their minds—that that was the only way——"

"Just tell me again exactly what occurred."

"It was perfectly simple. I threw open the window, whistled to the man, threw down a copper, and he tossed me up the paper. And there it is, you see—the only possible way the diamond could have left the room—thrown by me to an accomplice waiting in the street below."

"Not the *only* possible way," said Mr. Parker Pyne.

"What other way can you suggest?"

"If you didn't throw it out, there *must* have been some other way."

"Oh, I see. I hoped you meant something more definite than that. Well, I can only say that I *didn't* throw it out. I can't expect you to believe me—or anyone else."

"Oh, yes, I believe you," said Mr. Parker Pyne.

"You do? Why?"

"Not a criminal type," said Mr. Parker Pyne. "Not, that is, the particular criminal type that steals jewelry. There are crimes, of course, that you might commit—but we won't enter into that subject. At any rate, I do not see you as the purloiner of the Morning Star."

"Everyone else does, though," said Llewellyn bitterly.

"I see," said Mr. Parker Pyne.

"They looked at me in a queer sort of way at the time. Marroway picked up the paper and just glanced over at the window. He didn't say anything. But Pointz cottoned on to it quick enough! I could see what they thought. There hasn't been any open accusation, that's the devil of it."

Mr. Parker Pyne nodded sympathetically.

"It is worse than that," he said.

"Yes. It's just suspicion. I've had a fellow round asking questions—routine inquiries, he called it. One of the new dress-shirted lot of police, I suppose. Very tactful—nothing at all hinted. Just interested in the fact that I'd been hard up and was suddenly cutting a bit of a splash."

"And were you?"

"Yes—some luck with a horse or two. Unluckily my bets were made on the course—there's nothing to show that that's how the money came in. They can't disprove it, of course—but that's just the sort of easy lie a fellow would invent if he didn't want to show where the money came from."

"I agree. Still they will have to have a good deal more than that to go upon."

"Oh! I'm not afraid of actually being arrested and charged with the theft. In a way that would be easier—one would know where one was. It's the ghastly fact that all those people believe I took it."

"One person in particular?"

"What do you mean?"

"A suggestion—nothing more——" Again Mr. Parker Pyne waved his comfortable-looking hand. "There *was* one person in particular, wasn't there? Shall we say Mrs. Rustington?"

Llewellyn's dark face flushed.

"Why pitch on her?"

"Oh, my dear sir—there is obviously someone whose opinion matters to you greatly—probably a lady. What ladies were there? An American flapper? Lady Marroway? But you would probably rise, not fall, in Lady Marroway's estimation if you had brought off such a *coup*. I know something of the lady. Clearly then, Mrs. Rustington."

Llewellyn said, with something of an effort, "She—she's had rather an unfortunate experience. Her husband was a down-and-out rotter. It's made her unwilling to trust anyone. She—if she thinks——"

He found it difficult to go on.

"Quite so," said Mr. Parker Pyne. "I see the matter is important. It must be cleared up."

Evan gave a short laugh.

"That's easy to say."

"And quite easy to do," said Mr. Parker Pyne.

"You think so?"

"Oh, yes—the problem is so clear-cut. So many possibilities are ruled out. The answer must really be extremely simple. Indeed, already I have a kind of glimmering——"

Llewellyn stared at him incredulously.

Mr. Parker Pyne drew a pad of paper towards him and picked up a pen.

"Perhaps you would give me a brief description of the party."

"Haven't I already done so?"

"Their personal appearance—color of hair and so on."

"But, Mr. Parker Pyne, what can that have to do with it?"

"A good deal, young man, a good deal. Classification and so on."

Somewhat unbelievingly, Evan described the personal appearance of the members of the yachting party.

Mr. Parker Pyne made a note or two, pushed away the pad, and said: "Excellent. By the way, did you say a wineglass was broken?"

Evan stared again.

"Yes, it was knocked off the table, and then it got stepped on."

"Nasty thing, splinters of glass," said Mr. Parker Pyne. "Whose wineglass was it?"

"I think it was the child's—Eve."

"Ah!—and who sat next to her on that side?"

"Sir George Marroway."

"You didn't see which of them knocked it off the table?"

"Afraid I didn't. Does it matter?"

"Not really. No. That was a superfluous question. Well"—
he stood up—"good morning, Mr. Llewellyn. Will you call
again in three days' time? I think the whole thing will be
quite satisfactorily cleared up by then."

"Are you joking, Mr. Parker Pyne?"

"I never joke on professional matters, my dear sir. It
would occasion distrust in my clients. Shall we say Friday at
eleven-thirty? Thank you."

Evan entered Mr. Parker Pyne's office on the Friday
morning in a considerable turmoil. Hope and skepticism
fought for mastery.

Mr. Parker Pyne rose to meet him with a beaming smile.

"Good morning, Mr. Llewellyn. Sit down. Have a cigarette?"

Llewellyn waved aside the proffered box.

"Well?" he said.

"Very well indeed," said Mr. Parker Pyne. "The police
arrested the gang last night."

"The gang? What gang?"

"The Amalfi gang. I thought of them at once when you
told me your story. I recognized their methods, and once you
had described the guests, well, there was no doubt at all in
my mind."

"Who are the Amalfi gang?"

"Father, son, and daughter-in-law—that is, if Pietro and
Maria are really married—which some doubt."

"I don't understand."

"It's quite simple. The name is Italian and no doubt the
origin is Italian, but old Amalfi was born in America. His
methods are usually the same. He impersonates a real busi-
nessman, introduces himself to some prominent figure in the
jewel business in some European country, and then plays his
little trick. In this case he was deliberately on the track of
the Morning Star. Pointz's idiosyncrasy was well known in
the trade. Maria Amalfi played the part of his daughter
(amazing creature, twenty-seven at least, and nearly always
plays a part of sixteen)."

"Not Eve!" gasped Llewellyn.

"Exactly. The third member of the gang got himself taken on as an extra waiter at the Royal George—it was holiday time, remember, and they would need extra ctuff. He may even have bribed a regular man to stay away. The scene is set. Eve challenges old Pointz and he takes on the bet. He passes round the diamond as he had done the night before. The waiters enter the room and Leathern retains the stone until they have left the room. When they do leave, the diamond leaves also, neatly attached with a morsel of chewing gum to the underside of the plate that Pietro bears away. So simple!"

"But I *saw* it after that."

"No, no, you saw a paste replica, good enough to deceive a casual glance. Stein, you told me, hardly looked at it. Eve drops it, sweeps off a glass too, and steps firmly on stone and glass together. Miraculous disappearance of diamond. Both Eve and Leathern can submit to as much searching as anyone pleases."

"Well—I'm——" Evan shook his head, at a loss for words. "You say you recognized the gang from my description. Had they worked this trick before?"

"Not exactly—but it was their kind of business. Naturally my attention was at once directed to the girl Eve."

"Why? I didn't suspect her—nobody did. She seemed such a—such a *child*."

"That is the peculiar genius of Maria Amalfi. She is more like a child than any child could possibly be! And then the plasticine! This bet was supposed to have arisen quite spontaneously—yet the little lady had some plasticine with her all handy. That spoke of premeditation. My suspicions fastened on her at once."

Llewellyn rose to his feet.

"Well, Mr. Parker Pyne, I'm no end obliged to you."

"Classification," murmured Mr. Parker Pyne. "The classification of criminal types—it interests me."

"You'll let me know how much—er——"

"My fee will be quite moderate," said Mr. Parker Pyne. "It will not make too big a hole in the—er—horse-racing profits. All the same, young man, I should, I think, leave the horses alone in the future. Very uncertain animal, the horse."

"That's all right," said Evan.

He shook Mr. Parker Pyne by the hand and strode from the office.

He hailed a taxi and gave the address of Janet Rustington's flat.

He felt in a mood to carry all before him.

PROBLEM AT POLLENSA BAY

THE STEAMER from Barcelona to Majorca landed Mr. Parker Pyne at Palma in the early hours of the morning—and straightaway he met with disillusionment. The hotels were full! The best that could be done for him was an airless cupboard overlooking an inner court in a hotel in the center of the town—and with that Mr. Parker Pyne was not prepared to put up. The proprietor of the hotel was indifferent to his disappointment.

"What will you?" he observed with a shrug.

Palma was popular now! The exchange was favorable! Everyone—the English, the Americans—they all came to Majorca in the winter. The whole place was crowded. It was doubtful if the English gentleman would be able to get in anywhere—except perhaps at Formentor, where the prices were so ruinous that even foreigners blenched at them.

Mr. Parker Pyne partook of some coffee and a roll and went out to view the cathedral, but found himself in no mood for appreciating the beauties of architecture.

He next had a conference with a friendly taxi driver in inadequate French interlarded with native Spanish, and they discussed the merits and possibilities of Soller, Alcudia, Pollensa, and Formentor—where there were fine hotels but very expensive.

Mr. Parker Pyne was goaded to inquire how expensive.

They asked, said the taxi driver, an amount that it would be absurd and ridiculous to pay—was it not well known that the English came here because prices were cheap and reasonable?

Mr. Parker Pyne said that that was quite so, but all the same what sums *did* they charge at Formentor?

A price incredible!

Perfectly—but WHAT PRICE EXACTLY?

The driver consented at last to reply in terms of figures.

Fresh from the exactions of hotels in Jerusalem and Egypt, the figure did not stagger Mr. Parker Pyne unduly.

A bargain was struck, Mr. Parker Pyne's suitcases were loaded on the taxi in a somewhat haphazard manner, and they started off to drive round the island, trying cheaper hostelries en route, but with the final objective of Formentor.

But they never reached that final abode of plutocracy, for after they had passed through the narrow streets of Pollensa and were following the curved line of the seashore, they came to the Hotel Pino d'Oro—a small hotel standing on the edge of the sea looking out over a view that in the misty haze of a fine morning had the exquisitive vagueness of a Japanese print. At once Mr. Parker Pyne knew that this, and this only, was what he was looking for. He stopped the taxi, passed through the painted gate with the hope that he would find a resting place.

The elderly couple to whom the hotel belonged knew no English or French. Nevertheless, the matter was concluded satisfactorily. Mr. Parker Pyne was allotted a room overlooking the sea, the suitcases were unloaded, the driver congratulated his passenger upon avoiding the monstrous exigencies of "these new hotels," received his fare, and departed with a cheerful Spanish salutation.

Mr. Parker Pyne glanced at his watch and, perceiving that it was, even now, but a quarter to ten, he went out onto the small terrace now bathed in a dazzling morning light and ordered, for the second time that morning, coffee and rolls.

There were four tables there, his own, one from which breakfast was being cleared away, and two occupied ones. At the one nearest him sat a family of father and mother and two elderly daughters—Germans. Beyond them, at the corner of the terrace, sat what were clearly an English mother and son.

The woman was about fifty-five. She had grey hair of a

pretty tone—was sensibly but not fashionably dressed in a tweed coat and skirt—and had that comfortable self-posses-sion which marks an Englishwoman used to much travelling abroad.

The young man who sat opposite her might have been twenty-five, and he too was typical of his class and age. He was neither good-looking nor plain, tall nor short. He was clearly on the best of terms with his mother—they made little jokes together—and he was assiduous in passing her things.

As they talked, her eye met that of Mr. Parker Pyne. It passed over him with well-bred nonchalance, but he knew that he had been assimilated and labelled.

He had been recognized as English and doubtless, in due course, some pleasant noncommittal remark would be ad-dressed to him.

Mr. Parker Pyne had no particular objection. His own countrymen and women abroad were inclined to bore him slightly, but he was quite willing to pass the time of day in an amiable manner. In a small hotel it caused constraint if one did not do so. This particular woman, he felt sure, had excellent "hotel manners," as he put it.

The English boy rose from his seat, made some laughing remark, and passed into the hotel. The woman took her let-ters and bag and settled herself in a chair facing the sea. She unfolded a copy of the *Continental Daily Mail*. Her back was to Mr. Parker Pyne.

As he drank the last drop of his coffee, Mr. Parker Pyne glanced in her direction, and instantly he stiffened. He was alarmed—alarmed for the peaceful continuance of his holi-day! That back was horribly expressive. In his time he had classified many such backs. Its rigidity—the tenseness of its poise—without seeing her face he knew well enough that the eyes were bright with unshed tears—that the woman was keeping herself in hand by a rigid effort.

Moving warily, like a much-hunted animal, Mr. Parker Pyne retreated into the hotel. Not half an hour before he had been invited to sign his name in the book lying on the desk. There it was—a neat signature—C. Parker Pyne, London.

A few lines above, Mr. Parker Pyne noticed the entries: Mrs. R. Chester, Mr. Basil Chester—Holm Park, Devon.

Seizing a pen, Mr. Parker Pyne wrote rapidly over his signature. It now read (with difficulty) Christopher Pyne.

If Mrs. R. Chester was unhappy in Pollensa Bay, it was not going to be made easy for her to consult Mr. Parker Pyne.

Already it had been a source of abiding wonder to that gentleman that so many people he had come across abroad should know his name and have noted his advertisements. In England many thousands of people read the *Times* every day and could have answered quite truthfully that they had never heard such a name in their lives. Abroad, he reflected, they read their newspapers more thoroughly. No item, not even the advertisement columns, escaped them.

Already his holidays had been interrupted on several occasions. He had dealt with a whole series of problems from murder to attempted blackmail. He was determined in Majorca to have peace. He felt instinctively that a distressed mother might trouble that peace considerably.

Mr. Parker Pyne settled down at the Pino d'Oro very happily. There was a larger hotel not far off, the Mariposa, where a good many English people stayed. There was also quite an artist colony living all round. You could walk along by the sea to the fishing village, where there was a cocktail bar where people met—and there were a few shops. It was all very peaceful and pleasant. Girls strolled about in trousers with brightly colored handkerchiefs tied round the upper halves of their bodies. Young men in berets with rather long hair held forth in "Mac's Bar" on such subjects as plastic values and abstraction in art.

On the day after Mr. Parker Pyne's arrival, Mrs. Chester made a few conventional remarks to him on the subject of the view and the likelihood of the weather keeping fine. She then chatted a little with the German lady about knitting and had a few pleasant words about the sadness of the political situation with two Danish gentlemen who spent their time rising at dawn and walking for eleven hours.

Mr. Parker Pyne found Basil Chester a most likeable

young man. He called Mr. Parker Pyne "sir" and listened most politely to anything the older man said. Sometimes the three English people had coffee together after dinner in the evening. After the third day, Basil left the party after ten minutes or so and Mr. Parker Pyne was left tête-à-tête with Mrs. Chester.

They talked about flowers and the growing of them, of the lamentable state of the English pound and of how expensive France had become, and of the difficulty of getting good afternoon tea.

Every evening when her son departed, Mr. Parker Pyne saw the quickly concealed tremor of her lips, but immediately she recovered and discoursed pleasantly on the above-mentioned subjects.

Little by little she began to talk of Basil—of how well he had done at school—"he was in the First XI, you know"—of how everyone liked him, of how proud his father would have been of the boy had he lived, of how thankful she had been that Basil had never been "wild." "Of course, I always urge him to be with young people, but he really seems to prefer being with me."

She said it with a kind of nice modest pleasure in the fact.

But for once Mr. Parker Pyne did not make the usual tactful response he could usually achieve so easily. He said instead: "Oh, well, there seem to be plenty of young people here—not in the hotel, but roundabout."

At that, he noticed, Mrs. Chester stiffened. She said: Of course, there were a lot of artists. Perhaps she was very old-fashioned—*real* art, of course, was different, but a lot of young people just made that sort of thing an excuse for lounging about and doing nothing—and the girls drank a lot too much.

On the following day Basil said to Mr. Parker Pyne: "I'm awfully glad you turned up here, sir—especially for my mother's sake. She likes having you to talk to in the evenings."

"What did you do when you were first here?"

"As a matter of fact, we used to play piquet."

"I see."

"Of course, one gets rather tired of piquet. As a matter of fact, I've got some friends here—frightfully cheery crowd. I don't really think my mother approves of them———" He laughed as though he felt this ought to be amusing. "The mater's very old-fashioned. . . . Even girls in trousers shock her!"

"Quite so," said Mr. Parker Pyne.

"What I tell her is—one's got to move with the times. . . . The girls at home round us are frightfully dull. . . ."

"I see," said Mr. Parker Pyne.

All this interested him well enough. He was a spectator of a miniature drama, but he was not called upon to take part in it.

And then the worst—from Mr. Parker Pyne's point of view—happened. A gushing lady of his acquaintance came to stay at the Mariposa. They met in the teashop in the presence of Mrs. Chester.

The newcomer screamed: "Why—if it isn't Mr. Parker Pyne—the one and only Mr. Parker Pyne! And Adela Chester! Do you know each other? Oh, you do? You're staying at the same hotel? He's the one and only original wizard, Adela—the marvel of the century—all your troubles smoothed out while you wait! What? Didn't you *know?* You must have *heard* about him? Haven't you read his advertisements? *'Are you in trouble? Consult Mr. Parker Pyne.'* There's just nothing he can't do. Husbands and wives flying at each other's throats and he brings 'em together—if you've lost interest in life he gives you the most thrilling adventures. As I say, the man's just a *wizard!*"

It went on a good deal longer—Mr. Parker Pyne at intervals making modest disclaimers. He disliked the look that Mrs. Chester turned upon him. He disliked even more seeing her return along the beach in close confabulation with the garrulous singer of his praises.

The climax came quicker than he expected. That evening, after coffee, Mrs. Chester said abruptly, "Will you come into the little salon, Mr. Pyne? There is something I want to say to you."

He could but bow and submit.

Mrs. Chester's self-control had been wearing thin—as the door of the little salon closed behind them, it snapped. She sat down and burst into tears.

"My boy, Mr. Parker Pyne. You must save him. *We* must save him. It's breaking my heart!"

"My dear lady, as a mere outsider——"

"Nina Wycherley says you can do *anything*. She said I was to have the utmost confidence in you. She advised me to tell you everything—and that you'd put the whole thing right."

Inwardly Mr. Parker Pyne resented the obtrusive Mrs. Wycherley.

Resigning himself, he said: "Well, let us thrash the matter out. A girl, I suppose?"

"Did he tell you about her?"

"Only indirectly."

Words poured in a vehement stream from Mrs. Chester. The girl was dreadful. She drank, she swore—she wore no clothes to speak of. Her sister lived out here—was married to an artist—a Dutchman. The whole set was most undesirable. Basil was completely changed. He had always been so quiet, so interested in serious subjects. He had thought at one time of taking up archaeology——

"Well, well," said Mr. Parker Pyne. "Nature will have her revenge."

"What do you mean?"

"It isn't healthy for a young man to be interested in serious subjects. He ought to be making an idiot of himself over one girl after another."

"Please be serious, Mr. Pyne."

"I'm perfectly serious. Is the young lady, by any chance, the one who had tea with you yesterday?"

He had noticed her—her grey-flannel trousers—the scarlet handkerchief tied loosely around her breasts—the vermilion mouth and the fact that she had chosen a cocktail in preference to tea.

"You saw her? Terrible! Not the kind of girl Basil has ever admired."

"You haven't given him much chance to admire a girl, have you?"

"I?"

"He's been too fond of *your* company! Bad! However, I daresay he'll get over this—if you don't precipitate matters."

"You don't understand. He wants to marry this girl—Betty Gregg—they're *engaged*."

"It's gone as far as that?"

"Yes. Mr. Parker Pyne, you *must* do something. You must get my boy out of this disastrous marriage! His whole life will be ruined."

"Nobody's life can be ruined except by themselves."

"Basil's will be," said Mrs. Chester positively.

"I'm not worrying about Basil."

"You're not worrying about the *girl?*"

"No, I'm worrying about *you*. You've been squandering your birthright."

Mrs. Chester looked at him, slightly taken aback.

"What are the years from twenty to forty? Fettered and bound by personal and emotional relationships. That's bound to be. That's living. But later there's a new stage. You can think, observe life, discover something about other people and the truth about yourself. Life becomes real—significant. You see it as a whole. Not just one scene—the scene you, as an actor, are playing. No man or woman is actually himself (or herself) till after forty-five. That's when individuality has a chance."

Mrs. Chester said: "I've been wrapped up in Basil. He's been *everything* to me."

"Well, he shouldn't have been. That's what you're paying for now. Love him as much as you like—but you're Adela Chester, remember, a person—not just Basil's mother."

"It will break my heart if Basil's life is ruined," said Basil's mother.

He looked at the delicate lines of her face, the wistful droop of her mouth. She was, somehow, a lovable woman. He did not want her to be hurt. He said: "I'll see what I can do."

He found Basil Chester only too ready to talk, eager to urge his point of view.

"This business is being just hellish. Mother's hopeless—prejudiced, narrow-minded. If only she'd let herself, she'd *see* how fine Betty is."

"And Betty?"

He sighed.

"Betty's being difficult! If she'd just conform a bit—I mean, leave off the lipstick for a day—it might make all the difference. She seems to go out of her way to be—well—modern when Mother's about."

Mr. Parker Pyne smiled.

"Betty and Mother are two of the dearest people in the world; I should have thought they would have taken to each other like hot cakes."

"You have a lot to learn, young man," said Mr. Parker Pyne.

"I wish you'd come along and see Betty and have a good talk about it all."

Mr. Parker Pyne accepted the invitation readily.

Betty and her sister and her husband lived in a small dilapidated villa a little way back from the sea. Their life was of a refreshing simplicity. Their furniture comprised three chairs, a table, and beds. There was a cupboard in the wall that held the bare requirements of cups and plates. Hans was an excitable young man with wild blond hair that stood up all over his head. He spoke very odd English with incredible rapidity, walking up and down as he did so. Stella, his wife, was small and fair. Betty Gregg had red hair and freckles and a mischievous eye. She was, he noticed, not nearly so made up as she had been the previous day at the Pino d'Oro.

She gave him a cocktail and said with a twinkle: "You're in on the big bust-up?"

Mr. Parker Pyne nodded.

"And whose side are you on, big boy? The young lovers —or the disapproving dame?"

"May I ask you a question?"

"Certainly."

"Have you been very tactful over all this?"

"Not at all," said Miss Gregg frankly. "But the old cat put my back up" (she glanced round to make sure that Basil was out of earshot). "That woman just makes me feel mad. She's kept Basil tied to her apron strings all these years —that sort of thing makes a man look a fool. Basil isn't a fool really. Then she's so terribly *pukka sahib*."

"That's not really such a bad thing. It's merely 'unfashionable' just at present."

Betty Gregg gave a sudden twinkle.

"You mean it's like putting Chippendale chairs in the attic in Victorian days? Later you get them down again and say, 'Aren't they marvelous?' "

"Something of the kind."

Betty Gregg considered.

"Perhaps you're right. I'll be honest. It was Basil who put my back up—being so anxious about what impression I'd make on his mother. It drove me to extremes. Even now I believe he might give me up—if his mother worked on him good and hard."

"He might," said Mr. Parker Pyne. "If she went about it in the right way."

"Are you going to tell her the right way? She won't think of it herself, you know. She'll just go on disapproving, and that won't do the trick. But if you prompted her——"

She bit her lip—raised frank blue eyes to his.

"I've heard about you, Mr. Parker Pyne. You're supposed to know something about human nature. Do you think Basil and I could make a go of it—or not?"

"I should like an answer to three questions."

"Suitability test? All right, go ahead."

"Do you sleep with your window open or shut?"

"Open. I like lots of air."

"Do you and Basil enjoy the same kind of food?"

"Yes."

"Do you like going to bed early or late?"

"Really, under the rose, early. At half-past ten I yawn—

and I secretly feel rather hearty in the mornings—but, of course, I daren't admit it."

"You ought to suit each other very well," said Mr. Parker Pyne.

"Rather a superficial test."

"Not at all. I have known seven marriages at least, entirely wrecked, because the husband liked sitting up till midnight and the wife fell asleep at half-past nine and vice versa."

"It's a pity," said Betty, "that everybody can't be happy. Basil and I, and his mother giving us her blessing."

Mr. Parker Pyne coughed.

"I think," he said, "that that could possibly be managed."

She looked at him doubtfully.

"Now I wonder," she said, "if you're double-crossing me?"

Mr. Parker Pyne's face told nothing.

To Mrs. Chester he was soothing but vague. An engagement was not marriage. He himself was going to Soller for a week. He suggested that her line of action should be noncommittal. Let her appear to acquiesce.

He spent a very enjoyable week at Soller.

On his return he found that a totally unexpected development had arisen.

As he entered the Pino d'Oro the first thing he saw was Mrs. Chester and Betty Gregg having tea together. Basil was not there. Mrs. Chester looked haggard. Betty, too, was looking off color. She was hardly made up at all, and her eyelids looked as though she had been crying.

They greeted him in a friendly fashion, but neither of them mentioned Basil.

Suddenly he heard the girl beside him draw in her breath sharply as though something had hurt her. Mr. Parker Pyne turned his head.

Basil Chester was coming up the steps from the sea front. With him was a girl so exotically beautiful that it quite took your breath away. She was dark and her figure was marvellous. No one could fail to notice the fact since she wore nothing but a single garment of pale-blue crepe. She was heavily made up with ochre powder and an orange-scarlet mouth—but the unguents only displayed her remarkable beauty in a more pronounced fashion. As for young Basil, he seemed unable to take his eyes from her face.

"You're very late, Basil," said his mother. "You were to have taken Betty to Mac's."

"My fault," drawled the beautiful unknown. "We just drifted." She turned to Basil. "Angel—get me something with a kick in it!"

She tossed off her shoe and stretched out her manicured toenails, which were done emerald green to match her fingernails.

She paid no attention to the two women, but she leaned a little towards Mr. Parker Pyne.

"Terrible island this," she said. "I was just dying with boredom before I met Basil. He *is* rather a pet!"

"Mr. Parker Pyne—Miss Ramona," said Mrs. Chester.

The girl acknowledged the introduction with a lazy smile.

"I guess I'll call you Parker almost at once," she murmured. "My name's Dolores."

Basil returned with the drinks. Miss Ramona divided her conversation (what there was of it—it was mostly glances) between Basil and Mr. Parker Pyne. Of the two women she took no notice whatever. Betty attempted once or twice to join in the conversation, but the other girl merely stared at her and yawned.

Suddenly Dolores rose.

"Guess I'll be going along now. I'm at the other hotel. Anyone coming to see me home?"

Basil sprang up.

"I'll come with you."

Mrs. Chester said: "Basil, my dear——"

"I'll be back presently, Mother."

"Isn't he the mother's boy?" Miss Ramona asked of the world at large. "Just toots 'round after her, don't you?"

Basil flushed and looked awkward. Miss Ramona gave a nod in Mrs. Chester's direction, a dazzling smile to Mr. Parker Pyne, and she and Basil moved off together.

After they had gone, there was rather an awkward silence. Mr. Parker Pyne did not like to speak first. Betty Gregg was twisting her fingers and looking out to sea. Mrs. Chester looked flushed and angry.

Betty said: "Well, what do you think of our new acquisition in Pollensa Bay?" Her voice was not quite steady.

Mr. Parker Pyne said cautiously: "A little—er—exotic."

"Exotic?" Betty gave a short bitter laugh.

Mrs. Chester said: "She's terrible—terrible. Basil must be quite mad."

Betty said sharply: "Basil's all right."

"Her toenails," said Mrs. Chester with a shiver of nausea.

Betty rose suddenly.

"I think, Mrs. Chester, I'll go home and not stay to dinner after all."

"Oh, my dear—Basil will be so disappointed."

"Will he?" asked Betty with a short laugh. "Anyway, I think I will. I've got rather a headache."

She smiled at them both and went off. Mrs. Chester turned to Mr. Parker Pyne.

"I wish we had never come to this place—never!"

Mr. Parker Pyne shook his head sadly.

"You shouldn't have gone away," said Mrs. Chester. "If you'd been here this wouldn't have happened."

Mr. Parker Pyne was stung to respond, "My dear lady, I can assure you that when it comes to a question of a beautiful young woman, I should have no influence over your son whatever. He—er—seems to be of a very susceptible nature."

"He never used to be," said Mrs. Chester tearfully.

"Well," said Mr. Parker Pyne with an attempt at cheerfulness, "this new attraction seems to have broken the back of his infatuation for Miss Gregg. That must be some satisfaction to you."

"I don't know what you mean," said Mrs. Chester. "Betty is a dear child and devoted to Basil. She is behaving extremely well over this. I think my boy must be mad."

Mr. Parker Pyne received this startling change of face without wincing. He had met inconsistency in women before.

He said mildly: "Not exactly mad—just bewitched."

"The creature's impossible."

"But extremely good-looking."

Mrs. Chester snorted.

Basil ran up the steps from the sea front.

"Hullo, Mater, here I am. Where's Betty?"

"Betty's gone home with a headache. I don't wonder."

"Sulking, you mean."

"I consider, Basil, that you are being extremely unkind to Betty."

"For heaven's sake, Mother, don't jaw. If Betty is going to make this fuss every time I speak to another girl, a nice sort of life we'll lead together."

"You *are* engaged."

"Oh, we're engaged all right. That doesn't mean that we're not going to have any friends of our own. Nowadays people have to lead their own lives and try to cut out jealousy."

He paused.

"Look here, if Betty isn't going to dine with us—I think I'll go back to Mariposa. They did ask me to dine. . . ."

"Oh, Basil——"

The boy gave her an exasperated look, then ran off down the steps.

Mrs. Chester looked eloquently at Mr. Parker Pyne.

"You see," she said.

He saw.

Matters came to a head a couple of days later. Betty and Basil were to have gone for a long walk, taking a picnic lunch with them. Betty arrived at the Pino d'Oro to find that Basil had forgotten the plan and gone over to Formentor for the day with Dolores Ramona's party.

Beyond a tightening of the lips, the girl made no sign. Presently, however, she got up and stood in front of Mrs. Chester (the two women were alone on the terrace).

"It's quite all right," she said. "It doesn't matter. But I think—all the same—that we'd better call the whole thing off."

She slipped from her finger the signet ring that Basil had

given her—he would buy the real engagement ring later.

"Will you give him back this, Mrs. Chester? And tell him it's all right—not to worry. . . ."

"Betty dear, don't! He *does* love you—really."

"It looks like it, doesn't it?" said the girl with a short laugh. "No—I've got some pride. Tell him everything's all right and that I—I wish him luck."

When Basil returned at sunset he was greeted by a storm. He flushed a little at the sight of his ring.

"So that's how she feels, is it? Well, I daresay it's the best thing."

"Basil!"

"Well, frankly, Mother, we don't seem to have been hitting it off lately."

"Whose fault was that?"

"I don't see that it was mine particularly. Jealousy's beastly and I really don't see why *you* should get all worked up about it. You begged me yourself not to marry Betty."

"That was before I knew her. Basil—my dear—you're not thinking of marrying this other creature."

Basil Chester said soberly: "I'd marry her like a shot if she'd have me—but I'm afraid she won't."

Cold chills went down Mrs. Chester's spine. She sought and found Mr. Parker Pyne, placidly reading a book in a sheltered corner.

"You must *do* something! You *must* do something! My boy's life will be ruined."

Mr. Parker Pyne was getting a little tired of Basil Chester's life being ruined.

"What can I do?"

"Go and see this terrible creature. If necessary, buy her off."

"That may come very expensive."

"I don't care."

"It seems a pity. Still there are, possibly, other ways."

She looked a question. He shook his head.

"I'll make no promises—but I'll see what I can do. I have handled that kind before. By the way, not a word to Basil—that would be fatal."

"Of course not."

Mr. Parker Pyne returned from the Mariposa at midnight. Mrs. Chester was sitting up for him.

"Well?" she demanded breathlessly.

His eyes twinkled.

"The Señorita Dolores Ramona will leave Pollensa tomorrow morning and the island tomorrow night."

"Oh, Mr. Parker Pyne! How did you manage it?"

"It won't cost a cent," said Mr. Parker Pyne. Again his eyes twinkled. "I rather fancied I might have a hold over her —and I was right."

"You are wonderful. Nina Wycherley was quite right. You must let me know—er—your fees——"

Mr. Parker Pyne held up a well-manicured hand.

"Not a penny. It has been a pleasure. I hope all will go well. Of course, the boy will be very upset at first when he finds she's disappeared and left no address. Just go easy with him for a week or two."

"If only Betty will forgive him——"

"She'll forgive him all right. They're a nice couple. By the way, I'm leaving tomorrow, too."

"Oh, Mr. Parker Pyne, we shall miss you."

"Perhaps it's just as well I should go before that boy of yours gets infatuated with yet a third girl."

Mr. Parker Pyne leaned over the rail of the steamer and looked at the lights of Palma. Beside him stood Dolores Ramona. He was saying appreciatively: "A very nice piece of work, Madeleine. I'm glad I wired you to come out. It's odd when you're such a quiet stay-at-home girl really."

Madeleine de Sara, alias Dolores Ramona, alias Maggie Sayers, said primly: "I'm glad you're pleased, Mr. Parker Pyne. It's been a nice little change. I think I'll go below now and get to bed before the boat starts. I'm such a bad sailor."

A few minutes later a hand fell on Mr. Parker Pyne's shoulder. He turned to see Basil Chester.

"Had to come and see you off, Mr. Parker Pyne, and give you Betty's love and her and my best thanks. It was a grand stunt of yours. Betty and Mother are as thick as thieves.

Seemed a shame to deceive the old darling—but she *was* being difficult. Anyway, it's all right now. I must just be careful to keep up the annoyance stuff a couple of days longer. We're no end grateful to you, Betty and I."

"I wish you every happiness," said Mr. Parker Pyne.

"Thanks."

There was a pause, then Basil said with somewhat overdone carelessness: "Is Miss—Miss de Sara—anywhere about? I'd like to thank her, too."

Mr. Parker Pyne shot a keen glance at him.

He said: "I'm afraid Miss de Sara's gone to bed."

"Oh, too bad—well, perhaps I'll see her in London sometime."

"As a matter of fact, she is going to America on business for me almost at once."

"Oh!" Basil's tone was blank. "Well," he said. "I'll be getting along. . . ."

Mr. Parker Pyne smiled. On his way to his cabin he tapped on the door of Madeleine's.

"How are you, my dear? All right? Our young friend has been along. The usual slight attack of Madeleinitis. He'll get over it in a day or two, but you *are* rather distracting."

TOMMY AND TUPPENCE   PARTNERS IN CRIME

Tommy and Tuppence are, in private life, Mr. and Mrs. Thomas Beresford, a gay young married couple, inveterate readers of mystery stories and, at the moment, in temporary charge of The International Detective Agency, whose earlier manager, Theodore Blunt, has been indiscreet and is being detained by Scotland Yard. The Watson referred to by Tommy is, of course, the famous medical doctor of the Sherlock Holmes stories, and Inspector French, whose specialty is the breaking down of alibis, is the hero of several excellent detective novels by Freeman Wills Crofts. The **A.B.C.** in which Tuppence immerses herself in the story is that reliable British institution, the **Alphabetical Railway Guide.**

THE UNBREAKABLE ALIBI

TOMMY AND TUPPENCE were busy sorting correspondence. Tuppence gave an exclamation and handed a letter across to Tommy.

"A new client," she said importantly.

"Ha!" said Tommy. "What do we deduce from this letter, Watson? Nothing much, except the somewhat obvious fact that Mr.—er—Montgomery Jones is not one of the world's best spellers, thereby proving that he has been expensively educated."

"Montgomery Jones?" said Tuppence. "Now what do I know about a Montgomery Jones? Oh, yes, I have got it now. I think Janet St. Vincent mentioned him. His mother was Lady Aileen Montgomery, very crusty and high church, with gold crosses and things, and she married a man called Jones, who is immensely rich."

"In fact, the same old story," said Tommy. "Let me see, what time does this Mr. M. J. wish to see us? Ah, eleven-thirty."

At eleven-thirty precisely a very tall young man with an amiable and ingenuous countenance entered the outer office and addressed himself to Albert, the office boy.

"Look here—I say. Can I see Mr.—er—Blunt?"

"Have you an appointment, sir?" said Albert.

"I don't quite know. Yes, I suppose I have. What I mean is, I wrote a letter——"

"What name, sir?"

"Mr. Montgomery Jones."

"I will take your name in to Mr. Blunt."

He returned after a brief interval.

"Will you wait a few minutes please, sir? Mr. Blunt is engaged on a very important conference at present."

"Oh—er—yes—certainly," said Mr. Montgomery Jones.

Having, he hoped, impressed his client sufficiently, Tommy rang the buzzer on his desk, and Mr. Montgomery Jones was ushered into the inner office by Albert.

Tommy rose to greet him and, shaking him warmly by the hand, motioned towards the vacant chair.

"Now, Mr. Montgomery Jones," he said briskly, "what can we have the pleasure of doing for you?"

Mr. Montgomery Jones looked uncertainly at the third occupant of the office.

"My confidential secretary, Miss Robinson," said Tommy. "You can speak quite freely before her. I take it that this is some family matter of a delicate kind?"

"Well—not exactly," said Mr. Montgomery Jones.

"You surprise me," said Tommy. "You are not in trouble of any kind yourself, I hope?"

"Oh, rather not," said Mr. Montgomery Jones.

"Well," said Tommy, "perhaps you will—er—state the facts plainly."

That, however, seemed to be the one thing that Mr. Montgomery Jones could not do.

"It's a dashed odd sort of thing I have got to ask you," he said hesitatingly. "I—er—I really don't know how to set about it."

"We never touch divorce cases," said Tommy.

"No," said Mr. Montgomery Jones. "I don't mean that. It is just, well—it's a deuced silly sort of a joke. That's all."

"Someone has played a practical joke on you of a mysterious nature?" suggested Tommy.

But Mr. Montgomery Jones once more shook his head.

"Well," said Tommy, retiring gracefully from the position, "take your own time and let us have it in your own words."

There was a pause.

"You see," said Mr. Jones at last, "it was at dinner. I sat next to a girl."

"Yes?" said Tommy encouragingly.

"She was a—oh, well, I really can't describe her, but she was simply one of the most sporting girls I ever met. She's an Australian over here with another girl, sharing a flat with her in Clarges Street. She's simply game for anything. I absolutely can't tell you the effect that girl had on me."

"We can quite imagine it, Mr. Jones," said Tuppence.

She saw clearly that if Mr. Montgomery Jones's troubles were ever to be extracted, a sympathetic feminine touch was needed, as distinct from the businesslike methods of Mr. Blunt.

"We can understand," said Tuppence encouragingly.

"Well, the whole thing came as an absolute shock to me," said Mr. Montgomery Jones, "that a girl could, well—knock you over like that. There had been another girl—in fact, two other girls. One was awfully jolly and all that, but I didn't much like her chin. She danced marvellously though, and I have known her all my life, which makes a fellow feel kind of safe, you know. And then there was one of the girls at the 'Frivolity.' Frightfully amusing, but of course there would be a lot of ructions with the mater over that, and anyway I really didn't want to marry either of them, but I was thinking about things, you know, and then— slap out of the blue—I sat next to this girl and——"

"The whole world was changed," said Tuppence in a feeling voice.

Tommy moved impatiently in his chair. He was by now somewhat bored by the recital of Mr. Montgomery Jones's love affairs.

"You put it awfully well," said Mr. Montgomery Jones. "That is absolutely what it was like. Only, you know, I fancy she didn't think much of me. You mayn't think it, but I am not terribly clever."

"Oh, you mustn't be too modest," said Tuppence.

"Oh, I do realize that I am not much of a chap," said Mr. Jones with an engaging smile. "Not for a perfectly marvellous girl like that. That is why I just feel I have got to put this thing through. It's my only chance. She's such a sporting girl that she would never go back on her word."

"Well, I am sure we wish you luck and all that," said

Tuppence kindly. "But I don't exactly see what you want us to do."

"Oh!" said Mr. Montgomery Jones. "Haven't I explained?"

"No," said Tommy. "You haven't."

"Well, it was like this. We were talking about detective stories. Una—that's her name—is just as keen about them as I am. We got talking about one in particular. It all hinges on an alibi. Then we got talking about alibis and faking them. Then I said—no, she said—now which of us was it that said it?"

"Never mind which of you it was," said Tuppence.

"I said it would be a jolly difficult thing to do. She disagreed—said it only wanted a bit of brainwork. We got all hot and excited about it and in the end she said, 'I will make you a sporting offer. What do you bet that I can produce an alibi that nobody can shake?'

" 'Anything you like,' I said, and we settled it then and there. She was frightfully cocksure about the whole thing. 'It's an odds-on chance for me,' she said. 'Don't be so sure of that,' I said. 'Supposing you lose and I ask you for anything I like?' She laughed and said she came of a gambling family and I could."

"Well?" said Tuppence as Mr. Jones came to a pause and looked at her appealingly.

"Well, don't you see? It is up to me. It is the only chance I have got of getting a girl like that to look at me. You have no idea how sporting she is. Last summer she was out in a boat and someone bet her she wouldn't jump overboard and swim ashore in her clothes, and she did it."

"It is a very curious proposition," said Tommy. "I am not quite sure I yet understand it."

"It is perfectly simple," said Mr. Montgomery Jones. "You must be doing this sort of thing all the time. Investigating fake alibis and seeing where they fall down."

"Oh—er—yes, of course," said Tommy. "We do a lot of that sort of work."

"Someone has got to do it for me," said Montgomery Jones. "I shouldn't be any good at that sort of thing myself. You have only got to catch her out and everything is all right. I daresay it seems rather a futile business to you, but it means a lot to me and I am prepared to pay——er——all necessary whatnots, you know."

"That will be all right," said Tuppence. "I am sure Mr. Blunt will take the case on for you."

"Certainly, certainly," said Tommy. "A most refreshing case, most refreshing indeed."

Mr. Montgomery Jones heaved a sigh of relief and pulled a mass of papers from his pocket and selected one of them. "Here it is," he said. "She says, 'I am sending you proof I was in two distinct places at one and the same time. According to one story, I dined at the Bon Temps Restaurant in Soho by myself, went to the Duke's Theatre, and had supper with a friend, Mr. le Marchant, at the Savoy——*but* I was also staying at the Castle Hotel, Torquay, and only returned to London on the following morning. You have got to find out which of the two stories is the true one and how I managed the other.' "

"There," said Mr. Montgomery Jones. "Now you see what it is that I want you to do."

"A most refreshing little problem," said Tommy. "Very naïve."

"Here is Una's photograph," said Mr. Montgomery Jones. "You will want that."

"What is the lady's full name?" inquired Tommy.

"Miss Una Drake. And her address is 180 Clarges Street."

"Thank you," said Tommy. "Well, we will look into the matter for you, Mr. Montgomery Jones. I hope we shall have good news for you very shortly."

"I say, you know, I am no end grateful," said Mr. Jones, rising to his feet and shaking Tommy by the hand. "It has taken an awful load off my mind."

Having seen his client out, Tommy returned to the inner office. Tuppence was at the cupboard that contained the classic library.

"Inspector French," said Tuppence.

"Eh?" said Tommy.

"Inspector French, of course," said Tuppence. "He always does alibis. I know the exact procedure. We have to go

over everything and check it. At first it will seem all right
and then when we examine it more closely we shall find the
flaw."

"There ought not to be much difficulty about that," agreed
Tommy. "I mean, knowing that one of them is a fake to start
with makes the thing almost a certainty I should say. That is
what worries me."

"I don't see anything to worry about in that."

"I am worrying about the girl," said Tommy. "She will
probably be let in to marry that young man whether she
wants to or not."

"Darling," said Tuppence, "don't be foolish. Women are
never the wild gamblers they appear. Unless that girl was
already perfectly prepared to marry that pleasant but
rather empty-headed young man, she would never have let
herself in for a wager of this kind. But, Tommy, believe me,
she will marry him with more enthusiasm and respect if he
wins the wager than if she has to make it easy for him some
other way."

"You do think you know about everything," said her
husband.

"I do," said Tuppence.

"And now to examine our data," said Tommy, drawing
the paper towards him. "First the photograph—h'm—quite
a nice-looking girl—and quite a good photograph I should
say. Clear and easily recognizable."

"We must get some other girls' photographs," said Tuppence.

"Why?"

"They always do," said Tuppence. "You show four or five
to waiters and they pick out the right one."

"Do you think they do?" said Tommy. "Pick out the right
one, I mean."

"Well, they do in books," said Tuppence.

"It is a pity that real life is so different from fiction,"
said Tommy. "Now, then, what have we here? Yes, this is
the London lot. Dined at the Bon Temps seven-thirty. Went
to Duke's Theatre and saw *Delphiniums Blue*. Counter-
foil of theatre ticket enclosed. Supper at the Savoy with

Mr. le Marchant. We can, I suppose, interview Mr. le Marchant."

"That tells us nothing at all," said Tuppence, "because if he is helping her to do it, he naturally won't give the show away. We can wash out anything he says now."

"Well, here is the Torquay end," went on Tommy. "Twelve o'clock train from Paddington, had lunch in the restaurant car, receipted bill enclosed. Stayed at Castle Hotel for one night. Again receipted bill."

"I think this is all rather weak," said Tuppence. "Anyone can buy a theatre ticket; you need never go near the theatre. The girl just went to Torquay and the London thing is a fake."

"If so, it is rather a sitter for us," said Tommy. "Well, I suppose we might as well go and interview Mr. le Marchant."

Mr. le Marchant proved to be a breezy youth who betrayed no great surprise on seeing them.

"Una has got some little game on, hasn't she?" he asked. "You never know what that kid is up to."

"I understand, Mr. le Marchant," said Tommy, "that Miss Drake had supper with you at the Savoy last Tuesday evening."

"That's right," said Mr. le Marchant. "I know it was Tuesday because Una impressed it on me at the time and, what's more, she made me write it down in a little book."

With some pride he showed an entry faintly pencilled: "Having supper with Una. Savoy. Tuesday 19th."

"Where had Miss Drake been earlier in the evening? Do you know?"

"She had been to some rotten show called *Pink Peonies* or something like that. Absolute slosh, so she told me."

"You are quite sure Miss Drake was with you that evening?"

Mr. le Marchant stared at him.

"Why, of course. Haven't I been telling you?"

"Perhaps she asked you to tell us," said Tuppence.

"Well, for a matter of fact, she did say something that was rather dashed odd. She said—what was it now? 'You think you are sitting here having supper with me, Jimmy, but really I am having supper two hundred miles away in Devonshire.' Now that was a dashed odd thing to say, don't you think so? Sort of astral body stuff. The funny thing is that a pal of mine, Dicky Rice, thought he saw her there."

"Who is this Mr. Rice?"

"Oh, just a friend of mine. He had been down in Torquay staying with an aunt. Sort of old bean who is always going to die and never does. Dicky had been down doing the dutiful nephew. He said, 'I saw that Australian girl one day— Una something or other. Wanted to go and talk to her, but my aunt carried me off to chat with an old pussy in a bath chair.' I said, 'When was this?' And he said, 'Oh, Tuesday about teatime.' I told him, of course, that he made a mistake, but it was odd, wasn't it? With Una saying that about Devonshire that evening."

"Very odd," said Tommy. "Tell me, Mr. le Marchant, did anyone you know have supper near you at the Savoy?"

"Some people called Oglander were at the next table."

"Do they know Miss Drake?"

"Oh, yes, they know her. They are not frightful friends or anything of that kind."

"Well, if there's nothing more you can tell us, Mr. le Marchant, I think we will wish you good morning."

"Either that chap is an extraordinary good liar," said Tommy as they reached the street, "or else he is speaking the truth."

"Yes," said Tuppence. "I have changed my opinion. I have a sort of feeling now that Una Drake was at the Savoy for supper that night."

"We will now go to the Bon Temps," said Tommy. "A little food for starving sleuths is clearly indicated. Let's just get a few girls' photographs first."

This proved rather more difficult than was expected. Turning into a photographer's and demanding a few assorted photographs, they were met with a cold rebuff.

"Why are all the things that are so easy and simple in books so difficult in real life?" wailed Tuppence. "How horribly suspicious they looked. What do you think they thought we wanted to do with the photographs? We had better go and raid Jane's flat."

Tuppence's friend Jane proved of an accommodating disposition and permitted Tuppence to rummage in a drawer and select four specimens of former friends of Jane's who had been shoved hastily in to be out of sight and mind.

Armed with this galaxy of feminine beauty, they proceeded to the Bon Temps, where fresh difficulties and much expense awaited them. Tommy had to get hold of each waiter in turn, tip him, and then produce the assorted photographs. The result was unsatisfactory. At least three of the photographs were promising starters as having dined there last Tuesday. They then returned to the office, where Tuppence immersed herself in an *A.B.C.*

"Paddington twelve o'clock. Torquay three thirty-five. That's the train, and le Marchant's friend, Mr. Sago or Tapioca or something, saw her there about teatime."

"We haven't checked his statement, remember," said Tommy. "If, as you said to begin with, le Marchant is a friend of Una Drake's, he may have invented this story."

"Oh, we'll hunt up Mr. Rice," said Tuppence. "I have a kind of hunch that Mr. le Marchant was speaking the truth. No, what I am trying to get at now is this. Una Drake leaves London by the twelve o'clock train, possibly takes a room at a hotel, and unpacks. Then she takes a train back to town, arriving in time to get to the Savoy. There is one at four-forty gets up to Paddington at nine-ten."

"And then?" said Tommy.

"And then," said Tuppence, frowning, "it is rather more difficult. There is a midnight train from Paddington down again, but she could hardly take that; that would be too early."

"A fast car," suggested Tommy.

"H'm," said Tuppence. "It is just on two hundred miles."

"Australians, I have always been told, drive very recklessly."

"Oh, I suppose it could be done," said Tuppence; "she would arrive there about seven."

"Are you supposing her to have nipped into her bed at

the Castle Hotel without being seen? Or arriving there explaining that she been out all night and could she have her bill, please?"

"Tommy," said Tuppence. "We are idiots. She needn't have gone back to Torquay at all. She has only got to get a friend to go to the hotel there and collect her luggage and pay her bill. Then you get the receipted bill with the proper date on it."

"I think on the whole we have worked out a very sound hypothesis," said Tommy. "The next thing to do is to catch the twelve o'clock train to Torquay tomorrow and verify our brilliant conclusions."

Armed with a portfolio of photographs, Tommy and Tuppence duly established themselves in a first-class carriage the following morning and booked seats for the second lunch.

"It probably won't be the same dining-car attendants," said Tommy. "That would be too much luck to expect. I expect we shall have to travel up and down to Torquay for days before we strike the right ones."

"This alibi business is very trying," said Tuppence. "In books it is all passed over in two or three paragraphs. Inspector Something then boarded the train to Torquay and questioned the dining-car attendants and so ended the story."

For once, however, the young couple's luck was in. In answer to their question, the attendant who brought their bill for lunch proved to be the same one who had been on duty the preceding Tuesday. What Tommy called the ten-shilling-note touch then came into action and Tuppence produced the portfolio.

"I want to know," said Tommy, "if any of these ladies had lunch on this train on Tuesday last?"

In a gratifying manner worthy of the best detective fiction the man at once indicated the photograph of Una Drake.

"Yes, sir, I remember that lady, and I remember that it was Tuesday, because the lady herself drew attention to the fact, saying it was always the luckiest day in the week for her."

"So far, so good," said Tuppence as they returned to their

compartment. "And we will probably find that she booked at the hotel all right. It is going to be more difficult to prove that she travelled back to London, but perhaps one of the porters at the station may remember."

Here, however, they drew a blank, and, crossing to the up platform, Tommy made inquiries of the ticket collector and of various porters. After the distribution of half crowns as a preliminary to inquiring, two of the porters picked out one of the other photographs with a vague remembrance that someone like that travelled to town by the four-forty that afternoon; but there was no identification of Una Drake.

"But that doesn't prove anything," said Tuppence as they left the station. "She may have travelled by that train and no one noticed her."

"She may have gone from the other station, from Torre."

"That's quite likely," said Tuppence; "however, we can see to that after we have been to the hotel."

The Castle Hotel was a big one overlooking the sea. After booking a room for the night and signing the register, Tommy observed pleasantly: "I believe you had a friend of ours staying here last Tuesday. Miss Una Drake."

The young lady in the bureau beamed at him.

"Oh, yes, I remember quite well. An Australian young lady, I believe."

At a sign from Tommy, Tuppence produced the photograph.

"That is rather a charming photograph of her, isn't it?" said Tuppence.

"Oh, very nice, very nice indeed, quite stylish."

"Did she stay here long?" inquired Tommy.

"Only the one night. She went away by the express the next morning back to London. It seemed a long way to come for one night but, of course, I suppose Australian ladies don't think anything of travelling."

"She is a very sporting girl," said Tommy, "always having adventures. It wasn't here, was it, that she went out to dine with some friends, went for a drive in their car afterwards, ran the car into a ditch, and wasn't able to get home till morning?"

"Oh, no," said the young lady. "Miss Drake had dinner here in the hotel."

"Really," said Tommy, "are you sure of that? I mean—how do you know?"

"Oh, I saw her."

"I asked because I understood she was dining with some friends in Torquay," explained Tommy.

"Oh, no, sir, she dined here." The young lady laughed and blushed a little. "I remember she had on a most sweetly pretty frock. One of those new flowered chiffons all over pansies."

"Tuppence, this tears it," said Tommy when they had been shown upstairs to their room.

"It does rather," said Tuppence. "Of course, that woman may be mistaken. We will ask the waiter at dinner. There can't be very many people here just at this time of year."

This time it was Tuppence who opened the attack.

"Can you tell me if a friend of mine was here last Tuesday?" she asked the waiter with an engaging smile. "A Miss Drake, wearing a frock all over pansies, I believe." She produced a photograph. "This lady."

The waiter broke into immediate smiles of recognition.

"Yes, yes, Miss Drake. I remember her very well. She told me she came from Australia."

"She dined here?"

"Yes. It was last Tuesday. She asked me if there was anything to do afterwards in the town."

"Yes?"

"I told her the theatre, the Pavilion, but in the end she decided not to go and she stayed here listening to our orchestra."

"Oh, damn," said Tommy under his breath.

"You don't remember what time she had dinner, do you?" said Tuppence.

"She came down a little late. It must have been about eight o'clock."

"Tommy," said Tuppence as they left the dining room, "this is all going wrong. It seemed so clear and lovely."

"Well, I suppose we ought to have known it wouldn't all be plain sailing."

"Is there any train she could have taken after that, I wonder?"

"Not one that would have landed her in London in time to go to the Savoy."

"Well," said Tuppence, "as a last hope I am going to talk to the chambermaid. Una Drake had a room on the same floor as ours."

The chambermaid was a voluble and informative woman. Yes, she remembered the young lady quite well. That was her picture right enough. A very nice young lady, very merry and talkative. Had told her a lot about Australia and the kangaroos.

The young lady rang the bell about half-past nine and asked for her bottle to be filled and put in her bed and also to be called the next morning at half-past seven—with coffee instead of tea.

"You did call her and she was in her bed?" asked Tuppence.

The chambermaid stared at her.

"Why, yes, ma'am, of course."

"Oh, I only wondered if she was doing exercises or anything," said Tuppence wildly. "So many people do in the early morning."

"Well, that seems cast-iron enough," said Tommy when the chambermaid had departed. "There is only one conclusion to be drawn from it. It is the London side of the thing that *must* be faked."

"Mr. le Marchant must be a more accomplished liar than we thought," said Tuppence.

"We have a way of checking his statements," said Tommy. "He said there were people sitting at the next table whom Una knew slightly. What was their name—Oglander, that was it. We must hunt up these Oglanders and we ought also to make inquiries at Miss Drake's flat in Clarges Street."

The following morning they paid their bill and departed somewhat crestfallen.

Hunting out the Oglanders was fairly easy with the aid of the telephone book. Tuppence this time took the offensive and assumed the character of a representative of a new illustrated paper. She called on Mrs. Oglander asking for a few details of their "smart" supper party at the Savoy on Tuesday evening. These details Mrs. Oglander was only too willing to supply. Just as she was leaving, Tuppence added carelessly: "Let me see, wasn't Miss Una Drake sitting at the table next you? Is it really true that she is engaged to the Duke of Perth? You know her, of course."

"I know her slightly," said Mrs. Oglander. "A very charming girl, I believe. Yes, she was sitting at the next table to ours with Mr. le Marchant. My girls know her better than I do."

Tuppence's next port of call was the flat in Clarges Street. Here she was greeted by Miss Marjory Leicester, the friend with whom Miss Drake shared a flat.

"Do tell me what all this is about?" asked Miss Leicester plaintively. "Una has some deep game on and I don't know what it is. Of course she slept here on Tuesday night."

"Did you see her when she came in?"

"No, I had gone to bed. She has got her own latchkey, of course. She came in about one o'clock, I believe."

"When did you see her?"

"Oh, the next morning about nine—or perhaps it was nearer ten."

As Tuppence left the flat she almost collided with a tall, gaunt female who was entering.

"Excuse me, miss, I'm sure," said the gaunt female.

"Do you work here?" asked Tuppence.

"Yes, miss, I come daily."

"What time do you get here in the morning?"

"Nine o'clock is my time, miss."

Tuppence slipped a hurried half crown into the gaunt female's hand.

"Was Miss Drake here last Tuesday morning when you arrived?"

"Why, yes, miss, indeed she was. Fast asleep in her bed and hardly woke up when I brought her in her tea."

"Oh, thank you," said Tuppence, and went disconsolately down the stairs.

She had arranged to meet Tommy for lunch in a small restaurant in Soho, and there they compared notes.

"I have seen that fellow Rice. It is quite true he did see Una Drake in the distance at Torquay."

"Well," said Tuppence, "we have checked these alibis all right. Here, give me a bit of paper and a pencil, Tommy. Let us put it down neatly like all detectives do."

1:30	Una Drake seen in luncheon car of train.
4 o'clock	Arrives at Castle Hotel.
5 o'clock	Seen by Mr. Rice.
8 o'clock	Seen dining at hotel.
9:30	Asks for hot-water bottle.
11:30	Seen at Savoy with Mr. le Marchant.
7:30 A.M.	Called by chambermaid at Castle Hotel.
9 o'clock	Called by charwoman at flat at Clarges Street.

They looked at each other.

"Well, it looks to me as if Blunt's Brilliant Detectives are beat," said Tommy.

"Oh, we mustn't give up," said Tuppence. "Somebody *must* be lying!"

"The queer thing is that it strikes me nobody was lying. They all seemed perfectly truthful and straightforward."

"Yet there must be a flaw. We know there is. I think of all sorts of things like private aeroplanes, but that doesn't really get us any forwarder."

"I am inclined to the theory of an astral body."

"Well," said Tuppence, "the only thing to do is to sleep on it. Your subconscious works in your sleep."

"H'm," said Tommy. "If your subconscious provides you with a perfectly good answer to this riddle by tomorrow morning, I take off my hat to it."

They were very silent all that evening. Again and again Tuppence reverted to the paper of times. She wrote things on bits of paper. She murmured to herself, she sought perplexedly through *Rail Guides*. But in the end they both rose to go to bed with no faint glimmer of light on the problem.

"This is very disheartening," said Tommy.

"One of the most miserable evenings I have ever spent," said Tuppence.

"We ought to have gone to a music hall," said Tommy. "A few good jokes about mothers-in-law and twins and bottles of beer would have done us no end of good."

"No, you will see this concentration will work in the end," said Tuppence. "How busy our subconscious will have to be in the next eight hours!" And on this hopeful note they went to bed.

"Well," said Tommy next morning, "has the subconsious worked?"

"I have got an idea," said Tuppence.

"You have. What sort of an idea?"

"Well, rather a funny idea. Not at all like anything I have ever read in detective stories. As a matter of fact, it is an idea that *you* put into my head."

"Then it must be a good idea," said Tommy firmly. "Come on, Tuppence, out with it."

"I shall have to send a cable to verify it," said Tuppence. "No, I am not going to tell you. It's a perfectly wild idea, but it's the only thing that fits the facts."

"Well," said Tommy, "I must away to the office. A roomful of disappointed clients must not wait in vain. I leave this case in the hands of my promising subordinate."

Tuppence nodded cheerfully.

She did not put in an appearance at the office all day. When Tommy returned that evening about half-past five it was to find a wildly exultant Tuppence awaiting him.

"I have done it, Tommy. I have solved the mystery of the alibi. We can charge up all these half crowns and ten-shilling notes and demand a substantial fee of our own from Mr. Montgomery Jones, and he can go right off and collect his girl."

"What is the solution?" cried Tommy.

"A perfectly simple one," said Tuppence. *"Twins."*

"What do you mean—twins?"

"Why, just that. Of course, it is the only solution. I will

say you put it into my head last night talking about mothers-in-law, twins, and bottles of beer. I cabled to Australia and got back the information I wanted. Una has a twin sister, Vera, who arrived in England last Monday. That is why she was able to make this bet so spontaneously. She thought it would be a frightful rag on poor Montgomery Jones. The sister went to Torquay and she stayed in London."

"Do you think she'll be terribly despondent that she's lost?" asked Tommy.

"No," said Tuppence. "I don't. I gave you my views about that before. She will put all the kudos down to Montgomery Jones. I always think respect for your husband's abilities should be the foundation of married life."

"I am glad to have inspired these sentiments in you, Tuppence."

"It is not a really satisfactory solution," said Tuppence. "Not the ingenious sort of flaw that Inspector French would have detected."

"Nonsense," said Tommy. "I think the way I showed these photographs to the waiter in the restaurant was exactly like Inspector French."

"He didn't have to use nearly so many half crowns and ten-shilling notes as we seem to have done," said Tuppence.

"Never mind," said Tommy. "We can charge them all up with additions to Mr. Montgomery Jones. He will be in such a state of idiotic bliss that he would probably pay the most enormous bill without jibbing at it."

"So he should," said Tuppence. "Haven't Blunt's Brilliant Detectives been brilliantly successful? Oh, Tommy, I do think we are extraordinarily clever. It quite frightens me sometimes."

"The next case we have shall be a Roger Sheringham case and you, Tuppence, shall be Roger Sheringham."

"I shall have to talk a lot," said Tuppence.

"You do that naturally," said Tommy. "And now I suggest that we carry out my programme of last night and seek out a music hall where they have plenty of jokes about mothers-in-law, bottles of beer, *and twins*."

INSPECTOR EVANS   SCOTLAND YARD

This is probably the most pitiless—and the best—short story that Agatha Christie has written. Indeed, to the casual mystery reader, its implications may be quite frightening. If, therefore, you have met the cold-blooded murder it describes—while you have been reading alone or perhaps even at midnight—do not become unduly upset or alarmed. Just remember that **such people really do exist!** And remember, too, that in the long run only a very foolish person arouses the relentless suspicions of Scotland Yard.

ACCIDENT

"AND I TELL YOU THIS—it's the same woman—not a doubt of it!" Captain Haydock looked into the eager, vehement face of his friend and sighed. He wished Evans would not be so positive and so jubilant. In the course of a career spent at sea, the old sea captain had learned to leave things that did not concern him well alone. His friend Evans, late C.I.D. Inspector, had a different philosophy of life. "Acting on information received—" had been his motto in early days, and he had improved upon it to the extent of finding out his own information. Inspector Evans had been a very smart, wide-awake officer, and had justly earned the promotion which had been his. Even now, when he had retired from the force, and had settled down in the country cottage of his dreams, his professional instinct was still active.

"Don't often forget a face," he reiterated complacently. "Mrs. Anthony—yes, it's Mrs. Anthony right enough. When you said Mrs. Merrowdene—I knew her at once."

Captain Haydock stirred uneasily. The Merrowdenes were his nearest neighbors, barring Evans himself, and this identifying of Mrs. Merrowdene with a former heroine of a *cause célèbre* distressed him.

"It's a long time ago," he said rather weakly.

"Nine years," said Evans, accurate as ever. "Nine years and three months. You remember the case?"

"In a vague sort of way."

"Anthony turned out to be an arsenic eater," said Evans, "so they acquitted her."

"Well, why shouldn't they?"

"No reason in the world. Only verdict they could give on the evidence. Absolutely correct."

"Then, that's all right," said Haydock. "And I don't see what we're bothering about."

"Who's bothering?"

"I thought you were."

"Not at all."

"The thing's over and done with," summed up the Captain. "If Mrs. Merrowdene at one time of her life was unfortunate enough to be tried and acquitted of murder——"

"It's not usually considered unfortunate to be acquitted," put in Evans.

"You know what I mean," said Captain Haydock, irritably. "If the poor lady has been through that harrowing experience, it's no business of ours to rake it up, is it?"

Evans did not answer.

"Come now, Evans. The lady was innocent—you've just said so."

"I didn't say she was innocent. I said she was acquitted."

"It's the same thing."

"Not always."

Captain Haydock, who had commenced to tap his pipe out against the side of his chair, stopped, and sat up with a very alert expression:

"Hullo-ullo-ullo," he said. "The wind's in that quarter, is it? You think she wasn't innocent?"

"I wouldn't say that. I just—don't know. Anthony was in the habit of taking arsenic. His wife got it for him. One day, by mistake, he takes far too much. Was the mistake his or his wife's? Nobody could tell, and the jury very properly gave her the benefit of the doubt. That's all quite right and I'm not finding fault with it. All the same—I'd like to know."

Captain Haydock transferred his attention to his pipe once more.

"Well," he said comfortably, "it's none of our business."

"I'm not so sure. . . ."

"But, surely——"

"Listen to me a minute. This man, Merrowdene—in his

laboratory this evening, fiddling round with tests—you remember——"

"Yes. He mentioned Marsh's test for arsenic. Said you would know all about it—it was in your line—and chuckled. He wouldn't have said that if he'd thought for one moment——"

Evans interrupted him.

"You mean he wouldn't have said that if he knew. They've been married how long—six years, you told me? I bet you anything he has no idea his wife is the once notorious Mrs. Anthony."

"And he will certainly not know it from me," said Captain Haydock stiffly.

Evans paid no attention, but went on.

"You interrupted me just now. After Marsh's test, Merrowdene heated a substance in a test tube, the metallic residue he dissolved in water and then precipitated it by adding silver nitrate. That was a test for chlorates. A neat, unassuming little test. But I chanced to read these words in a book that stood open on the table. 'H_2SO_4 decomposes chlorates with evolution of Cl_2O_4. If heated, violent explosions occur, the mixture ought therefore to be kept cool and only very small quantities used.' "

Haydock stared at his friend. "Well, what about it?"

"Just this. In my profession we've got tests, too—tests for murder. There's adding up the facts—weighing them, dissecting the residue when you've allowed for prejudice and the general inaccuracy of witnesses. But there's another test for murder—one that is fairly accurate, but rather—dangerous! A murderer is seldom content with one crime. Give him time and a lack of suspicion and he'll commit another. You catch a man—has he murdered his wife or hasn't he?—perhaps the case isn't very black against him. Look into his past—if you find that he's had several wives—and that they've all died, shall we say—rather curiously?—then you know! I'm not speaking legally, you understand. I'm speaking of moral certainty. Once you know, you can go ahead looking for evidence."

"Well?"

"I'm coming to the point. That's all right if there is a past to look into. But suppose you catch your murderer at his or her first crime? Then that test will be one from which you get no reaction. But the prisoner acquitted—starting life under another name. Will or will not the murderer repeat the crime?"

"That's a horrible idea."

"Do you still say it's none of our business?"

"Yes, I do. You've no reason to think that Mrs. Merrowdene is anything but a perfectly innocent woman."

The ex-Inspector was silent for a moment. Then he said slowly:

"I told you that we looked into her past and found nothing. That's not quite true. There was a stepfather. As a girl of eighteen she had a fancy for some young man—and her stepfather exerted his authority to keep them apart. She and her stepfather went for a walk along a rather dangerous part of the cliff. There was an accident—the stepfather went too near the edge—it gave way and he went over and was killed."

"You don't think——"

"It was an accident. Accident! Anthony's overdose of arsenic was an accident. She'd never have been tried if it hadn't transpired that there was another man—he sheered off, by the way. Looked as though he weren't satisfied even if the jury were. I tell you, Haydock, where that woman is concerned I'm afraid of another—accident!"

The old captain shrugged his shoulders.

"Well, I don't know how you're going to guard against that."

"Neither do I," said Evans ruefully.

"I should leave well enough alone," said Captain Haydock. "No good ever came of butting into other people's affairs."

But that advice was not palatable to the ex-Inspector. He was a man of patience but determination. Taking leave of his friend, he sauntered down to the village, revolving in his mind the possibilities of some kind of successful action.

Turning into the post office to buy some stamps, he ran into the object of his solicitude, George Merrowdene. The ex-chemistry professor was a small, dreamy-looking man, gentle and kindly in manner, and usually completely absent-minded. He recognized the other and greeted him amicably, stooping to recover the letters that the impact had caused him to drop on the ground. Evans stooped also and, more rapid in his movements than the other, secured them first, handing them back to their owner with an apology.

He glanced down at them in doing so, and the address on the topmost suddenly awakened all his suspicions anew. It bore the name of a well-known insurance firm.

Instantly his mind was made up. The guileless George Merrowdene hardly realized how it came about that he and the ex-Inspector were strolling down the village together, and still less could he have said how it came about that the conversation should come round to the subject of life insurance.

Evans had no difficulty in attaining his object. Merrowdene of his own accord volunteered the information that he had just insured his life for his wife's benefit and asked Evan's opinion of the company in question.

"I made some rather unwise investments," he explained. "As a result, my income has diminished. If anything were to happen to me, my wife would be left very badly off. This insurance will put things right."

"She didn't object to the idea?" inquired Evans casually. "Some ladies do, you know. Feel it's unlucky—that sort of thing."

"Oh, Margaret is very practical," said Merrowdene, smiling. "Not at all superstitious. In fact, I believe it was her idea originally. She didn't like my being so worried."

Evans had got the information he wanted. He left the other shortly afterwards, and his lips were set in a grim line. The late Mr. Anthony had insured his life in his wife's favor a few weeks before his death.

Accustomed to rely on his instincts, he was perfectly sure in his own mind. But how to act was another matter. He wanted, not to arrest a criminal red-handed, but to prevent a crime being committed and that was a very different and a very much more difficult thing.

All day he was very thoughtful. There was a Primrose League Fête that afternoon held in the grounds of the local squire, and he went to it, indulging in the penny dip, guessing the weight of a pig, and shying at coconuts, all with the same look of abstracted concentration on his face. He even indulged in half a crown's worth of Zara the Crystal Gazer, smiling a little to himself as he did so, remembering his own activities against fortune-tellers in his official days.

He did not pay very much heed to her singsong, droning voice till the end of a sentence held his attention.

"—and you will very shortly—very shortly indeed—be engaged on a matter of life or death—life or death to one person."

"Eh—what's that?" he asked abruptly.

"A decision—you have a decision to make. You must be very careful—very, very careful. . . . If you were to make a mistake—the smallest mistake——"

"Yes?"

The fortune-teller shivered. Inspector Evans knew it was all nonsense, but he was nevertheless impressed.

"I warn you—you must not make a mistake. If you do, I see the result clearly, a death. . . ."

Odd! A death. Fancy her lighting upon that!

"If I make a mistake a death will result? Is that it?"

"Yes."

"In that case," said Evans, rising to his feet and handing over half a crown, "I mustn't make a mistake, eh?"

He spoke lightly enough, but as he went out of the tent, his jaw set determinedly. Easy to say—not so easy to be sure of doing. He mustn't make a slip. A life, a valuable human life depended on it.

And there was no one to help him. He looked across at the figure of his friend Haydock in the distance. No help there. "Leave things alone," was Haydock's motto. And that wouldn't do here.

Haydock was talking to a woman. She moved away from

him and came towards Evans, and the Inspector recognized her. It was Mrs. Merrowdene. On an impulse he put himself deliberately in her path.

Mrs. Merrowdene was rather a fine-looking woman. She had a broad serene brow, very beautiful brown eyes, and a placid expression. She had the look of an Italian Madonna which she heightened by parting her hair in the middle and looping it over her ears. She had a deep, rather sleepy voice.

She smiled up at Evans, a contented, welcoming smile.

"I thought it was you, Mrs. Anthony—I mean Mrs. Merrowdene," he said glibly.

He made the slip deliberately, watching her without seeming to do so. He saw her eyes widen, heard the quick intake of her breath. But her eyes did not falter. She gazed at him steadily and proudly.

"I was looking for my husband," she said quietly. "Have you seen him anywhere about?"

"He was over in that direction when I last saw him."

They went side by side in the direction indicated, chatting quietly and pleasantly. The Inspector felt his admiration mounting. What a woman! What self-command! What wonderful poise! A remarkable woman—and a very dangerous one. He felt sure—a very dangerous one.

He still felt very uneasy, though he was satisfied with his initial step. He had let her know that he recognized her. That would put her on her guard. She would not dare attempt anything rash. There was the question of Merrowdene. If he could be warned. . . .

They found the little man absently contemplating a china doll which had fallen to his share in the penny dip. His wife suggested home and he agreed eagerly. Mrs. Merrowdene turned to the Inspector.

"Won't you come back with us and have a quiet cup of tea, Mr. Evans?"

Was there a faint note of challenge in her voice? He thought there was.

"Thank you, Mrs. Merrowdene. I should like to very much."

They walked there, talking together of pleasant ordinary

things. The sun shone, a breeze blew gently, everything around them was pleasant and ordinary.

Their maid was out at the Fête, Mrs. Merrowdene explained, when they arrived at the charming Old World cottage. She went into her room to remove her hat, returning to set out tea and boil the kettle on a little silver lamp. From a shelf near the fireplace she took three small bowls and saucers.

"We have some very special Chinese tea," she explained. "And we always drink it in the Chinese manner—out of bowls, not cups."

She broke off, peered into a cup and exchanged it for another, with an exclamation of annoyance.

"George—it's too bad of you. You've been taking these bowls again."

"I'm sorry, dear," said the professor apologetically. "They're such a convenient size. The ones I ordered haven't come."

"One of these days you'll poison us all," said his wife with a half laugh. "Mary finds them in the laboratory and brings them back here and never troubles to wash them out unless they've something very noticeable in them. Why, you were using one of them for potassium cyanide the other day. Really, George, it's frightfully dangerous."

Merrowdene looked a little irritated.

"Mary's no business to remove things from the laboratory. She's not to touch anything there."

"But we often leave our teacups there after tea. How is she to know? Be reasonable, dear."

The professor went into his laboratory murmuring to himself, and with a smile Mrs. Merrowdene poured boiling water on the tea and blew out the flame of the little silver lamp.

Evans was puzzled. Yet a glimmering of light penetrated to him. For some reason or other, Mrs. Merrowdene was showing her hand. Was this to be the "accident"? Was she speaking of all this so as deliberately to prepare her alibi beforehand. So that when, one day, the "accident" hap-

pened, he would be forced to give evidence in her favor.
Stupid of her, if so, because before that——

Suddenly he drew in his breath. She had poured the tea
into the three bowls. One she set before him, one before
herself, the other she placed on a little table by the fire near
the chair her husband usually sat in, and it was as she placed
this last one on the table that a little strange smile curved
round her lips. It was the smile that did it.

He knew!

A remarkable woman—a dangerous woman. No waiting
—no preparation. This afternoon—this very afternoon—
with him here as witness. The boldness of it took his breath
away.

It was clever—it was damnably clever. He would be able
to prove nothing. She counted on his not suspecting—simply
because it was "so soon." A woman of lightning rapidity of
thought and action.

He drew a deep breath and leaned forward.

"Mrs. Merrowdene, I'm a man of queer whims. Will you
be very kind and indulge me in one of them?"

She looked inquiring but unsuspicious.

He rose, took the bowl from in front of her and crossed
to the little table where he substituted it for the other. This
other he brought back and placed in front of her.

"I want to see you drink this."

Her eyes met his. They were steady, unfathomable. The
color slowly drained from her face.

She stretched out her hand, raised the cup. He held his
breath.

Supposing all along he had made a mistake.

She raised it to her lips—at the last moment, with a shud-
der she leaned forward and quickly poured it into a pot
containing a fern. Then she sat back and gazed at him
defiantly.

He drew a long sigh of relief, and sat down again.

"Well?" she said.

Her voice had altered. It was slightly mocking—defiant.
He answered her soberly and quietly.

"You are a very clever woman, Mrs. Merrowdene. I think you understand me. There must be no—repetition. You know what I mean?"

"I know what you mean."

Her voice was even, devoid of expression. He nodded his head, satisfied. She was a clever woman, and she didn't want to be hanged.

"To your long life and to that of your husband," he said significantly and raised his tea to his lips.

Then his face changed. It contorted horribly . . . he tried to rise—to cry out. . . . His body stiffened—his face went purple. He fell back sprawling over the chair—his limbs convulsed.

Mrs. Merrowdene leaned forward, watching him. A little smile crossed her lips. She spoke to him—very softly and gently.

"You made a mistake, Mr. Evans. You thought I wanted to kill George. . . . How stupid of you—how very stupid."

She sat there a minute longer looking at the dead man, the third man who had threatened to cross her path and separate her from the man she loved. . . .

Her smile broadened. She looked more than ever like a Madonna. Unaware of the fate that waited her, she raised her voice and called.

"George—George. . . . Oh! do come here. I'm afraid there's been the most dreadful accident. . . . Poor Mr. Evans. . . ."

NOVELS OF MYSTERY AND SUSPENSE BY

AGATHA CHRISTIE

undisputed First Lady of Mystery Fiction,
with over 200 million copies of her books sold

THE BIG FOUR 50c

THE LABORS OF HERCULES 50c

THE MOUSE TRAP 50c

MURDER IN MESOPOTAMIA 50c

THE MYSTERIOUS MR. QUIN 50c

N OR M 50c

POIROT LOSES A CLIENT 50c

THE REGATTA MYSTERY 50c

13 FOR LUCK 50c

THEY CAME TO BAGDAD 60c

DELL BOOKS

If you cannot obtain copies of these titles from your local bookseller, just
send the price (plus 10c per copy for handling and postage) to Dell Books,
Box 2291, Grand Central Post Office, New York, N.Y. 10017. No postage or
handling charge is required on any order of five or more books.

If you enjoy the macabre,
the unexpected . . .
here are gems of death
and horror from the
world's most unfettered
imaginations.

ALFRED HITCHCOCK presents:

ALFRED HITCHCOCK'S DEATH BAG 60c
GAMES KILLERS PLAY 50c
HAPPINESS IS A WARM CORPSE 60c
A HARD DAY AT THE SCAFFOLD 50c
MORE STORIES FOR LATE AT NIGHT 50c
MORE STORIES NOT FOR THE NERVOUS 50c
NOOSE REPORT 50c
SKULL SESSION 60c
STORIES NOT FOR THE NERVOUS 50c

DELL BOOKS

If you cannot obtain copies of these titles at your local bookseller, just send the price (plus 10c per copy for handling and postage) to Dell Books, Box 2291, Grand Central Post Office, New York, N.Y. 10017. No postage or handling charge is required on any order of five or more books.

All the terror and suspense of
ROSEMARY'S BABY . . .

THE SURVIVORS

A spellbinding novel
by Anne Edwards

A beautiful and lost girl . . . a man obsessed with learning the undiscovered truth about the shocking slaughter of an entire family . . . a high-speed journey along the razor edge of madness into the jaws of unimaginable horror . . .

A novel that grips the imagination like a vise until the final shattering turn of the screw . . .

"You'll be reading THE SURVIVORS right to the breathless end."
— *Dallas Times Herald*

A DELL BOOK 95c

If you cannot obtain copies of this title at your local bookseller, just send the price (plus 10c per copy for handling and postage) to Dell Books, Box 2291, Grand Central Post Office, New York, N.Y. 10017. No postage or handling charge is required on any order of five or more books.

READ the book!   SEE the movie!

The Secret of Santa Vittoria

by
ROBERT CRICHTON

Robert Crichton's bestselling story concerns one million bottles of Italian wine. The Nazi invaders want it; the Italians hide it. How the people of Santa Vittoria make one million bottles of wine disappear into thin air is really what the SECRET is all about.

Don't miss the Stanley Kramer
production starring
Anthony Quinn, Virna Lisi,
Hardy Kruger, Sergio Franchi
and Anna Magnani as Rosa

A DELL BOOK   95c

If you cannot obtain copies of this title from your local bookseller, just send the price (plus 10c per copy for handling and postage) to Dell Books, Box 2291, Grand Central Post Office, New York, N.Y. 10017. No postage or handling charge is required on any order of five or more books.